Tamed

Hearts

Tamed Hearts

Bay Hearts #2

By Caz May

First Published 2022
Paperback ISBN 978-0-6488534-4-2

Published by Caz May

© Caz May 2021
Cover image from Shutterstock (VAndreas)
Cover editing by Caz May

Author's Preface

Hey lovely readers!

Please note this is book 2 in a Reverse Harem/
Menage romance duet in which there is
multiple love interests. Because of this some
parts of the story may seem like cheating. If
you're triggered by this or by MM, MMF or
MMFM which also involves scenes with cum
play, fisting and double penetration this book
may not be for you.
There is also mentions of self harm, suicide and
violence.
Also this story is set in Australia, where the
age of consent is sixteen. Please do not
comment on this in regard to the story in
reviews and such.

*As the author of this book I am not responsible for melted
reading devices or for any changes of underwear required when
reading the story.*

You have been warned!

Don't forget your tissues!

Enjoy the conclusion of Ariel and her b-boys!

Caz May

xx

Playlist

Featured Songs

Beat up Guitar-Darling Brando

I Won't Let You Go- Switchfoot

Follow You- Bring Me The Horizon

Popular Monster- Falling in Reverse

Paradise- MEDUZA, Dermot Kennedy

I Don't Need You-Asking Alexandria

Dark side of your room- All Time Low

Tear Me Down-Paul Rey

Animals-Maroon 5

Take Some Time- Asking Alexandria

This Year's Love- David Gray

Full playlist on Spotify

Also by Caz May

Secret Santa (A Christmas Rom-Com)

My Girl Duet

Bk 1-Not my Girl
Bk 2-Still my Girl

Always Only You Series

Bk 1-Roommates Don't Kiss & Tell
Bk 2-Friends Don't Say Goodbye
Bk 3-Feelings Don't Play Fair
Bk 4-Hearts Don't Steer Us Wrong

The Mackenney Family Saga

Bk 1-Country Secrets
Bk 2-Doctor Attraction
Bk 3-Unlawful Attachment

Lockgrove Bay Series

(Reading order as listed)

Be Tempted Duet

Bk 1-Loathing Temptation
Bk 2 Wicked Temptation

Bay Hearts Duet

Bk 1 Wild Hearts

A Holiday Romance Duet

Bk 1-Take Flight

You don't have to defend or explain your decisions to anyone.
It's your life.
Live it without apologies
Mandy Hale

Author's Preface
v

Playlist
vi

Also by Caz May
vii

Chapter One
18

Chapter Two
22

Chapter Three
26

Chapter Four
30

Chapter Five
34

Chapter Six
39

Chapter Seven
42

Chapter Eight
50

Chapter Nine
54

Chapter Ten
60

Chapter Eleven
65

Chapter Twelve
69

Chapter Thirteen
74

Chapter Fourteen
81

Chapter Fifteen
87

Chapter Sixteen
91

Chapter Seventeen
94

Chapter Eighteen
102

Chapter Nineteen
107

ChapterTwenty
112

Chapter Twenty-One
115

ChapterTwenty-Two
119

Chapter Twenty-Three
124

Chapter Twenty-Four
128

ChapterTwenty-Five
134

Chapter Twenty-Six
140

Chapter Twenty-Seven
151

ChapterTwenty-Eight
155

Chapter Twenty-Nine
164

Chapter Thirty
174

Chapter Thirty-One
191

Chapter Thirty-Two
195

Chapter Thirty-Three
201

Chapter Thirty-Four
204

Chapter Thirty-Five
209

Chapter Thirty-Six
218

Chapter Thirty-Seven
224

Chapter Thirty-Eight
227

Chapter Thirty-Nine
233

Chapter Forty
238

Chapter Forty-One
244

Chapter Forty-Two
247

Chapter Forty-Three
251

Chapter Forty-Four
254

Chapter Forty-Five
260

Chapter Forty-Six
263

Chapter Forty-Seven
267

Chapter Forty-Eight
276

Chapter Forty-Nine
282

Chapter Fifty
287

Chapter Fifty-One
293

Chapter Fifty-Two
299

Chapter Fifty-Three
303

Chapter Fifty-Four
311

Chapter Fifty-Five
317

Chapter Fifty-Six
323

Chapter Fifty-Seven
327

Chapter Fifty-Eight
332

Chapter Fifty-Nine
339

Chapter Sixty
345

Chapter Sixty-One
349

Chapter Sixty-Two
354

Chapter Sixty-Three
358

Chapter Sixty-Four
368

Chapter Sixty-Five
377

Chapter Sixty-Six
381

Epilogue
385

Acknowledgements
391

Stalk Me
392

Chapter One

Ariel

Hearing Braeden scream at me in a bellowing voice, without any care, "You need to leave!" rips my heart out. Tears are prickling my cheeks and I want to cry out in pain, as it feels as though he's ripping my heart out of my chest and serving it up to his brother for his own sick pleasure.

I'm practically naked, and even though Braeden attempts to give me my clothes back I can't take them. I can't be here a second longer.

Clasping my bra closed at the front I run without looking back, straight out of the caravan park. I don't have my phone, remembering I left that at home today. I left everything else at school, thinking that I'd be there tomorrow but right now all I want to do is run home and climb into bed with mum and cry my heart out until it stops hurting.

As though the universe is against me, punishing me for running home in my underwear the sky erupts, pouring rain suddenly drenching my shivering body, as thunder shakes around me.

I hate being out in thunderstorms, scared that the lightning will strike me down. And it also creeps me out how eerily quiet the streets are as well. That could partly be from being on the scummier side of town though. I feel a pang in my heart that Braeden has to live here, and I wish I could do something to help him get away from his brother, but I shove the feelings down as the hurt of him pushing me away digs deeper. I still love him, but he's hurt me one time too many and made me cry. If he wants to push me away, then I'm going to push him away and try to shut him out of my heart and mind.

With the rain still pelting down on me, I wrap my arms around my frozen body as I keep running. Passing Back beach a car exits the carpark, flashing it's headlights at me before it pulls up beside me. Panicking I wipe an arm across my cheeks, focusing on the make of car in the dark in front

Caz May

of me. The driver gets out, rushing to my side before I can even take another step forward to run away.

Sighing I take a deep breath when my best friends arms wrap around me in a crushing, but welcoming hug.

"Ar's what are you doing out here in the rain?" he asks me, pulling back from the hug and cupping my cheeks in his palms. His gaze is intense, stirring up even more emotions in my confused mind and heart.

Letting out a loud sob I try to let words fall out of my mouth, but nothing comes out. Briston takes that as a cue, stepping back to open the passenger door of his jeep with one hand, holding my hand in his other.

He helps me in, kissing my forehead sweetly before he gets back into the drivers side.

Driving off, he looks at me out of the corner of his eye.

"Ar's, you gonna tell me what happened? You're in your damn underwear." His tone is angry, as though he's pissed off with my lack of words.

"Braeden and I slept together."

"That doesn't tell me why you're practically naked and running home in a damn storm, Ar's," Briston says in the same angry tone.

I gulp, not sure what I want to confess beyond that admission, but Briston's tone has me scared. Concern paints his pretty face as well.

"He kicked me out when his brother came home."

"Seriously Ariel. What the actual fuck?"

"I know, but his brother was really angry..."

"Don't make excuses for him, Ariel. He shouldn't have let you run out in your damn knickers."

Tamed Hearts

"I know, Bris," I say solemnly, putting my head down and letting the tears fall down my cheeks like rain cascading down outside the bubble of Briston's jeep.

For the rest of the drive back to mine, Briston is silent. I don't say anything either, and when he pulls up outside my house, I sniff back my tears. "Thanks for driving me home, Bris."

"Anytime, Ar's baby. I'll see you at school," he tells me with a soft smile. I get out of the car without another word, running towards the front door to not get drenched from the storm that's still raging. Thankfully the front door is unlocked, and I rush straight into mums room again, crawling into bed with her and crying my heart out.

Braeden has shattered the piece of my heart that was his.

Caz May

Chapter Two

Briston

Driving home after dropping Ariel off, I'm raging. My blood is boiling hot with pent up anger, and slamming down the accelerator I consider going to confront Braeden. The only thing stopping me though is not knowing where he lives. Ariel knows, but she wouldn't tell me now when I'm irate, and she's a wreck because of his actions. My heart is aching for my best friend, and pulling up in my driveway I hold back my scream of anguish and annoyance I want to let out.

Mum is in the kitchen, making something for dinner that smells utterly divine. She's such a good cook, and I honestly never go hungry.

Her glance rakes my body, my soaked t-shirt that's clinging to my abs.

"Hi, baby boy. Did you get caught in the rain?"

"Yeah, I had to give Ariel a ride home," I reply softly, swallowing the rest of the words I want to say. As usual mum can see right through my demeanour, knowing I'm upset and angry.

"Go wash up, baby boy. Dinner will be ready soon."

"Ok, is dad working tonight?" I ask, hoping she replies yes. I don't dislike my dad, but I need to talk to mum alone.

"Yes, he's head chef tonight," she informs me, slapping my butt with a tea towel as I head out of the kitchen to go to have a shower.

STRIPPING FROM MY WET CLOTHES I wait for the water to warm up, before slipping under the spray of water. As I wash away the salt and sand from my skin my mind is torturing me with angry thoughts of what I want to do to Braeden for hurting my Ariel.

I'm angry at myself for loving him too, and angry at Ariel for letting him in to hurt us both. When he hurts her, he hurts me in the process.

Caz May

Getting out of the shower, I feel a little calmer and get dressed into some check pj pants before I head back into the kitchen for dinner.

Inhaling the smell of mum's famous chicken pie, I sit down on a stool as she slides a plate to me and takes a seat herself. We never eat at the dining table when dad isn't home, and I like the intimate feeling just eating with mum in the kitchen gives me.

After swallowing a few mouthfuls she gives me a soft smile.

"So baby boy, is something bothering you?"

"Yeah, I'm really confused about my feelings. I love Ariel, but I love Braeden to, even though he's hurting us both."

"I'm not going to ask you for details, baby. But you need to trust your heart."

"Yeah, my heart is confused," I tell her and she smiles at me again.

"You're lucky to have found two loves in your life, but give them both some space."

"Why do you say that?" I ask worriedly.

"Well, dear, I don't know what's happened but it sounds like you all need to sort out your feelings for each other."

I finish up my food, lifting the plate to my chin, and licking it clean before I jump off the stool.

"I'm going to go to bed. Thank you for dinner, mum."

I'm about to head to my room when she says, "Bris baby?"

I turn my head back to look at her.

"Yeah, Mumma?"

Tamed Hearts

"I always knew you loved Ariel," she says sweetly before adding, "own your sexuality baby. You're graight!" Her tone is giddy, infectious laughter lingering.

I give her a side eye look.

"What's that mean?"

"Not gay, not straight," she informs me with the same chuckle in her tone. "Bisexual, my boy. And that's graight!"

I laugh then, rushing back to give her a quick hug.

"Awesome, Mumma. I love it and you."

I tell her, "Goodnight," as I kiss her on the cheek.

"Goodnight Bris, baby," she tells me with another sweet smile.

Heading up to bed, I fall against the mattress.

Closing my eyes I think about her words, feeling a mix of emotions that follow me into sleep.

I fell in love with two people, and my heart is breaking for them both.

Caz May

Chapter Three

BRAEDEN

Coming to I shake my head to make myself more aware of my surroundings.

I'm still in the caravan, but don't know how much time has passed.

My whole body aches, making me wonder what my brother had been doing to me whilst I was out cold.

Tamed Hearts

Carson is kicking me now, so I move back on the floor to try and get away from the toe of his boots. The steel toe blundstones are going to leave bruises on my skin.

He curses at me, "Get up fucker!"

I try to speak but only a gasp comes out, a raspy gasp from my hoarse throat. I force myself to swallow hard.

"You're a piece of shit little brother," Carson tells me with a menacing laugh.

Stumbling to my feet, I groan, finding my voice.

"Fuck off Carson," I spit at him. "You're the only piece of shit around here."

He chuckles loudly, filling the whole caravan with his heinous laughter.

"I'm not the fucking dipshit bringing a girl here. At least I fuck broads on the down-low." His words disgust me, making my stomach twist.

"She's not just a girl arsehole," I again spit angrily at my older brother, invading his personal space.

"What? She's your girlfriend?" he questions with the same menacing laugh.

I shake my head, confused with my own thoughts.

"Well, no...but I'm in love with her," I tell Carson, even though I feel like a complete idiot at my admission.

"Seriously little brother," he replies, scoffing at me, and shaking his head. "Grow the fuck up. Love is for weak men."

I'm not sure if he's referring to anyone specifically or about love in general but I reply, "Dad wasn't weak, Carson. And he loved us."

Carson is almost laughing again, replying, "Whatever," with a callous uncaring tone that has me in knots, worried

Caz May

he knows something I don't. "At least tell me you wrapped ya wang?"

Biting down on my lip, I shake my head remembering back to being with Ariel. I know I didn't put on a condom, too wrapped up in the heat of the moment of finally getting to be with her and I stupidly came inside her.

"Oh fuck, dipshit," Carson practically bellows. "You better hope she's infertile because us Chappell men sure as hell are good for spreading our seed." He cackles then.

"You're such an arsehole!" I shout at him, shaken up by his consistent cackling.

"I'll own it, but daddy wasn't as innocent as you think Braeden," he tells me a little more calmly which rattles me.

"What's that supposed to fucking mean?" I question. He clearly knows something I don't about our family.

"Dig little brother," he tells me with the same eerily calm tone. "You might not like the answers. And lay low until you look like a human again."

"Or what?" I goad him.

"You don't want to find out," he threatens, before adding, "I'm going out for a deal."

He leaves without another word between us and groaning I lie down in bed, shifting from side to side to get comfortable.

My ribs and stomach ache, stabbing pain gripping me as I move.

My phone is on the bed beside me, having fallen out of my pants pocket when I took them off with Ariel. I want to text her, but the look in her eyes when she left shattered me and I honestly don't think she'll want to hear from me.

Tamed Hearts

Instead, I text Briston, hoping he'll answer and not push me away.

BRO I NEED YOU

Go fuck yourself. You hurt her.

I don't know what to reply back to that. Clearly Ariel has seen him, or is with him. And I'm alone.

Pulling the sheets up to my chin, I can still smell Ariel on them.

Inhaling the sweet scent of the girl I love, I close my eyes, letting tears slip down my cheeks as I cry myself to sleep.

Caz May

Chapter Four

Ariel

For the last few days—since I left Braeden's van in the rain—I've been in bed, under the covers bawling my eyes out.

I'm completely broken by Braeden pushing me away.

Nothing has ever hurt this much, and all I want to do is tear into my flesh to feel something other than my heart

Tamed Hearts

being ripped out of my damn chest, every damn time I think of him.

I've texted him but he hasn't replied, and that tears at my broken heart even more because even though I'm angry and broken from his actions, I'm worried about him. I want to see him—confront him—but I'm scared to go there. The bruise his brother inflicted with his harsh touch is still on my hip, still sore and my stomach is throbbing with the cut's I've inflicted on myself. They hadn't taken away the pain like I'd hoped they would, and I want to cut more, to bleed out and not wake up to more of this nightmare.

I'm angry with myself for falling in love with Braeden as well. I knew it was a bad idea, but my stupid wild heart took me down.

MY ALARM BLARES, waking me up to again tell me it's a school day. The thought of going to school, and possibly seeing Braeden has my stomach in knots. But it's also aching today for a completely different reason, that I'm beyond fucking thankful for.

Period cramps are shoving my insides around and rushing to the dunny I've never been gladder to see blood in my knickers. I was scared after realising I'd fucked Braeden without a condom. And Bris as well.

Getting back in bed,I pull the covers back over my head, only to have them pulled off completely barely a minute later when Bris barges in.

He pulls me out of bed, much to my own reluctance.

He glares at me.

Caz May

"You have to come to school, Ar's."

I groan in frustration.

"Don't want to. Don't want to see him," I reply belligerently.

Briston scoffs at me, guffawing before he replies, "He hasn't been at school. And if he was he'd meet my fists."

I laugh at him then. Laughing feels so good.

"You hit like a girl, Bris."

"Still," Briston defends. "He hurt you Ar's, which means he hurt me."

Defensively I plead with him, "But Briston. You weren't there. His brother..."

Again he laughs, throwing my spare uniform at me from where it's been discarded over my desk chair. A pang of longing hits me, as I remember that my other uniform is still at Braeden's. Gulping down my feelings I sniff back my tears when Briston says cheekily, "Get dressed. We'll be late."

Quickly putting my clothes on and grabbing my bag I've barely got my shoes on before Briston is dragging me out the door to his jeep.

The tears are still stinging my eyes and Briston gives me a concerned look as he starts the engine to drive away.

"Ar's you ok?"

I shake my head, sniffing back the tears. "No...I...love... him and he won't reply to my messages."

Briston blushes, biting his lip, and muttering, "That might be my fault. I told him to go fuck himself."

"Bris! Why?!" I shriek at him, annoyed.

"He let you run out into the storm at night in your underwear Ariel," Briston replies angrily.

Tamed Hearts

"Because of his brother," I defend. "I don't think he meant his words to me."

"I don't believe you," Briston says. "I'm going to protect you from his secrets Ariel," he tells me with a caring tone that I don't like. I don't want him to be all protective best friend.

Angrily I request of him, "Let me out of the car Briston."

"We aren't at school yet," he tells me, stating the obvious.

He pulls up the car on the curb, and opening the door I tell my best friend, "I'm walking. I don't want to be around you right now."

About to slam the door as I get out I scream at him, "You're heartless, Briston!"

He watches me getting out of his car, not saying a word.

"I hate you right now Briston." I give him an up yours and he drives off, skidding the tyres on the road.

I start walking to school, thinking about Braeden and how much I still love him. I'm still desperately in love with Briston too but they both hurt me. The urge to cut to let out the emotions is plaguing me again.

Feeling in the tiny pocket of my skirt I get out the razor blade I've tucked in there. It's cold against the palm of my hand, and the edge is sharp when I slice my palm with it.

Hurting myself is the only thing that feels right.

Caz May

Chapter Five

Drake

*D*riving to school, I spot Ariel walking slowly and scuffing her feet. She's looking down at the ground, clenching her fists and clearly seems as though she's sad about something and has been crying.

Pulling up at the curb, I let the window down. Leaning over the console, I question her loudly, "Ariel, do you need a ride?"

"No, leave me alone," she snaps at me, not even battering an eyelid or turning to look at me.

Serendipitously a thunderclap reverberates around us, rain starting to drizzle.

"It's starting to rain," I yell to her. "You'll freeze."

"Good," she snaps again, wrapping her arms around her body tighter.

Putting the car in park I get out as more thunder erupts around us.

Running up to her, I plead, "Please Ariel, just get in the car. You can tell me what's upset you."

She sobs, sniffing back her tears. Seeing her upset tugs at my heart, my heart that is still hers, still broken for her.

Without thinking I pull her into hug, that she doesn't refuse. Her sobs meet my shoulder, and pulling back a little so I can see her face my heart breaks all over again. I wish I could kiss her to make her feel better but I know I shouldn't because i'd gone on a date with Polly and honestly I like her.

That doesn't stop the crazy beating of my heart right now, my feelings for Ariel still apparent and hitting me in the chest like a lightning bolt at seeing her so sad.

The rain starts coming down harder, pelting us with icy cold droplets.

Ariel breaks the hug, stepping back and giving me a soft smile.

"I guess a ride is needed," she says as she steps towards my car.

Following I'm being all gentlemanly, opening the door for her to get in.

As we drive off she says softly, "Thanks for this, Drake."

Caz May

"Anytime Ariel. We might have broken up but I still care about you," I tell her adding in my head, *'Actually, I still love you.'*

"Yeah," Ariel mutters still sniffing back tears.

"You want to share why you're crying and walking to school in the rain?" I ask, hoping I don't upset her more.

"I um...had a fight with Briston," she tells me letting out an almost wail.

"Oh yeah, that's shit. What about?"

She shrinks back into the seat, crossing her arms over her chest and turning to look out the window when she mumbles, "Um...it was about...um..."

Touching her thigh, I gaze at her out of the corner of my eye.

"It's cool. You don't have to tell me if you don't want to."

"No, I need to tell someone."

I give her a sweet smile.

"Ok, lay it on me," I tease with a laugh.

"It was about Braeden," she tells me, looking across at me again with a frown. "He pushed him away, and Braeden isn't talking to me. I miss him so bad. I feel like my heart has been ripped out."

"That sucks, Ariel. I'm sorry, but neither of them are worth your tears."

"I know, but Briston is my best friend and he completely disregarded my feelings. That hurts just as much."

"Yeah, I don't know what I can say to make you feel better, but it will work out I'm sure."

Tamed Hearts

"I know. Just wish getting my heart broken didn't hurt so much."

I laugh, knowing exactly how heartbreak feels because she broke my heart a few months ago.

"I feel you. You broke my heart, but it gets better. Hearts heal."

Ariel smiles at me then, sighing when she replies, "I'm sorry Drake. I never meant to hurt you. I hope you find a girl who loves you completely."

I can't help but smile, chuckling softly and blushing when I answer, "Yeah, I'm...um...I just started seeing someone."

Ariel's face lights up.

"Ooo, who? Tell me. Do I know her?"

"Yeah, probably. It's Polly Baker."

"Oh Drake, she's a sweetie. Really smart and talented. She's in my art class."

"Yeah, it's new, but I like her. Don't tell anyone yet, please."

"My lips are sealed, and yours too about my boys."

"Of course. And we're friends still yeah?"

"Of course. Thanks again for the ride," she says, leaning over to kiss me on the cheek when we pull up at school.

"Do you need a ride home after school?"

"Yeah, that would be great. Thanks, Drake. Have a good day."

She grabs her bag and gets out of the car, heading inside the school gate, passing Polly who's waiting for me. She gives Polly a smile.

Caz May

Getting out of the car myself I casually walk up to Polly. She's seething when I step closer to her for a kiss.

"Why did Ariel get out of your car?" she questions me, with a sassy tone.

"I just gave her a ride, because of the storm. That's all, Pol. I promise."

"So nothing happened?"

"No, Pol. I like you. And I have a date planned for Friday you're going to love."

"Ok, I trust you. But only cause you're cute," she teases me with a giggle. I give her a quick kiss, a peck that's just a brush of our lips for a moment. It gives me butterflies that both scare and excite me.

"You going to sit with me at lunch today still?" I ask excitedly.

"You betcha," she sing songs when the bell goes, and she skips off waving at me with a cheeky smile.

Walking into school, I think about my feelings. This morning has shown me I'm definitely still in love with Ariel, but things are looking up with Polly. She gives me the butterflies I haven't felt in forever, and I love her cheeky sassiness. I'm not ready to completely out us as a couple, but I like having her around and this time I'm not going to go all guns blazing. Polly will have to prove she wants me before I jump on the commitment train.

Chapter Six

BRAEDEN

Heading into school for the first time in about a week, I'm trying to tamp down my intense anger from the way Carson has been treating me. He's been hurling angry words at me, lashing out at me whilst high and nearly

Caz May

beating me again. I'd slept outside in the locked car so he couldn't get to me the last few nights.

I SPOT ARIEL AT HER LOCKER. Just one look at her is tearing my heart out. I want her so much but it hurts to even look at her. This past week all I've thought about is her, how much I love her and miss her. Living without her is literal hell on earth, but after everything that happened I know I can't be with her.

With my arms full of books for first period, I'm not looking where I'm going when I feel someone step into my personal space. The breath I've just taken in is stolen from my lungs, when I look up to find Ariel confronting me. The bell hasn't rung and she pulls me into a classroom with a firm grip on my arm. I'm so shocked I'd let her willingly take me anywhere, even if it was to jump off a cliff together.

Inhaling a deep breath she says softly, "I...miss you Brae."

I don't say anything as I put my books down on the desk behind her, stepping into her personal space. The tension in the air is buzzing with us being so close again. And I need to be closer to her, even if I'm going to get burnt.

I kiss her, feeling suddenly overwhelmed by how much I love her. The kiss is brief.

I want more—so much more—but I pull back, breaking the kiss.

I curse at her, "Stop, little bitch, just fucking stop."

"Why Brae?" she questions me, anguish on her beautiful face that breaks my heart. "I love you and you keep pushing me away."

Tamed Hearts

"Because I have to. We can't be together."

Tears break through that she's been holding back and she mutters through her sobs, "Are you telling me you don't love me?"

Cupping her cheeks I resist the urge to kiss her again.

"Of course I fucking love you. So much that pushing you away is completely shattering me."

"Then stop pushing me away."

"I can't. I have to," I defend with as much conviction as I can muster. I need her to hear me.

Her eyes are streaked with unshed tears, and even though it's stupid—reckless—I kiss her again, murmuring against her lips.

"One last kiss, please darling," I murmur against her lips, making her give in and kiss me harder as though she can't get enough and will never kiss me again. That thought completely shatters me.

The bell goes and when the door flies open I callously shove her away yelling, "Fuck off little bitch! Leave me alone!"

Ariel is cut, sobbing as she runs out the door, giving me an angry glare that cuts me deep.

Again I broke my heart but this time it's gone out the door with her. Ariel has my heart in her hands. It's wild and I want her to tame it. I need her to fix my broken heart.

Caz May

Chapter Seven

Ariel

Running to art after the bell I'm in tears. I feel like cutting. Miss Canning sees me when I come in a little later than usual. She gives me a worried look, asking, "Ariel, are you ok?"

"No...he...my...he..." I stutter out the words through my tears.

Tamed Hearts

She pulls me aside, so my classmates can't listen in to the conversation.

"Calm down, hun. Tell me what's wrong."

Miss Canning is glaring at me, like she's concerned. I don't want to say Braeden's name, because it hurts to much, but also because despite how much he's hurt me I don't want to throw him under the bus and get him in trouble.

"He doesn't love me," I blurt out sniffing back the tears still stinging my eyes.

"Well, hun, I don't know who he is but if he doesn't love you and you love him he doesn't deserve your tears or your heart."

"I know Miss Canning, but it still hurts that he's being so cruel."

"Yeah boys suck," she says to me with a chuckle and a caring smile.

"Yeah, thanks Miss C. Could I go to sickbay?"

"Yeah, tell Ms Tanner you've got girl problems and go home. Have a treat yourself day."

I want to hug her, but give her a smile instead as I head out of the classroom.

AT HOME, in the bath, spooning mint choc chip ice cream into my mouth straight from the tub. The warm water is soothing, but it's not taking away the thoughts of cutting. The thoughts of bleeding out in the bath like I nearly did all those years ago. I hate feeling so many emotions, hate that even though he's being a complete bastard to me I still love Braeden desperately. His kisses from this morning are still

Caz May

on replay in my mind and I don't want to believe his words are true.

Getting out of the bath I quickly dry off, trudging to my bedroom in just a towel. As I'm getting dressed into some pj's I text him, fully prepared to be cursed out or for no reply to come.

I don't believe that you don't love me

Surprisingly his reply is instant, but it still shocks me.

I HATE YOU LITTLE BITCH. FUCKING YOU MEANT NOTHING TO ME.

I DON'T REPLY BUT burst into tears, throwing my phone on the bed. In a daze I'm startled by the doorbell reverberating through the house.

I'm not expecting anyone, and dad never forgets his key, so I'm kinda panicking, wondering if I should even go to open the door.

Swallowing that panic down I go to the front door, taking in a deep breath as I open it slowly to find Briston standing on the threshold.

Looking at my best friend on my doorstep after our fight last week breaks me. I'm still angry at him, but I'm hurting and still crying tears that won't stop.

He fixes his gaze on mine. "Aww, Ar's, don't cry. I'm sorry."

"I know Bris. I'm not upset with you," I tell him, even though it's only half the truth. I honestly can't stay mad at my best friend.

"Brae? Did he hurt you?" Briston questions, shuffling side to side on the balls of his feet.

"Well, yeah, but no..." I mumble, not ready to tell Briston that Braeden kissed me again, let alone shoved me away without a care.

"I'll kill him Ar's," Briston threatens. "Tell me what he did."

"Come inside first. It's freezing."

Briston follows me inside to my bedroom and taking his hand I pull him down to the bed with me.

He doesn't say anything as he wraps his arms around me to hold me close.

I love being close to him, feeling the warmth of his body, knowing that he's the one person that has always cared about me. Being with Briston has never been complicated, even when we were figuring out how we truly felt about each other and crossing that line from best friends to more.

"Bris, can we just be together. I need you."

He shifts on the bed a little, glaring at me.

"You sure you don't wanna talk about it?"

"No, I just want to feel and forget for awhile."

"Yeah, I get you," he tells me softly, before telling me the words I'll never tire from hearing him say, "I love you Ar's."

"I love you too Bris, but please stop talking and just kiss me."

Caz May

Briston doesn't hesitate, rolling over so he's on top of me, and kissing me. As our lips meet, I play with his lip ring with my tongue, biting down on it and making him murmur against my lips.

I can feel his dick hardening against my belly, and breaking the kiss I gaze up at him with a smile. "Bris, I want to feel you inside me."

"Fuck Ar's, really?" he asks, taking his lip ring in between his teeth.

"Yeah, please Briston," I beg, adding a moan as I sit up and pull off my pj top, throwing it on the floor.

He groans, leaning over my body to kiss my boobs. Licking my nipples, his lip brushes across my sensitive skin, and I can't help but moan from the pleasure that pulses through me.

Gazing over my body, he frowns a moment, questioning me, "Have you been cutting again, Ar's?"

"Yeah," I admit, feeling guilty and crossing my arms over my stomach.

"Ariel, baby, it breaks my heart that you do that to your beautiful body."

"I'm sorry, Bris," I tell him, before pulling him down to kiss me again by grabbing his luscious hair in my fist.

"Do you really think I'm beautiful?" I ask as a whisper against his lips.

He gives me a soft kiss before replying, "Absolutely Ariel. You're the only girl I'd ever call beautiful, and I love you."

I giggle, cupping his cheeks and kissing him again.

"Make love to me, Briston," I whisper to him.

Tamed Hearts

Again he groans, moving on the bed a little so he can yank off his t-shirt. I moan, admiring his perfect abs and the smatter of hair that leads right into his trackies.

"You're perfection Briston," I tell him, as he slides my pj pants down, leaving me completely exposed to him.

"Back at you, baby," he jeers, before pulling his trackies off over his hips, and kicking them off at his ankles. His dick is hard, and I tease him, "I think you like kissing me, Bris."

"I fucking love kissing you, Ar's."

"Yeah, and what else do you like doing, Briston?" I taunt him with a wicked sweet smile. He shifts on the bed, lining up the tip of his dick with my clit. He teases me, rubbing the tip over my sensitive spot.

"Being inside you," he teases, sliding down and entering me.

Falling against me, he starts rocking his hips in and out in a slow, steady rhythm that feels incredible. Again cupping his cheeks I pull his lips to mine, to kiss him as our bodies rock together in bliss.

Nothing even comes close to the feeling of having sex with my best friend. Not even cutting gives me this kinda pleasure, and this feeling is all I need.

Breaking the kiss, I moan loudly, as Briston looks down at me, thrusting deeper inside me.

"Harder, Bris," I say, moaning as he pumps his dick harder and faster into me.

"Fuck, Ariel, fuck you feel so good around my dick," he curses out loudly, kissing me again.

My body starts to tremble, and I can feel Briston pulsing inside me as he gets close to letting go.

Caz May

"Fuck, Ariel. I'm coming," he calls out, about to pull out when my release hits me with a sudden shake, keeping Briston inside me as we come together.

He rolls off and lays down beside me, completely silent except for his panting breaths. I roll onto my side, and touch his cheek to turn his gaze to me.

His expression is worried, and confused.

"Bris? What's wrong?"

"Why didn't you let me pull out, Ar's?"

It's a good question. We didn't use a condom, and I'm not on the pill yet.

"I...ar...wanted to feel you come inside me, and I was coming too. It just felt so good."

"Yeah, but Ar's you could get pregnant."

"I won't Bris. My period just finished."

"Ok, I guess. Maybe I could lick your pussy? Suck it out." His tone is serious, and my body tingles at the thought.

"Really?" I question.

"Yeah, Ar's. Sit on my face, baby." His eyes light up with the words, sparkling like sapphires.

Moving so I'm straddling his waist, Briston grabs my hips, guiding my body so my vag is over his lips. He doesn't give me a moment to think before he's sucking my clit, his whole mouth over my sensitive spot, kissing and licking every last drop of our come. He's moaning and it makes his lips vibrate against my vag lips, as his tongue darts in and out.

Pulling back a moment he licks his lips and says, "Fucking delicious, baby."

Tamed Hearts

I don't even get to voice a reply, before he's biting my clit again, licking me again. It feels so good, and makes me rock my pelvis over his chin to fuck his tongue.

"Fuck, Bris, I'm going to come," I call out, my thighs shaking as I start to tremble with my release. Briston keeps licking me, lapping up every last drop of my come until my trembling subsidies and I climb off to lie beside him again.

He smiles at me, once more licking his lips, rolling his tongue over his lip ring.

Murmuring I kiss him, tasting my come on his lips as I deepen the kiss.

He breaks the kiss, gazing at me as he gets out of bed.

"I should probably go before your dad gets home," he declares with a grin.

"Yeah, probably. He'll kill you if he finds you naked in my bed."

Rising to my knees he kisses me once more before he gets dressed. "I love you Bris. Thanks for making me forget for awhile."

"Anytime Ar's. I love you too."

I watch him walk out of my room, as I put my pj's back on and snuggle under the covers. I honestly still love Braeden, but right now I'd be happy just being with Briston.

Caz May

Chapter Eight

Briston

After leaving Ariel's last night, all I've thought about is how angry I am at Braeden for hurting her; again. It seems as though that's all the cunt can do. I probably shouldn't call him that, even in my mind, but I'm so angry my thoughts are menacing. I could kill him, whack him hard on the back of the head with my surfboard.

I don't really want to kill him, but...well I could. Today, even being out in the surf isn't calming me down, like usual. And as I stand on my board, catching a killer wave my eyes lock on a figure running along the foreshore.

Curse the fucker for looking so damn sexy in grey trackies and a black ripped tank top. All his clothes—other than his school uniform—seem like they're ripped. It makes me wonder about Braeden sometimes.

Riding the wave into shore, I tuck my board under my arm and sprint up the sand to catch him.

"Braeden!" I call out angrily. He stops in his tracks, panting as he puts his hands on his knees and turns to look at me. My traitorous mind goes straight to the gutter, thinking about him panting as I fuck him.

I can't be thinking of that now when I need to give him a piece of my mind about hurting Ariel.

Standing up straight, he's staring me down, following me to the Jeep when I don't say anything else.

"Briston, what's up man?"

"What's up?!" I bellow at him, standing my surfboard up and leaning against it. "What's up is you hurting Ariel for the hundredth fucking time!"

"I'm sorry, Bris. I didn't intentionally hurt her. And she won't let me explain."

His apology seems sincere, but it's not me that needs to hear it. I'm not going to let him near her.

He leans forward trying to kiss me but I push him away, my hands failing out in front of me as my surfboard falls

Caz May

forward. I don't catch it--in time--and the edge hits Braeden's head, just above his eyebrow.

"Fuck man, you trying to kill me?" he curses at me, as the surfboard falls, bumping the back of his head before it hits the ground with a thud beside our feet.

"No, but I fucking thought about it. I'm so cut at you for the way you treated Ariel."

"I said I'm fucking sorry. What more do you want from me, man?"

"I don't know. Not some half-arsed apology, especially because you've been ignoring us for weeks."

His face falls, his hair flopping in his eyes when he looks down at the ground.

"Some shit is happening, Bris," he tells me, forlorn. I'm still angry, but his words cut deep. My damn heart is still in love with the sexy fucker, and it aches for him, seeing him broken.

"Please, man. I need you," he admits with a throaty groan that excites my aching dick and makes me ache for him. But I can't go there now. Not after everything with my best friend, who I love—honestly—even more than I love Braeden.

"I can't Braeden," I tell him, bending down to pick up my surfboard.

Standing back up I'm in his personal space, the temptation to kiss him hanging in the air. But I don't, instead, I say right against his face, "You hurt our girl. We're fucking done!"

He stumbles back then, sniffs and walks away without another word.

Tamed Hearts

Shoving my surfboard in the back of the jeep I get in, spark the ignition and gun it home, sniffing back the tears that are threatening to release from my eyes.

I will not cry over him.

I'm a dude, and I will not fucking cry over another dude.

Chapter Nine

Drake

*S*econd dates are even scarier than first dates, especially with a girl like Polly. A month or so ago, our first date was with my friends around, and not really an actual proper date as I didn't even pick her up from her house. I'm facing that prospect now, parking outside her house—the mayor's house—to pick her up, with my erratic nervous heartbeat in my throat.

Grabbing the gerberas I got for her from the seat beside me, I tentatively get out of the car, sauntering up to the front door whilst psyching myself up to possibly face meeting her dad officially.

Instead, before I can reach the door and knock, it swings open and Polly is sashaying across the porch towards me, looking absolutely gorgeous.

She's wearing a little—very little—as in a short little black dress with long sleeves that just hide her underwear. It's skin tight, with a v-neckline that shows the perfect amount of cleavage. Her caramel tinged chocolate hair is down, in waves that frame her face, and on her feet highlighting her sexy long legs she has black patent stilettos.

I know fashion, having my older sister sit me down to be her audience for her pretend model shows as kids. I miss Marissa with her living in the city with her husband now. All the more reason to get out of Lockgrove Bay at the end of the year. It honestly can't come sooner, with all the memories of my constant fuck up's with girls everywhere I go.

Polly is now standing in front of me, smiling sweetly as I hand her the flowers. I'm at a loss for words because she really does look stunning.

"Hey Drake, you look nice," she coos at me, looking me up and down to take in my outfit of double denim coupled with a white t-shirt.

Finding my voice, I stammer, "You are...a...knockout...Pol."

Caz May

"Thanks, just an old outfit, but it's a fave."

I mentally kick myself in the guts to stop being a damn idiot around a pretty girl. This isn't my first date.

"It looks great on you. Are you ready to go?"

"Yeah, so ready," she replies with a cheeky smile.

Taking her hand, I lead her to my car and open the door for her to get in. She mutters a courteous thanks as I close the door once she's daintily slid her legs inside, keeping them tightly together to not give me even a glimpse of her knickers. The dress is so tight I wonder if she's wearing a g-string underneath.

Getting in the car myself, and driving away my mind starts wandering to my last date with Ariel.

I'd fallen for Ariel on that date—kissing her on the Ferris wheel—even though it was weeks later that I told her how I felt, only for her to stomp on my heart.

I shouldn't be thinking of her, not now, or at all now things are starting to happen with Polly. She deserves my focus to be on her.

"Where are we going?" Polly asks, a little worried murmur in her voice.

I give her a cheeky smirk, my eyes just darting to her from the road for a moment when I reply, "Just wait until we get there, miss impatient."

"Fine, Mr no fun." She pouts, huffing and biting down on her lip. It's kinda sexy, a little thing that always gets to me, no matter what girl is doing the teasing gesture.

The thoughts that start running through my mind are dirty, and I'm stressing myself out that I'm going to use Polly and break her heart.

Tamed Hearts

ONCE AT THE BEACH MARKET, I take Polly's hand as I help her out of the car. She stumbles on the gravel, falling into my arms and laughing giddily.

"You caught me," she says with a laugh. "Can't half tell I don't wear heels."

"Sure, but I bet you just wanted an excuse to be close to me," I tease, smirking at her, whilst kicking myself in the guts mentally for being so flirtatious.

Words like that are going to get me in trouble.

Polly Baker is sassy, and she'll meet me tit for tat with teasing me.

Already I've got butterflies in my damn stomach from being near her, and they scare the damn shit out of me.

I can't let another girl in.

I can't fall for another girl, even one who seems to be falling for me.

Stepping back and closing my car door, I take her hand and lead her towards the market stalls. It's abuzz with people, enjoying the balmy evening.

There's not a cloud in the sky, and gazing at Polly as we weave between the crowd my heart leaps a little in my chest. Her smile is wide, as she takes in the stalls, one selling vintage clothing, and all manner of jewellery.

"Oh my gosh, Drake, look at this bracelet?" she coos, holding up a leather woven bracelet with a heart charm on it. "It's so simple but pretty," she continues with a smile.

"Get it," I encourage with a smile back.

"I don't have any cash on me," she tells me with a pout that breaks me.

Caz May

"Let me get it for you," I reply, grabbing my wallet out of my back pocket before I can take back my offer.

"You don't have to do that, Drake. It's fine," she tells me, still pouting.

"I want to," I tell her, handing over the twenty dollar note to the stall holder.

Polly slips the bracelet on her wrist, her whole face lighting up in the most beautiful smile.

Shoving my wallet back in my pocket, my heart leaps when she leans up to kiss me on the cheek.

"Thank you, Drake. You aren't always a dick."

"Good to know, Pol," I jeer, reaching for her hand again as we browse more of the stalls.

She's so happy she's bouncing on her heels, shrieking and smiling as she looks at more stalls.

Reaching the end, I pull her close for a hug, loving how her body feels against mine.

Polly is sassy, but still has an innocence about her. I know she's had a boyfriend before, but I've also heard the gossip that Polly didn't put out, and Marco broke up with her because she wouldn't sleep with him.

Polly has kissed me, and damn...but I'm not going to sleep with her or anyone until I leave Lockgrove Bay.

HEADING ACROSS THE SAND to take a walk along the beach before I take her home, she gives me another sweet smile, softly speaking, "Thanks for tonight Drake. This has been a really nice date."

As she says the words, she stumbles with her heels digging into the sand.

Tamed Hearts

Before I can stop her fall, she's on her butt on the sand, her legs in the air for a moment before her back hits the sand too, and she screams out in annoyance.

I'm holding in my laugh, and telling my dick to calm down from seeing the glimpse of her seamless knickers underneath her dress.

Her cheeks colour. She's absolutely mortified as I outstretch a hand to help pull her to her feet.

Again her body crashes into mine, and she mutters, "Did anyone see? That was so embarrassing."

"No one saw," I tell her with a smirk.

"Thank god, I thought for sure I'd shown everyone at the beach my knickers.

Looking straight into her eyes on mine, I slip my hand under the hem of her dress to between her thighs when I tease, "Well, actually I did, and damn Polly."

Again she blushes and giggles as I crash my lips to hers for a delicious, dick jolting kiss. Deepening it, my fingers brush over the seam of her pussy, finding she's wet for me. It scares and excites me, and pulling back I lift my finger to her lips. Cheekily she licks it, and steps back from me.

"Don't get ideas, Mr touchy feely."

"Of course not, Miss wet knickers." She gives me a cheeky up yours, bending down to yank her heels off her feet before running off down the beach, holding them in a tight grip.

She looks back at me smiling and following I can't help but smile.

Polly Baker is sure something.

Caz May

Chapter Ten

BRAEDEN

This feeling that's overwhelming me is utter bullshit.
The two people I love the most in this fucked up world
have brushed me off, discarding me as though I meant
nothing to them and it hurts like a fucking punch to the
guts, like Carson has laid into me with his fists.

I still want to talk to Ariel—and Briston—but they're ignoring me, giving me cold stares when they see me in the hallways at school.

It's breaking my heart and fuelling anger inside me that I need to release. I've been wanking so much thinking of them both, that when Carson caught me out he chastised me, telling me my dick would fall off.

I need that release to be a root. A release without feelings. Too bad I don't really want to fuck anyone other than Ariel and Briston.

And for fucks sake I now have a hard on at school for everyone to see whilst I'm at my locker.

Pushing my pelvis against the cold metal I take a deep breath to calm myself, sensing when someone steps up behind me.

A waft of coconut shampoo assaults my nostrils as I exhale, and turning around, slamming my locker shut behind me I'm staring down Chastity *'fucks every guy'* Rogers.

"Hi Braeden," she coos at me, with a sweet flirty smile as she twirls a blonde ringlet in her fingers.

"Um, hi Chastity. Do you mind moving?"

She giggles, reaching down between us to cup my dick in her hand.

"I could but then everyone would see your hard on, Braeden."

"I'll take my chances," I tell her, pushing my back against the locker.

I've got nowhere to go, as she steps closer to me, caging me in.

Caz May

"You could do that or I could help you do something about it."

Her hazel eyes glow with her words, and even though I know it's stupid her suggestion isn't turning my guts.

Chastity isn't my Ariel, but she's pretty with plump kissable lips and her eyes are begging me to take her curvaceous body for a ride.

"I don't know if that's a good idea, Chasity. I'm in love with someone else."

Again she giggles, making her whole body that's still pressed against mine vibrate.

"Look Braeden, I've noticed you around. You're a sexy guy, and I want to fuck you." She says the last words against my lips, begging me to consider her brazen offer of sex.

I've heard the rumours, that she's a damn good root. And before I can tell my mind it's stupid, I'm kissing her. I'm fucking kissing the school slut in the middle of the hallway. But who the fuck cares?

She murmurs against my lips, before pulling back from the kiss and giving me a sexy smirk.

"Is that a yes?"

I nod, mentally kicking myself in the guts as I reply, "Your place?"

"You bet, gorgeous," she says flirtatiously as she takes my hand and leads me out of the school.

I gaze at her arse as she walks in front of me, dragging me.

Her pleated school skirt is so short I can practically see her pussy covered by lacy knickers.

Maybe fucking her won't be so bad.

The girl is hot.

❤

GETTING TO CHASITY'S HOUSE on the posh side of town after a rather awkward drive in her Audi A5 I'm feeling out of sorts, wondering if I should be even doing what I'm about to.

A kiss is one thing, but actually fucking another girl feels like I'm betraying Ariel. But then again, she's no doubt fucking Briston still.

Chasity hauls me inside hastily, we're barely through the front door before she's kissing me as though she wants to eat me alive.

I don't like a girl taking charge, but Chasity kissing me like a she devil on a mission is turning me on.

Clearly I need a root more than I thought.

Breaking the kiss, she starts to strip out of her school uniform, all the while her eyes on mine.

Once down to her underwear she giggles, sashaying up the stairs and looking back at me, just begging me to follow her.

I could leave, and run home or to Ariel's or Briston's but my dick is aching for release and Chasity is offering herself to me for a fuck and dump. I'd be an idiot to walk away from that.

Running up the stairs behind her, I stalk into her bedroom and she beckons me towards her bed she's sitting on, holding up a condom in her fingers.

Stumbling forward I undo my belt, pushing my slacks down to my feet.

Caz May

She stands up, sliding her knickers off and stepping closer to me to kiss me.

Breaking the kiss, I shrug off my blazer, leaving my shirt on as I shove her against the bed, snatching the condom from her fingers.

Opening it I sheath my dick, not even bothering to take my boxers off.

Chastity pulls me down by the neck for another kiss as I slide inside her pussy, starting to fuck her hard.

I'm regretting every thrust, but it's sex, and that's all that matters in this moment. I'll deal with the regret later.

I just need release.

Chapter Eleven

BRAEDEN

After soccer training, I hang back practising some drills when I spot Ava stalking across the soccer pitch towards me, with a scowl on her face as though she's set to murder me for something.

Stopping my drills with my foot on the ball I give her a smile, before I greet her, "Hey Ava, what's up?"

"What's up? What's up is you sticking your dick in Chasity *'fucks every guy'* Rogers."

Caz May

"How'd you find that out?" I ask, guilt and regret consuming me.

"The dirty bitch was bragging about it at lunch."

"Shit, I...fuck," I mutter under my breath.

"Does Ariel know? Was she there?"

"Thankfully not, but Braeden that was low."

I chuckle, trying to damp down my guilt. I don't even know what to say, as I've basically already admitted my guilt so no denying it now.

"Ariel loves you, Braeden, and will be distraught if she finds out."

I'm doubting that Ariel still loves me after the last few weeks. I'd hate me if the shoe was on the other foot. Without a doubt though—even after my fuck up with Chasity—I still love my little bitch.

"I know, I love her too but I'm not good enough for her," I tell Ava and she scoffs at me but doesn't say anything.

"And it's complicated because if I want Ariel I..." I can't finish the sentence. I'm not sure I should be admitting anything else to Ava, despite how good of a friend she's been to me.

"That's bullshit Braeden," she grunts at me. "And what do you mean by it's complicated?"

"I can't tell you," I retort, wanting this conversation to be over.

"Come on Brae, it's me. You know I won't tell anyone."

"Promise?" I question with my heart hammering in my chest.

"Of course my lips are sealed," Ava reassures me, giving me her sweet friendly smile.

Tamed Hearts

Not able to meet her eyes I mutter, "I...um...slept with Briston as well and we've all being together." I can't believe the words are out of my mouth, that I've admitted to not only being with a guy but having a threesome.

"So a threesome?" Ava enquires, with a quirk of her lips. She doesn't seem bothered by the prospect at all, which calms me and I reply, "Yeah and honestly I'm in love with Briston as well, so complicated."

"Well, Brae that's seriously hot," she tells me, giggling. "So are you bi?"

Shaking my head, I reply, "I don't know. I guess so. I love them both," I admit, biting down on my lip before adding, "I'm so fucking confused."

"Well, I haven't been in the exact situation but I get being confused about your feelings. You have to trust your heart."

Nodding I reply, "Yeah and my heart wants both of them as crazy as that is."

Ava smiles at me, reassuringly, telling me, "It's not crazy but love makes us feel crazy. I love Zeke so much it hurts."

I laugh in response. "I guess we both have secret loves huh?"

Again Ava gives me a sweet smile.

"Yeah, don't hide from how you feel about them Brae. It will only hurt you more."

Smiling at her I softly say, "You're sweet Ava. Thanks for listening."

Leaning forward I give her a kiss on the cheek.

"Anytime Brae, you're a good guy. Don't forget that."

"I'll try not to."

Caz May

She turns to walk away and picking up the soccer ball from under my foot, I head inside to grab my clothes.

No doubt I'm regretting my choice to fuck Chasity. It meant nothing to me, and now I've sunk to the lows of my fake reputation.

It feels horrible.

I don't want to be that guy.

I want to be the good guy Ava thinks I am, and the good guy Ariel deserves.

A good guy like Briston, a guy that won't hurt her and break her heart with words he doesn't mean.

Chapter Twelve

Briston

Sitting on my bed for our usual Friday movie night, things are a little different because Ariel and I have been doing everything but watching movies most nights we've been together.

Caz May

Not that I'm minding that happening. Kissing, touching and fucking my best friend is way better than watching shitty Netflix movies any day of the week.

We're definitely down with Netflix and chill.

Tonight though, we're watching a movie—a comedy—and Ariel isn't laughing even in the absolutely hilarious parts. She's really sad actually and squeezing her side I ask, "Ar's baby, what's up?"

Turning her head to look at me, she utters soft words, "He really hurt me Bris, but I miss him."

"I know Ar's," I affirm, kissing her forehead. "I do too."

Seeing my best friends' heart breaking over another guy is breaking my heart for her.

There's silence between us for a moment, and I just want to kiss her to take away the pain I see in her eyes.

"I love him Bris, but it hurts so bad."

Her words are so true, stab me in the heart true, and I respond, "Yeah, I love him too, but it wasn't meant to be."

She nods at me, and I kiss her lips.

"But you and me Ariel. I never dreamed we'd be together."

She gives me a sweet smile in response, causing my heart to explode in my chest in a crazy rhythm.

"Yeah me too, Briston. I've loved you for so long."

Again, I kiss her, harder this time as she cuddles closer to me.

"I love you, Ariel," I whisper against her lips.

Pulling back she repeats back, "I love you too, Briston."

Shifting on the bed, she rolls her hips so she's straddling me.

Tamed Hearts

Giving me pecking kisses, she asks between them, "Can we forget and feel for a bit?"

"Yeah, baby," I reply, kissing her fiercely and murmuring when she bites my lip, taking my lip ring between her teeth, and pulling back. Pleasure and pain from that gesture pulse through me.

"Damn, Ar's, you slay me baby."

"Fuck me, Briston," she demands, lifting her nightie off so she's naked except for her lacy knickers.

"Fuck, Ariel. You're so damn beautiful."

She laughs, giving me another kiss and rocking her still covered pussy over the front of my boxers.

My dick springs forward, the tip pressing against her clit. Sliding back she grabs the elastic of my boxers, yanking them down to my knees.

I grip her hips to pull her closer to my erection, and not giving a shit I rip the lacy knickers so her pussy is bare to me.

She playfully slaps me.

"Thanks Bris. Those were my favourites."

"Sorry Ar's, but I like you better without any knickers."

Laughing she replies, "I like you without any boxers and love seeing your dick hard for me."

"Is that so, sexy bestie?"

"Yeah, sexy bestie, so fuck me and I might forgive you for destroying my favourite knickers."

Again rocking her now bare pussy over my dick, I tease her clit with the tip. She slaps my abs once more, leaning over me to kiss me as she whispers, "Briston, fuck me please."

Caz May

"Well, only because you begged me, Ar's," I jeer at her, thrusting hard up inside her wet pussy.

Starting to ride my dick I watch my best friend in pleasure, loving how her perfect round tits bounce.

"Fuck, Bris, you feel so good inside me."

"Mmm, Ar's, you're so wet...ride me harder, baby."

Leaning over my chest, still bouncing her butt as she rides my dick her tits meet my lips and teasingly I suck a nipple into my mouth.

"Oh, god...Briston!" she calls out, stilling her hips a moment when she bears down all the way, taking my dick completely inside her channel.

Removing my mouth from her tit, I pull her lips to mine by grabbing a fistful of her hair.

"Kiss me whilst you fuck me, Ar's," I demand, smashing my lips to hers for a lustful kiss. Her moans against my lips as we kiss, and fuck have me teetering on the edge of release.

Tearing her mouth from mine she calls out, "Bris, fuck! I'm coming!" Her hips still, and I call out in response, "Fuck Ariel, I'm going to come!"

She stammers, "Bris, pull out...now." But it's to late for that, as my come spills inside her with my orgasm.

Shifting so she's beside me, she sniffs back a tear. It felt good to fuck her but I've made a bad choice.

"Bris, we didn't use protection. You came in me."

"I'm sorry, Ar's. It was too late to pull out."

"So, Briston, I could get pregnant."

"Don't stress, Ar's. If that happens we'll deal," I tell her pulling her against my side and kissing her forehead.

Tamed Hearts

"I love you Ariel Jane Findley."

She smiles then, and replies whilst looking directly at me, "I love you too, Briston Elijah Nicholls."

Once more I kiss her, shoving worries of her getting pregnant aside and just enjoying being with her, my best friend, and the girl I've always been in love with, even before I knew it.

Chapter Thirteen

Ariel

*D*espite no longer being with Drake, at most lunchtimes, I still sit with his friends. They've become my friends as well, and having girlfriends like Ava and Dakota is definitely welcome.

Today, my stomach is in knots. It's been well over a month since I got my period last. And I've had constant cramps for the last two weeks, turning my stomach so much I've vomited a number of times. I'm terrified I'm pregnant, as the last time Briston and I had sex he carelessly came inside me.

Taking a bite of my cheese sandwich, I try to swallow it down without throwing up. Doing so makes me cough, nearly spitting it out with the vomit that rises into my throat.

Not again.

STANDING UP, and throwing my sandwich on the table in front of me I rush to the dunnies with a hand to my mouth, the other clutching my stomach.

I'm going to chunder—everywhere—if I don't get to the dunnies, like right now.

Reaching the outside dunnies I use the hand not clutching my stomach to push the door open, and barely make it into a cubicle before my milo, and Vegemite toast from breakfast are making a second appearance.

Once the contents of my stomach is expelled into the dunny, I flush it and sit on the floor with my back against the cubicle wall.

Sighing I give into the tears that are stinging my eyes.

I don't want to move. And honestly, I can't move. I'm angry with myself for getting into this position, and angry at Briston for his actions that have put me in this position.

If I had anything to cut with, I'd slice into my skin and bleed out on the dunny floor.

I'm as good as dead anyway when dad finds out I'm pregnant.

Holy shit, I'm fucking pregnant.

Caz May

I really think I'm pregnant.

Letting out a wail I let the tears fall, startled when I hear the door creaking on its rusty hinges and a voice calling out, "Ariel? Are you ok?"

It's Ava. And she stops at the cubicle, her feet visible under the door.

I don't want to say anything, because I'm far from ok, but she's most likely heard my wailing sobs.

"I'm here," I say with a groan.

"Are you ok? You rushed in here so quick."

I shake my head, even though she can't see me.

"Yeah, I'm ok now."

"Did you vomit?" Ava asks worriedly. I don't reply, so she presses on, "Can you open the door?"

"Ok, I'll try," I say, standing up with another groan, and unlocking the cubicle latch to open the door.

Ava takes one look at me before pulling me into a hug. It's so sweet I start blubbering again with tears streaming down my cheeks, smearing my mascara down my cheeks.

Ava breaks the hug, stepping back towards the sinks when she says, "Oh Ariel, tell me what's wrong?"

Staring at my friend in the mirror as I wash my hands I tell her through sobs, "I think I'm pregnant."

"Oh shit, really? Are you late?"

"Yeah, a week or so. And I've been throwing up for at least a week."

Ava takes my hand, squeezing it.

"Have you taken a test?"

Shaking my head, I reply, "No, I have no idea what one to get, and dad will ask a thousand questions if I use the credit card without him knowing."

"Well, I'll go with you to the chemist after school. We'll use cash."

"Thanks, Ava. I'm so nervous about even buying a test," I tell her, letting out a strained laugh.

She laughs and replies, "Don't worry, I'll buy it. I have no shame, and honestly, I had a scare a month back with Zeke."

My mouth falls open.

"Oh my, really? Are you?"

"No!" she shrieks, laughing. "Was just stressed with exams and stuff. And I freaked because I missed a couple of pills and was a few days late."

"Oh, well I'm definitely later than that. But hopefully, I'm just stressed too."

"I'm sure that's all," she assures me as I turn back to the mirror and wipe my fingers across my mascara streaked cheeks as the bell goes.

We head out for class and Ava promises to meet me at the school gate when the end of day bell goes. My heart rate is through the roof, but I'll know soon enough.

❤

AFTER GETTING THE TEST at the chemist Ava comes home with me.

Thankfully dad is working night shift, and he'll be none the wiser.

Ava is sitting on my bed, reading the instructions of the First response pregnancy test she assured me were the best kind to get.

Nervously, I'm holding the pink wrapped stick of fate in my palm as I pace my room.

Ava looks up at me, telling me, "So you pee on it for like five seconds and we wait for three minutes for the result."

"Right, three minutes," I surmise, heading to the bathroom with Ava following me.

She stands outside the door. And I go in, unwrapping the test as I pull down my knickers from under my school dress.

Awkwardly I sit down on the dunny and pee on the stick, putting it down on the counter as I finish and flush the dunny.

I call out to Ava, "You can come in, Av's."

She opens the door, glaring at me before laughing. "Take a deep breath, Ar's. And cross your fingers and toes only one pink line comes up."

I laugh to hide my nervousness. "Don't jinx it, Ava," I jeer at her.

We both stare at the test, willing the minutes to go faster because quite frankly it's the longest three minutes of my life. Ava picks up the test, holding it up to me.

"See, I told you. Negative. Not pregnant."

"Thank god," I reply with a laugh. "This period is going to be a damn crime scene going by my symptoms then."

"Shark week from hell," Ava again says with her cheeky laugh.

"Yeah, thanks for today Ava. You're a really great friend."

"Anytime, Ariel. You going to tell Briston?"

"Yeah, he'd want to know. It's partly his fault to."

Tamed Hearts

"Yeah, you gonna be ok? I need to get home before Ash and Tem arrive from Melbourne."

"Yeah, I'll be fine. Thanks again."

She smiles at me, giving me a hug before she leaves.

Back in my bedroom, I grab my phone and text Bris.

Bris, need to tell you something.

What?

Can you call me?

Sure thing baby

Barely a second later my phone is ringing with my sexy best friend's face flashing on my screen.

Taking a moment to stare at the picture of him biting down on his lip ring, I answer, "Hey Briston."

His reply is defensive, "Hey Ariel. You right? You sound weird."

"I'm ok now. But Bris, I'm late."

"As in late, late? Like ya rags are late, late?" I laugh at his mixed up, stupid repeated words.

"Yes, that kinda late, Bris."

"Right, um...shit. So should I get a test or something?" I can hear the panic but concern in his voice.

"No, it's fine. Ava helped me get one. And it was negative."

Caz May

"So off the hook then?"

"Yes, shark week is just late. No shark on the hook."

"Good, but I would've helped you Ar's. Honest."

"I know Bris," I tell him, smiling into the phone. "We better get protection if you want to keep fucking."

He laughs, as though he's smiling into the phone and thinking about us fucking.

His tone drops low and deep when he replies, "Sorry we haven't. I...um...didn't have to with Braeden, and I get carried away in the moment forgetting it's different with a girl."

"Yeah, but fucking without protection has consequences Bris."

"I know Ar's. I'll go to the chemist and get some naked frangers."

"Good, I'll see you at school tomorrow."

"Of course, baby. Love you."

He makes a kissing sound into the phone and I laugh when I reply, "Love you too, Bris."

He hangs up and I lie down cuddling my teddy bear to my chest to fall asleep even though it's barely six pm.

Hopefully tomorrow I wake up with blood-stained sheets.

Chapter Fourteen

Ariel

*I*t's kinda strange to be in the Castello's house, with Ezekiel, Ashton and Tempany back for Ava's eighteenth.

Ava has invited our entire year level and the house is abuzz with music, and people laughing and chatting.

Ashton and Tempany are practically joined by either the hip, or their lips and Ava is downing countless cocktails scoffing at her older brother angrily.

Caz May

"Argh, why does he have to be so, urgh?!" she questions me, before downing the last few drops of her cocktail, licking the margarita glass with the tip of her tongue to get every last drop of alcohol.

She's very tipsy—borderline drunk—and so fired up at her brother and stepsister for being all cosy at her birthday party, I'm surprised steam isn't emanating off her barely covered body. Her outfit is a white crop top bandeau with sparkles across the breast line, and denim shorts that skim the very top of her butt cheeks. She's barefoot, and completely carefree showing so much of her body off.

If I could've worn long sleeves I would be, but it's still incredibly hot for this time of year, especially at this time in the evening. So, to cover my wrists I'm wearing a multitude of bangles on each arm with a baggy t-shirt style dress that skims the top of my knees. Briston thought it wasn't sexy enough for a birthday party, but he wasn't one to talk wearing a simple outfit of boardies and a t-shirt. He'd look sexy in anything though.

Following Ava towards the kitchen for yet another cocktail, I'm about to voice a reply to her previous question when she stops dead in her tracks, letting out a loud shriek.

"What the actual fuck! Zekey bear!"

Stepping up next to Ava, I see what she is seeing. Her boyfriend against the island counter, with Chastity pressed up against him, trying to kiss him.

Ezekiel has his palms gripping the edge of the counter, as though he's trying to get away from Chasity pouncing on him.

He certainly doesn't look as though he's enjoying the moment.

"It's not what it looks like, Av's. Slutty bitch here cornered me."

Ava storms closer, seething.

"She's practically fucking you, Ezekiel!" Ava bellows at her boyfriend, pulling the full name card on him for impact.

Chastity is cackling like a heinous bitch, clearly getting off on the exchange. She hasn't moved an inch.

"And you think I'm enjoying this shitshow, Ava?"

"I don't know Ezekiel. You're not making a move to leave."

"Does it look like I can move, Ava?" he questions with a raised, slightly angry voice.

Ava huffs, not replying to him as she steps up behind Chasity and grabs a fistful of her long blonde locks, yanking her backwards and away from Zeke.

My eyes dart to the front of Zeke's shorts, hoping for his sake he's not got an erection, as Ava would surely murder him if he did. He's in the clear, but Chasity isn't.

"You're going down bitch!" Ava squeals at Chasity, shoving her against the counter next to Zeke.

"He asked for it!" Chastity taunts Ava, her eyes darting between Ava and Zeke.

"Like hell I did, Chastity!" Zeke bellows at her, balling his fists as though he's fighting the urge to slap her. "I fucked you once, and that was one time too many."

Ava grabs the front of Chasity's tank top, and Chasity's eyes glare back at her before she turns to Zeke with a sexy pout.

Caz May

"You loved it, Ezekiel. And you'd have loved it this time around if your girlfriend here didn't interrupt."

"Yeah, nah. Go fuck yourself!" Zeke bellows. "And don't you ever call me Ezekiel again!" He's irate now, about to pull Ava off Chasity when she shoves her hard in the chest.

"You are a psycho, boyfriend stealing ho, Chastity!"

"Yeah, well, you're a stupid bitch..." Chasity doesn't get any more words out, as Ava slaps her across the cheek causing her to stumble backward, hitting the floor with a scream.

Ava is on her before any of us can stop her, the kitchen filling with the party guests to watch the bitch fight unfolding.

Ava starts slapping Chasity, pulling her hair and screaming at her incoherently.

"You're the only bitch around here! You touched my Zekey bear. And no one touches my Zekey bear!"

Chastity grunts, pushing her hands into Ava's chest.

"Seriously, fuck off, bitch! You can fucking have him."

Ava falls backwards, her bum hitting the floor as Chasity stumbles to her feet.

"No dick is worth getting set upon by a psycho bitch!" Chasity bellows as she storms out of the room in a huff, flipping off everyone who's laughing.

Zeke extends a hand to Ava, helping her up and pulling her close to kiss her forehead.

He whispers something in her ear that makes her giggle.

She gives him a kiss, again giggling as he grips her around the waist and throws her over his shoulder, making her squeal in delight as he stalks away with her delighted squeals trailing them.

Every one who was watching dissipates, getting back to the party even though the guest of honour is now otherwise occupied. We all know what the birthday girl is about to get up to. I grab a bottle of water from the counter when my best friend scoots up behind me, playfully slapping my butt.

"Hey, Ar's, that was quite a show, huh?"

"Yeah, it was. Ava took her down."

"Yeah, would you take a girl down for me?" he jeers, pressing me into the bench and kissing my neck.

"Nah, maybe a guy though," I tease, turning around, and cupping his cheeks as I kiss him.

He moans against my lips, breaking the kiss and giving me a sexy smirk.

"That'd turn me on, baby."

"You're a dirty boy, Briston," I tease him, giving him a peck of a kiss.

"Only for you, Ariel," he teases back, kissing me again. "Can we get out of here before I'm making a spectacle by fucking you on this bench?"

"Yeah, I guess. I don't think Ava will be down for a bit."

"By the moans I can hear, over the music right now, that would be a no."

He steps back, taking my hand, and I laugh at his words as we walk out of the party together.

At the front door, on the porch I spot Braeden, sipping on a bottle of beer. He's in another world, and my heart lurches in my chest just looking at him, at my broken boy who shattered my heart by being so careless and callous.

Part of me wants to rush over to hug him and kiss him, but I know that'll only break my heart more when he pushes me away again.

Instead, I kiss Briston, following him down the path to his jeep.

I love Briston, but my heart feels torn—incomplete— without the other part of me.

Braeden still has my heart, even though he doesn't deserve it. And I have no idea how I'm going to get over this feeling, as even being with my best friend in every way doesn't quell the feeling that something is missing.

Chapter Fifteen

Ariel

Getting back from the party—after stopping at Briston's for a quickie—I find dad is beside himself, pacing the living room.

He's holding a bottle of whiskey, sipping from it and muttering under his breath.

Walking into the living room I'm hesitant to say anything, so only a meek, "Dad?" comes out of my mouth.

Caz May

He stops the pacing, staring at me with tears in his eyes, but a scowl as he's seething.

"Where have you been young lady? It's after midnight."

"I was at Ava's eighteenth. I told you about that, and Briston just dropped me home."

"Was drinking involved?"

"I had a drink, yes, but Briston didn't. I promise we were safe, dad."

"Good, good, but you did break curfew, Ariel."

"I lost track of time. Eleven pm is a shit curfew for someone my age."

"Language, Ariel Jane. I'll let this time slide, but I will most definitely ground you next time."

"Thanks, dad," I reply sweetly, rushing to hug him. His arms come around me, and I feel the whiskey bottle hit my shoulder blade. It hurts but I try not to wince when I pull back from the hug, asking him, "Are you, ok dad?"

He shakes his head and takes another long sip of the whiskey.

"Not really, your mum is really going downhill."

"Oh, what's happening?"

"She's having more episodes, and refusing to take her medication."

"It will be ok, dad," I tell him, trying to sound confident when I'm beyond worried.

Dad has shielded me from Mum's schizophrenia, never letting me in on how sick she really is. It both upsets me and angers me. And worries me, as I wonder if there's some hereditary link, like mother, like daughter.

Dad gives me a nod, turning away to sit on the couch with his whiskey bottle as company. I hope he doesn't have work tomorrow, as he's clearly heading towards being drunk.

Heading down the hallway I go into Mum's room, breaking down into tears the moment I step across the threshold.

She's awake, but a little out of it and climbing into bed with her she cuddles me close, slipping into sleep, having taken her sedative medication tonight.

Thinking about that, as I watch her brings up memories of the past. The day, that day her psychosis hit breaking point. The look in her eyes was vacant, as though my mum had vanished from the bathroom where she was helping me wash my hair. I treasured those moments, even at age ten, as it showed that she cared about me. That day my stomach was cramping from some stomach bug I'd picked up at school. I was vomiting so much, feverish and she put me in a bath, so calmly before the switch went off and she tried to kill me, drown me by shoving me under the water by the shoulders.

My saliva still catches in my throat, as the memories flood my mind.

Other times she was always dressing me up, putting me in pretty dresses that itched, and making me dance around the living room. It pained her that I never wanted to be a ballerina, like she was when she was younger. I was too clumsy and that irritated mum.

She comes to a little, her eyes fluttering open and focusing on me.

Caz May

"Ariel, my darling," she murmurs.

"Hi, mum. You doing ok?"

"Yeah, baby girl. You?"

I put my head on her chest, looking up at her.

"Not really," I confess.

"Tell me, baby. Is it boy problems?"

"Yeah, things are good with Briston. I love him so much, but I really miss not talking to Braeden," I tell her, trying to not let the tears out.

"Have you spoken to him?"

"I've tried, but he either doesn't want to hear it or we're at a loss for words and end up kissing."

"That's not so bad though is it?" Mum asks with a smile.

"Well, no, but he hurt me mum, and I need to talk to him about it."

"Then write a letter to him to get your feelings out on paper," she suggests, running a hand over my hair. I sit up in the bed.

"Does that really work?"

"You can only try, baby girl."

"Yeah, that's true. Thanks mum," I tell her leaning over to kiss her on the forehead before I shuffle off her bed, and head back to my room.

Before I'm even out the door, she's drifted off again. And my heart breaks.

Despite everything I'm not ready to lose my mum, but something tells me time is not on my side.

Chapter Sixteen

Ariel

*W*rite him a letter. Let the words out on paper mum had said. I don't even know what to say, what to write with all the emotions swirling in my mind. Grabbing a piece of paper, and a pen I sit cross legged on my bed, ready to let the words out. To bleed onto the paper.

Caz May

Dear Braeden,

This is so damn hard, but I need to get the words out and find writing it down on paper is easier than talking. After we had sex, I literally saw ♡'s. Nothing had ever felt that amazing. And I knew my heart was yours. It's always been Briston's, but now a part of it is yours as well.

But you shattered it. Shoving me away when your brother came home as though I meant nothing to you. No one has ever hurt me that bad. How dare you?!

I don't know why I'm even writing this pointless letter. It's not like you honestly give a shit about me. You've probably moved onto someone who isn't damaged like me, someone who isn't scarred with letting her own emotions out. I can't fucking turn my feelings off for you though. You own a piece of my heart Braeden. A broken piece now, but it's still yours. And I want to hate you, but I don't. I could never really hate you. We could fix each other.

Love, Ariel

I WANT TO THROW THE LETTER OUT, not give it to him, but he needs to read the words from my heart, so I get up from the bed and put the letter in an envelope from my desk draw. I scrawl his name, 'Braeden' across the front and tuck it in the front pocket of my backpack, ready to put it in his locker tomorrow.

Caz May

Chapter Seventeen

BRAEDEN

After school—and soccer practice—I decide to go past my locker to grab some books for homework.

I'm struggling big time with English, but I'd been given a large print copy of Romeo and Juliet with some fancy text that was supposed to make it easier for my dyslexic brain to process.

It frustrates me getting special treatment with school work and exams. If I didn't need school to go to uni then I'd have quit years ago, the moment I turned sixteen. Carson wouldn't let me, as he wanted a better life for me than he has. His verbalising of those thoughts and wishes for me was the nicest thing he's ever said to me.

SAUNTERING up to my locker I notice something is sticking out of the side of the door. Getting closer I pull it out, and it's a white envelope with scrawly handwriting on it. It's practically illegible, but I'm pretty sure it says my name.

I want to rip it open, but also I'm scared of what might be inside, so folding it I shove it in my pocket before heading home. The entire trip home, the letter is burning a hole in my pocket.

SITTING DOWN ON MY BED—thankful Carson is nowhere to be found—I grip the letter in my sweaty palms. Sliding a finger under the seal I toss the envelope aside, sliding the letter out. The same scrawly handwriting hits me when I unfold it, all jumbled and with what appears to be a whole heap of number two's. I can't read it. My brain is just seeing a blur of lines on the page. It seems also like the i's are dotted with tiny hearts.

That's super cute, and despite not being able to read the words I know the letter is from Ariel. That very thought stabs at my heart. I truly want to know what the letter says. No one has ever written me a letter before, which makes me even more desperate to read it, but frustratingly I can't.

With my anger rising, gripping the letter in my fist I nearly rip it, but I restrain myself because I want to know

Caz May

what it says. There's only one way I can find out what it says, and even knowing she probably doesn't want to see me, I'm out the door in a rush, grabbing my guitar as I again shove the letter in my pocket.

I'T'S AWKWARD AS SHIT—holding my guitar case—sprinting through town to get to her house as quick as possible. It's just gone dark, but the streetlights in Ariel's neighbourhood give me just enough light to easily see as I sneak into her room.

Sliding the window up, I throw my guitar in first, not surprised that she lets out a shriek.

Crawling in afterwards, I stumble a little, smiling when I see her sitting on her bed with books spread out everywhere in front of her. She looks undeniably beautiful, momentarily making me forget about the reason I'm actually here.

"Braeden?" she questions, eyeing me as I cross the room towards her bed. "What are you doing here?"

I know why I'm standing in her bedroom, still in my school uniform, but I'm a little tongue-tied, struck dumb from seeing her looking so stunning without even trying when I miss her so much it hurts.

Stopping at the edge of her bed, I yank the letter out of my pocket and throwing it on the bed, muttering, "because of this."

"Did you read it?" she asks anxiously. That tone makes me nervous.

"I can't read it, Ariel."

"What do you mean?"

Tamed Hearts

"I can't read it. Your handwriting confuses me."

"Sorry, so um, you couldn't read it at all?"

I can feel the tears in my eyes, angry, frustrated tears full of the emotions I'm feeling from her pushing the fact about reading the letter.

Sinking to the floor, on my butt I mutter through my sobs, "I. Can't. Read. It."

"I don't understand what you're trying to say, Braeden. Are you telling me you can't read?" Her hand brushes my shoulder, lingering there and burning my skin even through my shirt. I turn to look up at her, wiping my sleeve across my eyes so I can focus on her face when I tell her, "I'm dyslexic. So I can read, but find handwriting and small text really confusing."

"Oh Braeden, I'm sorry I had no idea."

"It's ok, I don't really make it known. It's really embarrassing."

She shakes her head at me, her eyes showing her emotions.

"Thank you for sharing that with me, Brae."

"Don't go blabbing it," I tell her teasingly.

"It's not for me to tell people. Do you want me to read the letter to you?"

"Yeah, if it's not going to break my heart."

She smiles at me, making my heart pound in my chest.

"I can't guarantee that, but I really need you to hear the words."

Grabbing the letter, she slides off her bed to sit next to me on the floor. It feels really intimate when she takes my hand, holding it in hers as she starts reading softly,

Caz May

"Dear Braeden,

This is so damn hard, but I need to get the words out and find writing it down on paper is easier than talking. After we had sex, I literally saw star's.

Nothing had ever felt that amazing. And I knew my heart was yours."

She pauses, squeezing my hand and causing my heart to gallop in my chest. Her words mirror my feelings for her. I try to speak, but she gives me a soft smile, putting a finger to my lips to silence me. Darting my tongue out, I lick it, taking it in between my lips and her sexy little whimper makes my dick jolt.

"Braeden, stop, be serious," she chastises me with a cheekiness in her tone.

"Sorry, darling, continue, please," I tell her loving how her eyes light up with my term of endearment.

Leaning her head on my shoulder, she sighs and continues reading softly, "It's always been Briston's , but now a part of it is yours as well.

But you shattered it. Shoving me away when your brother came home as though I meant nothing to you. No one has ever hurt me that bad. How dare you?!

I don't know why I'm even writing this pointless letter."

Again stopping, she turns to stare at me, her gaze cutting right into my soul as though she can see right into my head, my heart.

"Is that all it says?" I ask her.

Shaking her head she gives me that heart shattering smile. She's silent for a moment, so when she speaks again my heart breaks,

Tamed Hearts

"It's not like you honestly give a shit about me. You've probably moved onto someone who isn't damaged like me, someone who isn't scarred with letting her own emotions out."

My heart breaks, shatters again. She's so wrong. I do give a shit about her, which is why I pushed her away. I couldn't let my brother hurt her. I couldn't have that on my conscience. My actions have hurt her regardless, and I've hurt myself in the process, scarring my heart this time.

"Ariel, I..."

She cuts my words off, I can't get them out when she's squeezing my hand tightly and staring right at me.

"Please Braeden, let me finish this," she pleads, shifting a little so her leg brushes against mine. It sends a jolt of electricity through me, and I nod.

Once more she sighs and speaks, "I can't fucking turn my feelings off for you though. You own a piece of my heart Braeden. A broken piece now, but it's still yours. And I want to hate you, but I don't. I could never really hate you. We could fix each other."

"Fuck Ariel, I...shit...I..."

She smiles and says sweetly, "Love, Ariel."

"Darling, " I murmur softly, not sure what I can even say. I'm not sure if she means 'love' in the 'I love you' way or just an ending to a letter.

She's again staring at me, begging me with her eyes to say something, but I don't have any words of reply. I want to tell her about Chastity, how I monumentally fucked up by sticking my dick in the school ho but decide not to. It's not the right time.

Caz May

"Braeden, please say something," Ariel pleads.

"I um...don't know what to say, Ariel."

She shrinks back from me, pulling her knees to her chest. She puts her head down, and sniffs back tears.

"Ariel, darling, please don't cry."

"But. You. Can't. Even..." she mutters wiping an arm across her tear stained cheeks.

She's breaking my heart. I want to get the words out, want to tell her that I love her with my completely fucked up heart, but I don't have those words.

There is only one way I can get the words out, and crawling on my hands and knees across her bedroom floor to my guitar case I unzip it, pulling out my guitar before I slide back to her side, holding my guitar in my lap as I start to strum 'Addict of magic' by Picture this.

It's one of the only songs I know by heart that expresses how I feel about her.

"Braeden..."

I'm humming the first part of the song, too scared to sing, but also because the chorus is the words I need her to hear.

Still strumming, I focus on her, my beautiful, damaged girl as I let the lilt of my voice out with the words of the song, *'Every inch of my body, Every part of my heart, Every corner of my mind. Wants you here when you're not. Because I get withdrawals when I can't kiss your lips. So come over here, darlin', 'Cause I can't resist...'*

I barely get the last words out, before she's leaning over me, kissing the final words away.

Pulling back I shove my guitar aside, taking ahold of her waist and settling her on my lap.

"Braeden, that was amazing. I didn't know you could sing like that."

"You're amazing, darling. And even though they aren't my words, I mean them."

"I know, Brae," she says softly as I grip her hair, yanking her closer to kiss her. A sensual, hot kiss that undoes me. I want to tell her I love her again, but now is not the time. When she breaks the kiss, I brush her hair from her cheeks aside.

"You're so beautiful, darling. We good?"

"Yeah, Brae. We're good."

"Good," I reply, giving her another kiss that makes her murmur against my lips.

Desperately I want to stay, and take things further, but I can't do that to her.

"I gotta go, darling. But i'll see you at school."

She gives me a peck of a kiss, climbing off my lap and helping me up. She climbs back into bed, and pulling the sheets over her body I kiss her forehead before I pick up my guitar, silently packing it up before I sneak back out.

Looking back at Ariel as I climb out the window of her room, she's already asleep. She looks so peaceful, and so damn beautiful.

I'm glad things are ok between us, but I know I really need to tell her about what I did.

Caz May

Chapter Eighteen

Briston

*I*t's a beautiful day, still warm but not super hot.

Practically our entire year level is at the beach, Ariel and some others with who she has become friends.

One person is missing, and I honestly don't know how I feel about him not being here.

Ariel seems a little off with the damn fairies, but she looks stunning, a lot more brazen with showing off her body.

She's wearing a one-piece bathing suit and a sarong tied over her hips. She never would have been caught dead exposing her wrists or her thighs before everything that happened with us, but she can see herself through my eyes now, through his eyes.

Standing on the beach, just at tide edge I openly kiss her, not caring that our friends are around to see us. She doesn't kiss me back, acting off and I'm wondering if it's because our friends are around or because of her being so exposed.

Breaking the kiss, I lift her chin up with a finger so our eyes catch.

"Ar's, what's wrong baby?"

Her face falls, her gaze dropping from mine when she tells me softly, "Braeden snuck in the other night and broke down Bris."

The reason she seems off is now clear, and I'm not sure I want to know what I'm about to ask.

"Yeah, something happened with you guys?"

She nods, stabbing me in the heart with her words, "He kissed me. And I shared the letter with him that I wrote for him because he couldn't read it."

Her words stab at me, but confuse me equally. "What do you mean, couldn't read it? Like your handwriting?" I question, thinking about how weird my best friends handwriting is, with a's that look like two's and little hearts

Caz May

instead of dot's on her i's. It confuses me, so I get it. But Ariel shakes her head at me, looking really sad.

"No, like actually couldn't read it. He's dyslexic and he broke down in tears when he told me."

That was definitely not what I'd expected her to say. "Shit, poor dude," I say, before adding with a shake of my head, "But that doesn't forgive his actions Ar's."

"I know. But he played a song for me after, poured his heart out to me. And I just couldn't help but kinda forgive him."

Her words make my stomach twist.

"Yeah, well good for you Ar's. But he's not forgiven for me yet."

She huffs at me, with a hint of defiance.

Grabbing her by the waist, I pull her sarong off. She shrieks, getting angry as I taunt her with it, slapping her butt playfully.

"Bris! People will see my thighs!"

"Not in the water, Ar's. And honestly, no one will even care," I tell her, glancing around the beach to show her what I mean.

She looks around the beach at our friends who are kicking a soccer ball around or playing in the water. No one is even looking at us.

"Fine," she says with a huff, "but I'm kicking your arse later."

I laugh, grabbing her by the waist again to pick her up and put her over my shoulder, carrying her into the water.

Tamed Hearts

Things quickly get playful as we splash each other and her carefree giggles fill the air. This is the Ariel I love, the sweet, playful, fun loving girl.

Diving under the waves together, coming back up I flick my hair back, before clutching Ariel close when she comes back up.

Stealing her gasps for air I kiss her, loving tasting the salt on her lips. After separating our lips, Ariel shivers.

"Cold, baby?" I question.

"Yeah, even though it's warm today, the water is damn icy."

"You're not used to it," I tell her with a laugh, gripping her hand with mine to stalk out of the waves.

Ava sees us together from her spot on the shore. She's smiling giddily when she rushes up to us.

"Looks like you guys made it official?" she questions us, looking between us with a cheeky smile.

"Yeah, you could say that," I reply, not able to stop myself from grinning.

Ava smiles. "I'm happy for you guys, but you should probably talk to Braeden."

I give her a quizzical look, then look to Ariel who's mirroring my questioned gaze at Ava.

"Yeah, why's that?" Ariel asks her, squeezing my hand.

"He shouldn't have, but he told me a bit about what happened with you all," Ava confesses, before adding with an even sadder concerned tone, "And he's pretty cut."

A bubble of annoyance boils in my guts, but I can't be angry at Ava, nor Braeden for confiding in someone. "Ok thanks Ava," I reply, again taking Ariel's hand to lead her up

Caz May

the beach towards the place I took Braeden to. I need to feel, and be alone with my girl without prying eyes.

She's smiling when she asks, "Where are we going Bris?"

"Somewhere private, where I can get you naked," I tell her with a smirk that makes her laugh as I lead her away.

My dick is throbbing in my board shorts already, and thoughts fill my mind of being at this exact place with Braeden.

I'm only about to share it with Ariel, but I'd love to share this dirty experience with them both.

I'm still angry with him, but thoughts of him make my body react, and my heart race.

Love sure hurts.

Chapter Nineteen

Ariel

*W*ith Briston's hand in mine, we're running to the cliffs at the other end of the beach from where we left our friends.

He pulls me into an alcove that's not visible from the main beach, and shoves me against a cliff face, kissing me fiercely and possessively. It's a dirty, hot kiss that sends a shockwave of pleasure through me.

Caz May

Pulling back I'm breathless, panting out words, "Damn, Bris. That was some kiss."

His breathing is heavy too, when he replies, "You turn me on, baby."

He captures my lips in another kiss, a little calmer but equally as thrilling. And breaking it, he whispers in my ear, "Are you wet for me, Ariel?"

Biting his earlobe I whisper back, "Always, Briston. What're you going to do about it?"

Leaning in, so his lips are a breath away from mine he purrs against them, "I'm going to fuck you right here, right now."

His words send the tingles south, and moving back a little I voice my concern, "We don't have protection."

He sighs, promising, "I'll pull out, baby. Don't stress."

I'm worried, given our track record but I'm also horny, so I reply, "Ok, Bris, I trust you."

Again he kisses me, slipping his hands into the straps of my bathers and sliding them down my arms so he can peel off the wet second skin.

The cool beach breeze sends a shiver through me, and Briston breaks the kiss to gaze over my body, admiring me naked.

Contemplating me, his hands lightly touch each scar on my body, before he's kissing my wrist scars, bringing my left wrist to his lips as he tells me, "I love you so much, Ariel."

His kiss on the sensitive skin of my wrist gives me goosebumps; everywhere my skin is exposed to his lingering gaze.

Tamed Hearts

"I love you too Briston," I tell him, giving him a soft kiss. "You make me feel beautiful."

He smiles at me, cheekily, but replying sincerely, "You are beautiful Ar's."

Without warning—whilst still staring at me—he drops his boardies to his ankles, gripping my waist as he kisses me once more.

His kiss is wild, the kind of kiss that shows how much we want each other, and can't get enough of each other.

Turning my body around, my hands are now against the rocks.

Rotating my head I watch as my best friend enters me from behind, slamming his dick inside my pussy.

Yes, my pussy.

Briston had told me to actually use the dirty word for my vagina during sex, and I don't hate it as much as I thought. I definitely don't hate it when he groans it out all raspy whilst fucking me.

His thrusts are hard, each one hitting a deeper spot inside my pussy. My hands are pressing into the cold cliff face, and Briston leans over my back, his hands above me, pressing into the cliff face as well.

The only sounds are the crash of the waves against the rocks at the other side of the cliffs and the slap of our bodies together.

"Fuck, Ariel, baby, you feel so good around my dick."

"Bris, fuck me harder, please..." I beg, pushing my arse back towards him. He obeys my request, thrusting harder and sending me over the edge of a sudden, pulsating release.

Caz May

"Bris, fuck, I'm coming!" I call out, as he pulls out and comes on my back. His cum is warm on my skin, and gazing at me with a cheeky grin he bends down, rubbing it over my skin with his fingers.

"You look so pretty with my cum all over your body, Ar's."

I don't reply, taking in a deep breath as Briston licks his lips, looking up at me as he licks his cum off my skin.

The sensation of his warm tongue over my goosebump prickled skin makes me moan and after cleaning every drop of his release from my body he stands up, turning me around so I'm facing him.

He brings his fingers to my lips, and darting my tongue out I taste his cum which makes him groan and kiss me again.

"That was dirty, Briston."

He chuckles.

"I'm a dirty boy," he replies giving me a wink that makes my stomach flip.

Once more he kisses me before stepping back and yanking up his boardies. He helps me slip my bathers back on, taking my hand and leading me back out onto the main beach. What we just did was dirty, and naughty, but it's made me fall deeper and harder—under the waves—for my best friend.

GETTING BACK TO THE BEACH, it's quiet—except for the crash of the waves—and empty as our friends have left.

"Looks like everyone cleared out. You ready to go?" Briston asks, smiling at me.

"Yeah, let's head back to yours," I reply, following my best friend to his jeep feeling giddy and in love.

Momentarily I'd forgotten about the other half of my heart, but as we drive back to Briston's, the song Braeden played for me comes on the radio and I fight back the tears that sting my eyes.

I don't need Briston seeing me upset, especially over Braeden. I need to guard my heart, and tamp down the hurt, even if it breaks my heart.

Caz May

Chapter Twenty

Briston

Ariel is in her own little world, off with the damn fairies when we get back to mine. She shrugs me off when I try to help her out of the jeep, and it irritates me, but I let her follow me inside rather than pushing the issue. My best friend hates it when I go all gentlemanly on her.

Heading into the kitchen—with Ariel trailing me—for a snack because I'm damn starving from being at the beach all day I find Mum pulling out some chocolate chip cookies from the oven. They smell utterly divine.

"Damn mum, they smell delish," I tell her, stepping into the kitchen to give her a kiss on the cheek.

"Thanks, baby boy, dig in," she says with a smile, her gaze turning to Ariel. "Hello, Ariel dear. It's lovely to see you."

"Hi Mrs Nicholls, it's lovely to see you too," Ariel says with a soft, melancholic tone.

Mum gives her a smile as Ariel takes a cookie.

"I'm happy to see you and Briston together," Mum tells her, winking at me.

"Shush, mum," I chastise, taking a big bite of the cookie in my hand.

"You're cute together, Briston. I always wanted you two together," Mum says happily.

It makes me want to spit out my cookie everywhere. Sometimes mum's over the top support of everything in my life annoys me. And Ariel's non reaction is also unsettling. Something is up with her.

"How's your mum doing, Ariel?" Mum asks with a sweet smile.

Ariel shrugs, swallowing her bite of cookie before replying, "Things aren't good. She's really been out of sorts lately."

Mum replies, "I'm sorry to hear that, dear. Let me know if I can help in any way."

Ariel nods, meekly responding, "Thanks."

Caz May

I take another couple of cookies, one in between my teeth and a couple in my hands.

"Thanks for the cookies mum. We're going to my room, so no interrupting."

"Of course not, baby boy," she responds with a wink that makes me roll my eyes at her. I tell her too much.

Ariel follows me to my room and lies down on the bed with me, without saying a word.

We're both silent, staring at the ceiling and munching on our cookies. The silence is so thick, but calm until I hear Ariel's sobs. She's started to cry, and my heart breaks.

Rolling onto my side, I put an arm over her waist to bring her closer to me, to comfort her.

"Ar's, baby, don't cry. Tell me what's wrong."

"Nothing. Just. Kiss. Me," she requests through her sobs.

I'm about to kiss her when her phone rings. I didn't even know she had it in her bag, nor that she'd brought her bag inside. I'm as much off with the damn fairies as she is.

"Shit," she curses out, panicking, and jumping off the bed.

Bending down to her bag on the floor, she plucks out her ringing phone, mouthing to me, *'it's my dad'*.

She answers it, meekly, and her face shatters.

Chapter Twenty-One

Ariel

*W*ith a soft tone I answer the phone to dad. His voice is deep, and he doesn't even say, 'hello' before yelling at me, "Where are you?"

"At Briston's," I tell him, sniffing back my sobs.

"You need to come home right now," dad roars at me, his voice breaking.

Caz May

I don't like his tone. I've done nothing wrong. He's never cared if I've been at Briston's before. But with him now silent, and breathing heavily I'm concerned, worried that something is wrong that has nothing to do with me being at Briston's.

"Dad is everything ok? Is it mum?"

Dad answers me, "Yes Ariel. You need to come home now."

Hanging up my heart shatters, my whole body becomes numb, and the tears are now streaming down my cheeks

"Bris. I. My. Mum. Have. To. Go," I stammer, barely able to get the words out coherently because I'm crying so hard.

"Do you need a ride?" Briston asks, jumping off his bed to come and envelope me in a hug as I stand.

"Yeah," I wail into his shoulder.

He doesn't waste a minute before he's helping me out to the car.

The entire trip home I'm on edge, bouncing my knees anxiously. The urge to cut is thrumming through my veins.

Bris pulls up outside my house, asking, "Do you want me to come in?"

Shaking my head I tell him, "No. But thanks for the ride."

Grabbing my bag from beside my feet, I give my best friend a kiss on the cheek before I'm racing to the front door.

INSIDE, I FIND DAD pacing the hallway outside mum's room.

Tamed Hearts

Rushing up to him I hug him, tightly wrapping my arms around him, crying into his shoulder. He kisses my hair, and pulling back I ask, "Can I see her?"

He nods at me, solemnly telling me, "Yeah, baby girl. But she's gone."

Again the tears break free, into sobs. Pulling back further from dad's embrace I scream, beating my fists against his chest as I wail, "Why?"

He reaches out to grab my fists, to stop me, calm me. "I didn't get to say goodbye."

"I'm sorry baby girl. I was too late," he tells me, sniffing back a sob himself. "She was fading when I called you."

"You should've done something!" I scream at him, softly adding under my breath, "Saved her."

"I know," he tells me, looking me in the eyes. "But I couldn't this time."

He breaks down into tears, walking away without another word. I'm scared, worried about what I'm about to confront.

Cautiously I go into the room to find mum laying on the bed with blood stained sheets. Her wrists are slit with wide gashes, and a knife is in one hand still.

A silent scream escapes my lips, knowing that she'd bled out by cutting her wrists. It makes my own wrists throb when I lay down with her, my head against her chest. I cry. And cry, letting out everything with my tears.

Brushing her hair back from her porcelain cheeks I tell her what's in my heart, "I'm in love with Briston, mum. I know you always wanted us together.

Caz May

"And Braeden too, mum. I wish you could've met him. I think you'd really have liked him. He's got tattoos, and piercings. And he's a sexy bad boy type."

Right now, I'd give anything for mum to reply. To be able to hear her reply and to tell her that I've forgiven her for trying to kill me by drowning me when I was little. But I'll never get the chance, and my heart is wrecked.

I MUST'VE FALLEN ASLEEP, as I wake up to dad carrying me —cradling me in his arms—to my room. He tucks me into bed, kissing my forehead as he pulls the sheets up to my chin.

"Goodnight, my darling girl."

I murmur in a sleepy voice, "Goodnight, daddy." And barely hear him close the door as he leaves, drifting into sleep that I don't want to wake up from.

Chapter Twenty-Two

Briston

After Ariel ignores me for the rest of the weekend and doesn't turn up at school on Monday or Tuesday, I'm standing on her doorstep on what has been a bitterly cold day with an armful of homework I gathered for her.

Caz May

My heart is aching, and I'm getting the feeling something horrible has happened. It's not like Ariel to ignore me, to not even reply to a text message.

Shifting on my feet, tentatively I knock on the door still awkwardly holding the books and papers in my other hand.

It swings open, to Dr Findley looking like he should be in the hospital for himself. His features are sunken, his eyes bloodshot, and his clothes dishevelled. He's a shell of himself.

Slowly I speak, "Hi Dr Findley. Is Ariel home?"

He nods, ushering me inside.

"Yes, Briston. She's in her room."

"Great, I've got some homework for her."

"Thanks, son. I'm not sure she'll be up to much of that at the moment, but certainly go through. She'd love to see you."

"Thank you," I reply with a nod, as he closes the door and I head down the hallway to Ariel's room. I don't bother knocking on her closed door, but open it to find her curled up in bed clutching her childhood—falling apart, furless—teddy bear to her chest, as she sobs into her pillow.

Stalking across her room, I softly say, "Ar's, are you ok?"

She looks up at me, as I'm putting her homework on her desk.

"I bought you some homework."

She still doesn't say a word, barely moving even when I sit at the end of her bed.

Seeing her so broken kills me inside. My stomach knots, with thoughts filling my mind of what might have happened.

Tamed Hearts

"Ar's, tell me what's wrong, baby please. I hate seeing you like this."

Rubbing a hand up and down her back, I wait a moment, before saying her name softly, "Ariel, baby, please."

She shifts, sitting up a little and staring at me, vacantly. Her lips part, as though she's going to speak, but only muttered breath comes out. And she falls against my chest, sobbing. Pulling her close, I rub her hair to comfort her.

"Ariel, you can tell me. I love you." Hearing those words she pulls back and looks up at me, dropping her teddy bear in her lap, and wiping her arm across her tear stained cheeks.

Caressing her cheek, with a brush of my thumb again I wait for her to speak.

"Mum. She...did it."

"Did what, baby?"

"Slit her wrists. She bled out Bris." And my heart breaks.

"I'm so sorry Ar's. I'm so fucking sorry."

I pull her back into a hug, comforting her with the same gesture of rubbing her hair. She sobs into my chest again, murmuring, "I...I...didn't even get to say goodbye."

"What do you mean?"

"She was gone when I got back from yours. I was too late."

"Oh Ariel, I'm sorry. God, you probably hate me for keeping you so late after the beach."

She shakes her head.

Caz May

"I could never hate you Bris. But...I...I'm just hurt that dad didn't tell me sooner how bad things were."

"Yeah, that's pretty shit."

"I told her though, when I lay with her before dad ripped me away."

"Told her what?" I question, quirking my lip ring between my teeth.

"About us, that I love you, and I told her about Braeden too. She was the one to tell me about writing him the letter."

"I'm sure she would've been happy to see you happy, us together."

"Yeah, she always wanted us together, even when she thought you were gay," she says with a laugh that lights up her face, memories of her mum hitting her mind.

"Yeah, you have to think of the good times, Ar's. Not the bad times, or memories of the bad things she did that gave you the physical scars."

"I know Bris. And I'm trying."

"Good, that's all you can do. You'll be ok."

"Yeah, I'm just scared."

"Of what?"

"Becoming her."

"You won't, Ariel. I promise I'm always here for you."

"Thanks, Bris, I love you sexy bestie," she teases with a sweet smile.

"Back at you, sexy bestie, with all my heart."

She giggles then, leaning forward to kiss me and we fall back on the bed together, kissing to feel, and show our love for each other.

There's still more to say, to find out when the funeral is and when she'll be back at school, but right now I get the sense that my best friend just wants to feel something other than hurt, and pain. And I'm down for kissing her anytime.

Caz May

Chapter Twenty-Three

Ariel

S tanding slumped over at the graveside I can barely see through my tears.

Briston has an arm around my shoulders—comforting me—but Dad can't even touch me, nor look at me. It hurts that he's shutting me out when I'm hurting—broken—too.

I get that he's lost his wife—for what feels like the second time—but I've lost my mum. And other than him, and Briston I have no one else.

No siblings to cry with, or to share good memories with. And I'm struggling with the emotions, having given myself a tonne of fresh cuts that will scar this past week.

The priest is reciting words that I honestly can't even hear. I can hear birds twittering in the trees, giving my heart a jolt because mum always loved birdsong. It makes me feel like she's here, watching over us as we say goodbye.

Looking up a moment, sure I heard the priest say my name, I notice that everyone is there—from school and most of the hospital staff and others dad knows from around town—including Braeden. My heart again jolts in my chest. I wasn't expecting him to be here. We've not said one word to each other since the letter reading night, and I've honestly not even seen him around school.

That worries me, considering how his brother lay into him that night. The thoughts break into my mind, making my body throb thinking about the bruises his brother left on my skin that have just faded, and I let out a pained whimper.

Briston looks at me, kissing my temple, mouthing, "You ok, baby?"

I nod at him, forcing a smile before I nod towards Braeden as discreetly as I can. I can't help but look at him, my eyes are drawn to him. And it doesn't help that he looks dashing in a suit. But that's not why my eyes are drawn to him, it's because he's crying. Tears have streaked his

Caz May

cheeks, and he's falling apart, crying so hard I can practically hear his tears from the other side of the grave.

And that has me worried—wondering—what Braeden has been through for him to be crying so wretchedly at a funeral of someone he never met. Others are crying, but not like Braeden is.

Looking at him is making my heart ache, for him, for the loss he's clearly experienced.

I'm going to fall apart.

I'm going to scream.

I need release.

Shifting out of Briston's embrace, I want to run towards Braeden, to hug him tight and cry with him.

But I don't.

I stand beside my best friend stiff as a board, until the funeral director woman stops in front of me holding a white rose. I take it from her, mouthing 'thank you' and sniffing back my tears as I step up to the side of Mum's grave.

The coffin is suspended on straps, ready to be lowered into the ground, and I lean over to see the bottom of the hole. It seems like a never ending pit, and stumbling on my feet a little I gasp. Arms pull me back, heating my skin under my dress. Dirt flies into the hole as I'm pulled back from falling into the abyss beside my mum.

Wouldn't be so bad to be honest.

The person holding me yanks me back, breathing heavily into my ear, and for a moment I think it's Briston. But glancing down I notice his tattooed fingers, actually noticing the words on them now, *'Lone Wolf'.*

Glancing up to his face, I see the tears still streaking his cheeks. There's so much pain in his eyes, and I want to take it away.

"Careful, darling," he whispers, licking his lips. It's not a dirty seductive gesture, but it stirs up the butterflies in my stomach.

"Brae, you came. You didn't have to come," I tell him shifting in his arms so I'm facing him. He brushes strands of hair off my cheeks, kissing my forehead softly.

"Of course I did, darling. I love you."

My heart shatters into a million pieces, my throat hoarse and dry with wanting to verbalise the reply of *'I love you, too, Brae.'* And swallowing I fight, tamp down the urge to kiss him.

I can feel hundreds of eyes on us, glaring at me as they whisper slurs of how much of a hussy I am for being in two boys arms at my mothers' funeral.

Braeden breaks my thoughts, "You ok?"

I nod, and shake my head, stepping back from him, and turning back towards the grave to throw the lone rose into the abyss.

The coffin is now covered with roses—white and pink—and I watch as it's lowered into the ground.

Tears break free again, and the tension in my body is enveloped by one person taking my hand, and one wrapping his tattooed arm around my waist.

My B-boys both offer comfort in their own ways, but now Braeden's touch is the one I want more. Something is telling me he knows the pain I'm feeling, and my heart breaks for him, even though it's a shattered mess.

Caz May

Chapter Twenty-Four

BRAEDEN

It's odd being in Ariel's house as someone who's kinda welcome and not intruding through her bedroom window in the middle of the night.

The funeral was damn hard, with all the emotions of dad's funeral hitting me head on, and seeing Ariel so broken.

Briston was comforting her, but being quite honest he did a shit job of it. Ariel melted into my arms, and I wanted to kiss her to take away the pain she was feeling. Being there though I couldn't do that. People at school knew--or had an idea--that Ariel and I had been together.

Still I don't think comforting her—kissing her—in the living room of her house with people around is a good idea. I'm watching her from across the room—like a creeper—glaring daggers at Briston who seems to be glued to her side. He kisses her temple, walking away for a moment to grab some food from the buffet table. Seems like overkill to have a buffet table at an after funeral wake, but I don't come from money like is in abundance in the Findley household. For a moment, I think about just leaving without talking to Ariel. But now is the time to tell her about my past. She needs the comfort from someone who understands.

When Briston's back is turned I shuffle through the crowd of people to Ariel. She smiles softly when she sees me, which makes me feel a little giddy. I've never seen her give Briston a smile like that, and I love that my Ariel has special smiles just for me. She sniffs back tears, whispering my name, "Brae…"

Stepping closer to her, touching her arm, I whisper in her ear, "Darling, can we talk in private?"

She inhales a breath, shivering with her exhale as I pull back to see her answer reflected in her pretty dark grey eyes.

Caz May

Her answer doesn't come with words, but with her taking my hand and leading me through the crowd, and down the hallway to her room.

Closing the door behind us, she drops my hand, breaking down into tears as she falls to the floor by her bed.

My heart both hammers in my chest, and shatters into pieces for her.

Dropping to my knees in front of her, wrapping my arms around her shaking body I kiss the top of her head, speaking softly, "You're ok, darling. I'm here."

Comforting her with my embrace, I wait until her sobs subside and she shifts in my arms, so I pull back to look at her.

"Thanks Brae. I'm sorry for breaking down again."

"Don't be sorry for letting out your emotions, darling. Especially about this."

I brush a thumb across her cheek to collect the tear droplets from her beautiful flushed cheeks. So many thoughts, and feelings are rushing through me, for her.

"It hurts so much," she declares, sniffing back her tears, and looking at me with a questioning gaze.

"I know, darling. Trust me, I know."

"How? How could you possibly know how this feels?" she blurts out with an angry tone that should irritate me, but doesn't.

I know this hurt, and know her reaction, having lived it myself.

Granted I was only six when dad and Edwin died, but I remember it as clear as though it happened yesterday.

Tamed Hearts

Grabbing Ariel's hands in mine, I plead, "Look at me please, Ariel?"

Her eyes dart from our interlocked fingers to my lips, and then lock on my eyes as she takes her lip between her teeth.

"I'm sorry…" she mumbles.

"You don't have to be sorry, but I do know how you feel."

"How Brae? Please tell me how you could possibly know how much it hurts to lose someone you loved so much."

"Because I lived it, when I was six."

Her eyes boggle at me, "What? Is that why you live with Carson?"

"Yeah, when I was six my life giver went insane, and murdered my dad and little brother, Edwin. He'd only just turned one. And I watched her…"

"Oh my god, Brae. That's horrible. I had no idea. I'm so sorry."

Without a word I grab her, yanking her onto my lap and kissing her.

She's my air, the only one who can take away the pain of the memories filling my brain.

Breaking the kiss, her hooded eyes are glaring at me, a thousand questions on the tip of her tongue.

"So you like saw it happen?"

"Yeah, and fuck…" I curse out, kissing her again to focus on something other than the heinous images in my mind.

Her kisses undo me, tears of pain and anguish but relief dripping down my cheeks.

Caz May

I break the kiss then, caressing her cheek with the pad of my thumb.

"Fuck, I love you, Ariel. I love you so fucking much, it hurts, darling."

"I...um..." she stammers, averting her gaze from mine for a moment. With a finger under her chin, I tip her head up to lock our eyes together, before kissing her again.

"You don't have to say it back, now. It's ok."

"Well, you're not forgiven, yet, " she tells me with that cheeky, sweet only for me smile. "But thanks you for being here for me and telling me about your dad as well."

"I'm always going to be here for you, darling. Don't be afraid to talk to me, ever."

"Thanks," she says giving me a kiss again that makes my heart hammer and my dick stir.

"You need to apologise to Briston as well," she tells me with a peck of a kiss. "He still cares about you, even if he's being a douche canoe."

"Yeah I know," I reply with a laugh, from her calling her best friend a douche canoe. "What's happening with you guys?"

She shifts, sliding off my lap and starting to stand up when she replies, "We're together, but kinda miss you."

"I've missed you both too," I tell her, standing as well, and gripping her hand, interlocking our fingers.

She gives me that smile again—the one I'm dubbing the dick stir smirk—and I give her another sweet kiss, before leaving her room.

She has a piece of my heart. A piece that no one else before her has ever had. I've never told anyone about what happened when I was six, when Lilith Chappell splintered my whole world to smithereens.

Ariel Findley makes what little is left of my shattered heart feel whole again, and it will never beat as hard for anyone but her.

I hope I can have her whole heart back again, that I'll be able to hear her say she loves me again.

Caz May

Chapter Twenty-Five

Briston

I watch Braeden leaving Ariel's room, and heading out of the house with a smug look on his face. Seeing red, hoping like hell he hasn't broken her again I go into her room, finding her sitting on the floor by her bed, with tear stained cheeks.

Tamed Hearts

He's hurt her again. I want to punch the gorgeous fucker. And then kiss him. Fuck.

Stalking into Ariel's room I sit down next to her, asking softly, "What happened, baby? You ok?"

She gives me a smile, her gaze turning to me, replying, "Yeah, Bris. I um...don't know what to say."

"About what? Did he hurt you? I swear I'll fuck him up, Ar's," I threaten, even though my stomach is in knots thinking about being close to Braeden again. He's hurt my girl, but I still want to kiss him; fuck him.

"No, nothing like that, but I think you need to talk to Braeden yourself."

She again smiles, sniffing back a sob, and pulling the sleeves of her cardigan down over her hands.

I'm confused, wondering what she's not telling me. I hate that we seem to be hiding secrets from each other now. We never used to.

"Yeah, are you guys good now? You kiss and make up?"

"Yeah, nah," she murmurs, shaking her head. "I'm still hurt, but I want to be with him again."

I shock myself with my reply, "You and me both," I tell her, helping her to her feet when I see my parents at the door of Ariel's bedroom. "I gotta go now though. The parentals are ready to head out it seems." Mum nods at me, and Ariel smiles at them, nodding a thanks to them for being here for her.

"Ok...I'll text you later," she tells me before I give her a kiss.

"Love you, Ar's baby," I tell her as I head to the door to leave with my parents.

Caz May

She calls back, "Love you too, Bris baby."

I smile at her, loving the sweet new nickname that she's given me. My girlfriend just called me 'baby' and I love it. Shit, is Ariel my girlfriend? That thought and label excites me a lot.

IN THE CAR, on the way home with the parentals, mum is staring back at me in the backseat with a smirk on her face.

She wants to say something, some piece of motherly advice no doubt. Or a snide comment about what's happening with me and Ariel.

"Briston, son?" Dad pipes up, my name as a question.

"Yeah, dad?" I question back, trying not to sound snarky and annoyed.

"How're things are going with Ariel? Is she your girlfriend?"

Fuck me dead. Telling mum is one thing, but telling dad is a whole other kettle of fish.

"Well, yeah. Not like officially but yeah."

"That's great, son. We love her like a daughter. And she needs all the love she can get right now," dad says wisely, pulling into the driveway.

More words are on the tip of my tongue. And getting out of the car, dad slaps me on the back.

"You still seeing that boy, as well?" he asks in a tone that I don't really understand.

Mum has obviously mentioned Braeden, and my sexuality has never been hidden from my parents, at least before it wasn't.

"Nah, not in that way. But I miss him."

Tamed Hearts

Dad gives me a wink, a fatherly I know what you felt and did gesture.

"You got close with him?"

"Yeah," I admit, as we head inside. "And then things went bad when he hurt Ariel."

Pushing the door open, Mum pipes up, "Oh that's not good to hear. Was there something happening with them as well?"

A blush rises up my cheeks, as I follow them inside and reply, "I'm not sure you wanna hear the details mum."

I follow her into the kitchen, as dad goes to the den giving me another nod.

I'm glad I don't have to say anything else, to respond to mum's incessant questions with him around. There are some things—despite dad knowing I'm gay, well bisexual now—that a father doesn't need to hear his son talking about.

Mum has always been more open than dad, even though they're both accepting of me.

Mum starts making us hot chocolate, her telltale sign that she's ready to listen whilst probably firing a thousand questions at me.

Waiting for the kettle to boil, she teases me, "Try me baby boy."

I sit on the breakfast bar stool, sighing and huffing, "Fine...we slept together, a threesome." Once the words leave my mouth, I cover my face with my hands, peering through my fingers to gauge her response.

"Ooo...sounds fun," mum teases, turning around to grab the two hot chocolates she finishes making before handing

Caz May

me one and giving me that tell me my boy glare that only a mother can give.

She leans on the bench, sipping her hot chocolate when I reply sheepishly, "It was. But aren't you going to give me a lecture? Tell me that I can't be in love with or be with two people?"

She shakes her head, smiling wide.

"Of course not, baby boy. Love is wonderful and most people are lucky to fall in love once, to have that great love. But it seems as though you've found two great loves." Her words hit me in the feels, a shot to heart.

"So you're not angry at me?" I ask, taking a big gulp of hot chocolate and nearly burning my tongue.

"No, baby boy. Not angry," she says pausing to take a sip of her hot chocolate before putting it down on the counter in front of her.

Stepping closer to me, she outstretches her arms to hug me.

"I'm proud of you for being so open and loving, especially now with Ariel. She needs you."

Hugging her back, as I stand up I reply, "Thanks mum. I'm going to head to bed."

She sets me free from her loving embrace, and smiles once more, saying, "Goodnight, baby boy," as I head down the hallway to bed, thinking about what mum said.

Ariel's words of telling me that I need to talk to Braeden is also on my mind.

My body is certainly missing him—despite being with Ariel—and I honestly still love him, even though it hurts.

Tamed Hearts

Getting into bed, pulling the covers up to my chin and settling into the mattress I decide to sleep on it and message him the next day. Actually talking to him now will hurt too much.

Caz May

Chapter Twenty-Six

BRAEDEN

Hearing the clattering of the knife against the kitchen floor, I slide on my socks across the tiles to see what's happened. Mum is standing by the kitchen counter, with a scary clown-like smile on her face. And dad and Edwin are on the floor and they aren't moving. Mum looks at me, before walking out of the kitchen. She doesn't even say anything, doesn't even care that I call out after her, "Mum!"

my voice sounds all husky. I don't even know if I made a sound because surely mum would care. But then dropping to my knees on the tiled floor, I cry from the cold floor on my knees and she still doesn't come to see if I'm ok. And I'm not ok, because there's blood on the floor. Lots of blood pouring out of daddy and Edwin's bodies all over the floor. Daddy gasps. He's barely breathing. "I love...you...Braeden..." he says between shaky breaths. "She...did...this," he says again, his eyes closing. He's not breathing at all, and neither is my baby brother. They're dead. And I think my mum killed them.

THRASHING MY ARMS about I wake up screaming, my whole body drenched in a cold sweat.

Sitting up in bed Carson curses at me, "Fucker, shut the fuck up!" He throws a pillow at my head.

And I scream again, panic hitting me as I get out of bed. I need to get out of here.

I need fresh air to stop my head from spinning, to rid my mind of the memories of that horrible night.

Grabbing my phone, awkwardly holding it I pull on a t-shirt and some shorts, running out of the caravan. At the door, I stretch my sneakers onto my feet and run.

There's only one place I want to be right now. I need to be with her, to forget and feel.

AS USUAL, getting to her bedroom window I sneak in, climbing into her open window. I love that even when it's freezing she has it open, as though she expects me to be all Romeo and scale all heights to get to her.

Caz May

Once I'm in her room I watch her a moment as she sleeps, murmuring softly when she rolls over and her eyes flutter open to focus on me standing by her bed.

A startled gasp escapes her lips, but she's not scared. She pulls back the covers, and I crawl into bed with her, hugging her close and inhaling the sweet vanilla coconut scent of her freshly washed hair.

We don't exchange words before I kiss her. She accepts the kiss, cupping my jaw as it gets heated, kicking my heart into high gear.

Kissing my Ariel is exactly what I needed.

Breaking the kiss, I smile at her, brushing stray strands of her hair aside so I can see her entire beautiful face.

"Hey darling," I murmur, kissing her forehead, and sniffing back the tears that are threatening to fall from my eyes.

"Hey Braeden," she says softly, gazing straight into my eyes in the darkness. "Are you ok?"

I shake my head.

"No. I. It all came back to me," I stammer, forcing out the words between shaky breaths.

"What? What came back to you?" she asks softly, cupping my jaw again so I look at her.

"Losing my dad and Edwin," I tell her, letting the tears slide down my cheeks. She brushes them away and I continue, "I had a nightmare about it. And my brother didn't give a fucking shit."

"I give a shit," she tells me, barely audible but I feel her words against my lips, and in my heart.

"I know, and I love you for that, darling."

She kisses me then, licking my lips and pulling me closer with her arms wrapping around my waist. Our legs entangle, and my dick jolts in my shorts, desperate for the connection between us to go to the next step once more.

Against my lips, Ariel whispers, "Brae?"

"Yeah, darling?" I enquire, pulling back from the kiss so I can look at her properly.

"I want to tell you about my scars. Why I cut."

"You don't have to," I reply, seeing the worry in her eyes.

"I want to," she responds, adding softer, "I haven't even told Briston."

"Oh, well, um...you don't have to tell me, but it's up to you."

Taking my hand, she sighs, opening and closing her mouth a few times.

Squeezing her hand, I kiss her forehead.

"I'm here darling. Take your time."

Again she sighs, and then says softly, "My mum was mentally ill. She had schizophrenia.

"And in one of her psychosis episodes, she tried to kill me by drowning me when I was sick with a stomach bug."

"Oh darling, that's horrible," I tell her squeezing her hand again, and pulling her closer as she's shivering.

"Yeah, and she was always dressing me up, and all sorts of other odd things.

"So I cut to feel, to feel closer to her. To understand and let out my emotions."

"Oh Ariel, darling I'm so sorry."

Caz May

I don't know what else I can say, what I can do when she shifts in my arms, continuing to let everything out, "And when I was thirteen and mum got diagnosed with breast cancer I tried to drown myself and I nearly bled out."

"Fuck Ariel, I..." I cut my own words off, not continuing but instead, I kiss her, pouring all of my love for her into the kiss.

She breaks the kiss, words again pouring out of her mouth, "My dad found me. And since then he's been super protective of me."

My heart breaks for her, how broken my girl is, how strong, and fierce she is.

"Understandable. Do you still cut?" I ask, adding, "Please tell me you don't, darling."

She nods in the darkness.

"I wasn't for ages...but then everything with you...and Bris happened. And I started to again to let out all the emotions."

"I'm sorry, Ariel. I'm so fucking sorry," I tell her, angry at myself for pushing her down that painful path again.

"It's not your fault Brae," she tells me sincerely, giving me a kiss that makes my heart pound, beating so loudly I'm sure she can hear it in the silence of her room.

"You make me ache for you, my heart, my soul aches for you. I love you, with every beat of my broken heart," I voice with conviction.

She starts to reply, but I silence her with a deep kiss. Breaking it she lifts her t-shirt off, exposing her gorgeous tits that have hardened with our kisses. I yank my own t-shirt off and she hums in appreciation, her gaze raking my torso.

Tamed Hearts

"What do all your tattoos mean?" she asks sweetly.

"So many things darling, a convo for another day, huh?"

"Ok, but only if you take off your shorts as well."

"You wanna see my birthday suit?"

She laughs sweetly.

"Yeah, Brae, I want to see you naked and hard."

Eagerly I shove my shorts down, my dick springing free and hitting her in the stomach.

I kiss her lips, hooking my thumbs into her knickers and sliding them down her legs. Kicking them off, she breaks the kiss, looking at me with lust in her eyes.

Starting at her collarbone, I lave kisses across her skin, down over her tits to her stomach, kissing all her scars. She writhes in pleasure, murmuring, sweet sexy moans escaping her lips.

"You're so beautifully broken, darling. Every inch, every scar shows how beautiful you are."

Once at her pussy, I kiss her clit, my tongue darting in and out of her wet folds, tasting her. She grabs a fist of my hair, yanking my head up to look her in the eyes.

"Brae, please, I need you. Make me feel."

Crawling up the bed I kiss her lips, whispering against them, "You sure, darling?"

"Yeah, Brae, fuck me."

I shake my head at her. I'm not fucking her right now. There's too much emotion in the room.

"No can do, darling. If we're having sex right now, I'm not fucking you."

Caz May

She pouts at me. And I laugh in response, kissing her again—deeper—teasing her by laving my tongue across her lips. Her hips buck up to meet mine, the tip of my dick brushing against her entrance.

Against my lips she moans, and curses as she breaks the kiss, "Fuck, Brae, please I need you, now."

Sliding a hand down between our bodies, I slip a finger inside her pussy, asking her, "Protection? Do you have any condoms?"

She shakes her head, and my heart falls. I don't want to go there again, to sleep with her again without protection.

"No, but I want to feel you Brae. Nothing between us, please." Her words are pleading, and I know I shouldn't but I need her so much right now.

"Fuck it," I call out, taking my finger out of her pussy and putting it to her lips as I glide inside her; bare.

Fuck.

I still inside her, overwhelmed with how incredible it feels. Starting to thrust slowly I cup her cheeks, leaning down to kiss her. Her moans meet my lips as we get lost in other. I've never had sex like this, emotional and deep in connection.

"Braeden," she murmurs my name against my lips, a soft beg for more as her hips meet my slow thrusts with force that's asking for more.

"Yeah, darling?" I ask breaking the kiss, and stilling my thrusts, still seated inside her.

"More, please," she begs, pulling me down for a kiss by grabbing my neck. I obey, pumping in and out of her wet pussy harder. She can't help the moans, and whimpers of

Tamed Hearts

pleasure that are escaping her lips. It's making my dick even harder inside her, hitting her g-spot, causing her to cry out my name, "Braeden, fuck!"

"Ariel, I love you," I call out, trying to keep my voice an octave lower than hers in case her dad hears.

With my dick still seated inside her, I grab her hips and pull her up, so she's sitting on my lap. I kiss her, and she wraps her arms around my neck, starting to bounce up and down on my dick.

Incredible doesn't even begin to describe how it feels. I'm seriously not fucking kidding when I'm saying it's the best sex of my damn life.

I've got sweat dripping down my back, my torso and cheeks. Ariel's hair is clinging to her cheeks with sweat as well, and her gorgeous tits are sweaty and her nipples hard. Bending down I kiss the buds, causing her to loudly moan, a 'fuck' barely audible but in my head.

Our bodies are rocking together, a sensual ride of pleasure. I'm so close to the edge, and I can tell Ariel is edging closer as well, with her pussy clenching tighter around my dick like a vice as she rides me harder and faster.

"Brae, I'm coming," she murmurs to me, her eyes on mine.

"Oh, yeah, darling. Come for me," I tell her as she bears down all the way on my dick, trembling as she comes.

"Fuck, Ariel, you look so fucking beautiful when you come."

She gives me a quick kiss, not making a move to get off my dick, so I push her back down onto the bed.

Caz May

Her legs bend at her knees, around me as I pump back inside her. She pants, and moans, her hips once more bucking up to meet mine, heading towards another orgasm. I moan out her name over and over again, as she pants and moans, her mouth open with her silent screams of pleasure. About to come, I pull out, spraying ropes of cum over her belly and tits.

Gazing up at me, she runs her fingers through the cum on her belly, rubbing it into her skin. "Mmm, Brae, you made me all messy."

"Ariel, darling. You better stop doing that or I'll be fucking you." She giggles, licking her fingers.

"Yummy," she taunts, grabbing my neck to pull me down for a kiss. A dirty, hot pash that's stirring up the lust in my belly, and love in my heart. Breaking the pash, I lick all my cum off her tits, and belly, and kiss her pussy until she comes again with a loud lascivious moan.

Kissing her again, I lay down beside her, neither of us saying a word as we fall asleep in each other's arms. I could honestly get used to the comfort being with her gives me.

❤

WAKING UP TOGETHER, her wrapped in my arms—naked—is sweet bliss. Murmuring I give her an endearing good morning kiss.

"Morning, darling," I coo at her with a smirk that makes her giggle and smile back when she purrs, "Morning, Brae."

"You ok?" I ask her, kissing her forehead.

"Yeah, I will be," she replies, not looking me in the eyes.

Tamed Hearts

"Something else on your mind?"

She nods, her gaze locking on mine when she softly says, "Bris."

I don't like hearing that her best friend is on her mind the morning after I made love to her.

"I…don't think he'll like us being back together," she confesses, hitting me in the guts with what she's implying.

Again I kiss her, to not let my emotions get the better of me. "Let me deal with Briston," I tell her after the kiss.

She stretches, arching her back and I get out of bed, finding all my clothes scattered across her bedroom floor. As I'm getting dressed Ariel rolls onto her side watching me.

"Do you still love him too?"

Pulling up my daks, I nod, looking at her when I reply, "Yeah, darling I do. So much it hurts."

Licking her lips, she smiles and says, "You should tell him. I want both of you…together you make my heart happy."

It's my turn to smile. She may not be able to voice that she loves me specifically but her actions when we were together last night and her other sweet words tell me my girl feels the same about me as I do about her.

"Back at you darling," I tell her leaning over to give her a kiss. "I love you. I'll see you at school soon yeah?"

"Yeah, I'll be back in a couple of days," she tells me, as I shrug my t-shirt on before leaving, by climbing out of her bedroom window into the cool morning air.

Sneaking a look back into Ariel's room I see her sprawled out naked in her bed, back to sleep.

Caz May

She looks so stunningly beautiful, and for a moment I just watch her, thinking about climbing back into bed with her, curse the damn consequences, but I'm also thinking about how I'm going to tell her about Chasity.

I fucked up by fucking the school whore, and I'm scared I'm going to lose Ariel when she finds out.

Just when I've gotten her back, I'm going to lose her all over again, and I don't know if my damaged heart can handle that.

Chapter Twenty-Seven

Ariel

*M*y phone chimes with a text and rolling over in bed I grab it from the beside table.

You still avoiding me?

My heart falls that it's a text from Briston, and not Braeden.

Never was avoiding you Bris.

Caz May

Can I come over?

Always. Dad's asleep. Night shift.

Even better. See you in fifteen

STILL IN MY PJ'S I STUMBLE to the front door when Briston arrives. He eyes me when I open the door, his lip quirking up in a cheeky smile.

"Damn, Ar's baby. Sexy Pj's," he teases, winking at me. Tugging the legs of my shorts down, I let Briston inside, elbowing him in the side.

"Stop it, Bris."

"Never," he teases again, following me back to my bedroom. He's trailing behind me, and I can tell he's watching my arse, so purposely I wiggle it and hear him moan.

Once in my room, I sit down on the bed, and he follows, leaning in to kiss me. I don't return his kiss, and he scowls at me.

"What's up with you, Ar's?"

Not able to meet his gaze, I stare down at the floor.

"I...slept...with..." I can't say it. I can hear Briston's heavy breathing. Maybe I should lie, but that would hurt my best friend, and I can't keep secrets from Briston anymore.

"Who with Ariel? Are you telling me you cheated on me?"

"Well, yeah, nah, I..." I stammer, looking up at him, and the heartbroken expression on his face. I've hurt him, but sleeping with Braeden wasn't a mistake, and sure as hell didn't feel like cheating.

"Ariel, please...just tell me," Briston begs.

Tamed Hearts

"Fine," I reply exasperated. "I slept with Braeden."

"Seriously!" Briston shrieks, loud enough to wake up dad down the hall when he sleeps like a log after night shift.

"Shh, Bris. you'll wake up my dad. And yes...I did. And I don't regret it."

"Come on Ar's. You cheated on me."

"How, Briston? It was Braeden, not some other guy."

"What's that matter? I thought we were like together, Ariel."

"We are, Bris, but I still love Braeden," I tell him, reaching out to touch his bare arm. He shies away, and I continue, "And things are different with him."

"Things like what, Ariel? Is he a better fuck?"

"How could you even ask me that?"

"So he is. Thanks for hitting a guy in the feels, Ariel."

"I'm not saying that Briston. It's just different with Brae because of other things."

"Like what things?" he asks, his eyebrow lifting as he stares at me.

"I can't tell you, but you should talk to him."

He stares daggers at me, an angry *'fuck you'* kinda expression on his face. I don't want to share those things about Brae without his knowledge.

"Can't you tell me?"

"No, you need to talk to Brae. He wants to talk to you, and he misses you."

Briston's gaze drops to the floor. And he mutters under his breath, "I miss him too."

"Then get your head out of your arse Bris, and talk to him."

Caz May

"Fine, I will," he promises leaning closer and kissing me. This time I accept his kiss, to the point of kissing him back until he's pushing me down onto the bed. Stopping him from taking things further, I push him off with my hands on his chest.

"Bris, please, not now."

"Fine, go fuck him then!" he bellows, standing up from the bed, and storming out of the room.

I have no words to say to my best friend—boyfriend?— as he stalks out of my bedroom.

He's being a tosser.

Hopefully, he talks to Braeden, and things can go back to the way they were before.

I miss my B-boys.

My heart only feels whole when it's all three of us together. And I'm scared that's not ever going to be a possibility again.

Chapter Twenty-Eight

Briston

What happened between Ariel and I on the weekend has been on my mind. Her being a bitch after sleeping with Braeden pissed me off, but mostly I'm jealous that she seems to be getting closer to him. And pushing me away in the process.

Caz May

I don't really know what to do, but before school I message him.

We need to talk, apparently

HEY MAN. SOUNDS RIPPER. WHEN YOU DOWN?

Come over after school.

Shoving my phone into my backpack, I head out the door to school. It's pissing down rain, and getting in the jeep I curse loudly from the dripping water on my head. It's only a tiny hole in the canvas top, but when it rains it comes in like waves.

Cements my mood right now. My pissy mood at my best friend, for putting me into this situation. I love her, but her making me feel like second best is a bitch move.

Pulling up at school, I see her walking in with Ava and Dakota. I'm angry at her still, but sneaking up behind her I embrace her from behind.

Hobbling forward, she turns her head to look at me, giving me a scowl.

"Hey, baby," I coo, giving her a smirk.

"You talking to me now, Briston?" she taunts, unable to stop her smile from breaking through.

"Just needed some space, baby," I tell her, giving her a kiss. Ava scoffs from beside us, laughing.

"Might I suggest the cleaning closet for a quickie?" she teases.

Tamed Hearts

"Not going to happen, Ava," Ariel replies. "I've got a big test in Maths today. And I don't want to be late."

Dropping my arms from around Ariel's waist, we continue walking inside, just in time for the bell.

At her locker I give Ariel a sweet dirty kiss goodbye, whispering in her ear, "I'm seeing Braeden after school."

She gives me a smile.

"Good, now get to class, dufus," she teases.

Giving her a playful slap on the butt, under her school skirt I back away whilst smiling at her.

It was stupid to accuse her of cheating on me.

I fucking love that girl, no matter what.

AFTER SCHOOL, nervously I'm pacing the lounge room waiting for Braeden to arrive.

I'd put on a t-shirt but no daks, just tight white boxers. I'm about to go and put on some trackies—because only wearing underwear is presumptuous—when the doorbell rings, and I'm struck stupid, glued to the floor for a moment in panic.

Holy shit.

He's here, and I'm in undies.

Fuck it.

Padding across the floor to the door I inhale deep breaths to calm myself, my racing heart, but also my threatening hard on.

Thinking about him—on my doorstep—after everything that's happened with him and Ariel shouldn't be making me feel this way.

Caz May

He hurt her—hurt me—but just thinking about being with him is sending me spiralling.

Opening the door, I gasp as I take in his sexy self right in front of me. He hasn't changed out of his soccer gear, and his hair is slicked with sweat.

God, he looks fucking edible.

But he's not here for that.

I need to take ahold of my damn balls.

"Hey man," he purrs at me, with a sexy husk to his voice that makes my traitorous dick jolt.

Opening my mouth, I start to say, 'hey' but think otherwise, screaming out, "You don't get to 'hey' me, you fucking arsehole."

He pouts, mouth agape like a fish out of water.

"What crawled up your arse, Briston?" he questions me harshly crossing the threshold like an angry bear on a mission.

My dick is stirring to life in my jocks, and god do I want to kiss him, slam his body against the wall and dry hump him until he's begging me.

Once he's inside I slam the door behind him.

"You hurt her," I bellow at him, clenching my fists.

His face falls again, and biting down on his thin lower lip he mutters, "I had to. I honestly had no choice."

"Yeah, right. Fuck off, Braeden. You made the wrong choice."

He nods, confirming, "Yeah I did, but things are good now."

"Yeah, she told me you fucked her again."

"I didn't fuck her Briston. It was more than that."

Tamed Hearts

"Oh, you making love now?" I question in a teasing sarcastic tone.

"Something like that, but seriously are things not good with you guys? Or are you just a jealous tosser?"

Those words hit me hard. I've never been good at hiding my emotions. And I'm sure my jealousy is written all over my face.

Of course I'm fucking jealous. He's a literal sexy god.

Laughing his comment off, I shove him in the chest and bad idea. A really fucking bad idea. Just touching him has my dick partying in my jocks.

"Who the fuck cares, Braeden. You fucking hurt her, and I hate you! I hate you for that!" I bellow at him, laying into him beating my palms against his chest.

Stumbling backwards he falls over the back of the couch, pulling me down with him so our bodies collide. His strong tattooed fingers grip my wrists, and he tries to jostle me off.

"You don't hate me, Briston," he taunts, smirking at me.

"Yes, I fucking do. I hate you, Braeden!"

"Yeah, then why is your dick hard?"

He pushes his crotch up to mine, his own hard dick creating friction between us.

"My dick is a traitor. Reflex memory."

"Sure. Or you don't hate me and want to..." his voice trails off, and I finish the thought in my head, 'to kiss me'.

"In your dreams, Braeden," I taunt, wrestling him more by gripping his hips. His arms wrap around me, pulling me down so our lips are a breath apart.

Caz May

"Prove it. Prove that you hate me," he says suggestively, raising his eyebrow.

And fuck it I kiss him. And fuck does it feel amazing to be kissing him again.

Kissing Braeden is so raw, and possessive, angry almost compared to kissing Ariel, and it makes my dick steel rod hard. He kisses me back, arching his back so our dicks collide against each other again harder. Moving my hips I kiss him harder, grinding against his erection.

I could come.

Pulling back I grip the waistband of his soccer shorts, whispering, "I don't hate you. Not at all."

He shifts so I can yank the shorts down, and I find he's commando and hard.

"Mmm, fuck Brae. Your dick is glorious," I tell him leaning down as I scoot backwards on the couch and take his length into my mouth.

He moans as I start sucking, and licking his hardness. His skin is silky and warm in my mouth.

Giving a gobby—when he's moaning so loud—is even better than actually getting one myself.

He looks up at me, murmuring, "Fuck you suck good dick, Bris."

Rewarding him for the praise I lick the tip, slit of his dick, tasting his salty precum. Bobbing up and down on his dick, I suck harder, taking him all the way into my mouth, pausing when I feel him hit the back of my throat.

"Fuck, Briston!" he calls out, his dick spasming as he fills my mouth with his load.

Sliding off his dick, I stretch up over his body and kiss him. He grabs my neck, a fistful of my hair, and pulls me closer, kissing me deeper.

"Fuck, Brae...I...I'm sorry...I" I stammer, caressing his cheek.

"You've got nothing to be sorry about man, but I do," he tells me, shifting so we both sit up on the couch.

"I'm sure you don't either," I tell him.

"Yeah I do, man. I did something really fucking stupid."

"Yeah? Other than breaking our girls heart?"

"Yep, I slept with Chastity. It was a mistake."

I hear his words, and absorb them, anger rising in my guts.

Raising my hand, I gulp, retracting it when he asks abruptly, "Bris, man, did you hear me?"

Again I raise my hand, edging it closer to his face.

"Yes, I fucking heard you, arsehole!" I bellow at him, slapping my hand firmly across his cheek.

"Fuck! Bris! That hurt man."

"Good, you deserved it. How could you do that?"

"It meant nothing. Ariel had pushed me away and it was a lapse in judgement."

"So it was just once? When?"

"Before Ar's mum died. And I honestly regretted it straight away."

"She's a ho, Brae. Ariel deserves better than a guy who sinks his dick into a girl like Chasity."

"Don't you think I know that, Briston? Ariel is the most amazing girl I've ever met. She's so beautifully broken. I love her so much."

Caz May

I scoff at his words, letting my sarcasm show.

"Yeah, you love her so much you slept with another girl."

"It was a fucking mistake. Seriously. I shouldn't have even told you since you guys are like, whatever the fuck you are."

"She's my girlfriend, Braeden. And I don't maybe yours to."

"Yeah I don't think we're at that point. The whole labelling us thing."

"You could be. You did make a shit choice, but I'm pretty sure Ar's still loves you."

"She hasn't said as much, but yeah. I know she loves you."

"Trust me, she might not have said it, but she loves you."

He sighs, standing from the couch, pulling up his shorts. "I'm an idiot for hurting her."

"Yeppers," I tell him, with a chuckle. "You should grovel to win her back properly. Show her you love her instead of just telling her."

"That sounds like a plan," he replies when I stand from the couch as well. "We good?"

"Yeah, Brae, we're good," I tell him with a kiss. "But you need to grovel and tell our girl about what you did."

"I will, I promise. No more secrets."

He kisses me then, and I fight the urge to push him down on the couch to ride his dick.

The front door creaks open anyway, and mum comes in, seeing Braeden and smiling like a damn Cheshire cat.

Tamed Hearts

"Hello, Braeden, dear. Lovely to see you."

"Hi Mrs Nicholls. Nice to see you as well."

Again she smiles, nodding to the bags on the porch.

"Briston, be a dear and help me bring in the groceries."

"Yeah, mum. I'll just see Brae out," I tell her, giving her a scowl, followed by a cheeky grin when she gives me a glare that tells me she means business.

Following Braeden to the door, he picks up his bag and slings it over his shoulder.

Stepping outside I shut the door, and shove him against the doorframe to give him a dirty, wish I could fuck you right now kiss.

Breaking it, he gives me a dirty, wicked smirk that makes my dick ache. Damn mum for coming home, and needing me.

"You sure you can't stay? Come up to my room?"

"Nah, I should be getting home. My brother will wonder where I am."

"Right, cool, well I'll see ya at school. Tell Ar's."

"I promise," he says giving me a final kiss before he leaves me with a throbbing dick, and thudding heart.

Yeah, I still fucking love him, despite the fuck up of him hurting Ariel without meaning to.

Hopefully he stands by his word, and tells her. I don't know if I could forgive him if Ariel finds out from someone else.

Caz May

Chapter Twenty-Nine

BRAEDEN

Briston had told me to show Ariel I love her without telling her. Pretty damn hard with barely a cent to my name, but after having raided my soccer ball money box I'm standing in the middle of Woolies on a cool Sunday arvo, staring at the array of boxed chocolates. They all seem so cliched, even just the thought of buying her chocolates and flowers seems cliched, but I'm doing it. I'd do anything to see her smile. Anything to not see pain showing on her beautiful face.

Firstly I pick up a yellow box of the Whitmans chocolates, flipping it over to see what it has in the box. And spotting the name 'cherry cordial' I nearly spit out my chewy in disgust. Those are the most disgusting chocolates ever invented. Just seeing the name on the packaging brings back memories of raiding the box of chocolates dad bought home for Lilith one night when he got home late. Edwin had begged me to get them off the counter, opening and shutting his little fists in his 'gimme, gimme' wordless speech. Secretly I wanted the chocolates as well. Lilith had said we couldn't have dessert again, because I didn't do my chores again. It wasn't fair, nothing ever was with her. Carson got everything he wanted, and even things he didn't want. She loved him the most. To Lilith I was pond scum, and the one who was her lackey around the house, because god forbid she ever lifted a finger.

Now I laugh at the thought of her cleaning dunnies in jail, like she made me do, just for one scoop of ice-cream as a Friday night treat. A treat that I barely ever earnt, because I liked to rebel against her, and leave a big shit in the toilet without flushing it. Blaming that on Carson never worked though, the damn golden child who never did no wrong. If only she knew the half of what my older brother did to me —as a kid—and now.

Shoving the box of Whitmans chocolates back on the shelf, I pick up a box of Roses chocolate, cliched but honestly the best ones.

Caz May

With them tucked under my arm, I go to pick out some flowers, nearly fainting when I see how much they are. How can a few roses, bunched up in cellophane cost twenty bucks? With buying the chocolates, I've only got another ten bucks.

And all I can afford is some ugly as shit, white daisy type flowers. I know they have some other long arse name, but I can't remember, and it's not important. Heading to check out at the self serve registers, I swallow down the anger that builds in me from the glare of the attendant staring at me, as though I'm going to steal something. I know I probably look like a criminal—a guy from the wrong side of town—with my hole filled t-shirt and trackies, but I'd never steal, no matter how desperate I was.

Clutching the chocolates and flowers, I yank the receipt out and throw it in the cocky idiots face, rushing out the store after giving him an up yours. He doesn't look too pleased, but I couldn't honestly give a fuck.

All I give a fuck about is seeing Ariel and giving her these, begging her to love me again.

GETTING TO HER FRONT DOOR, my feet are aching from running barefoot. The stupid gravel path up to her door has dug tiny spears of rock into my baby butt soft feet. Cursing myself, I knock on the foreboding wooden door, hoping Ariel answers and not her dad. He hasn't seen me, or acknowledged me since he found me half naked in his daughters bed.

A minute later the door swings open, and I'm greeted by my girl wearing only a lacy knicker and bra set. It shows her gorgeous body off, and I'm momentarily tongue tied.

"Hey, Brae," she purrs at me, ushering me inside as she says, "What are you doing here?"

"Bringing you these, to show you I love you."

"You didn't have to buy me flowers and chocolates to show me that, Brae," she sweetly replies, taking them from me.

"Well, yeah, nah, Bris told me I needed to show you how I feel in other ways."

Her eyes light up at my mentioning of Briston.

"You spoke to Briston?"

"Yeah, and we…" I cut my words off, following her into the kitchen.

"What? Did something happen with you guys?" she asks, putting the flowers in a vase on the counter that has roses that have seen better days in it.

"Yeah, we kissed, and he sucked me off."

"Oh, wow. So things are good with you both then?"

"Kinda, I'm still on his shit list for hurting you, but he'll forgive me," I say with a smile, thinking of taking her right on this counter.

"He will, and he probably already has," she tells me, smiling and opening the fridge, bending over to grab out a jug of water.

I gulp down the lump in my throat. She's not making this easy on me.

"Darling? You bending over like that…is…fuck…"

Turning back around, she gives me the dick hardening smirk, putting the jug on the counter.

"Is what, Brae?" she taunts, still with the sexy smirk. I gesture down to the rod in my trackies. Her gaze follows, and she licks her lips, stepping closer to me.

"Just begging me to fuck you, right here."

"Oh really?" she taunts again, stepping even closer, right into my personal space, and caging me against the counter.

"Dad isn't home. Night shift," she tells me hastily which causes me to gulp again, and not have a minute to think before she's kissing me.

Her kiss ignites every synapse in my body on fire, sending shockwaves through me as she murmurs and moans into the kiss. Deepening it, I grip her hips and take a step forward, guiding her with me, our lips still locked together in the most delicious kiss.

Breaking the kiss her lustful gaze meets mine, and I ask with a rasp, "Can I fuck you, darling? Right here on the kitchen counter?"

She nods, and still gripping her hips we swap places, turning around so I can hoist her up onto the edge of the marble countertop.

I barely have a moment to think before she grips my neck and brings my lips back to hers. Against them she whispers, "Fuck me now, Braeden."

Groaning I pull back, plunging my trackies, and boxers to the floor.

Tamed Hearts

A sweet gasp escapes her lips as her gaze falls to my hard dick, and she takes it in her hand, stroking it with her eyes locked on my face.

"Fuck, Ariel. I need you," I drawl out, grabbing her lace knickers, and edging them down.

She lifts her butt off the counter, and I slide her knickers over her thighs until they drop to her ankles.

Dipping my finger into her pussy she moans her pleasure, shifting on the bench when I pull it out and put it to her lips. Licking it she whimpers, and I silence her with kiss.

With our lips still dancing in a kiss, I snake my arms around her back, yanking her right to the edge of the counter, and breaking the kiss I stare right into her stormy eyes as I plunge my dick into her pussy.

Biting her lip, she groans, cursing out a raspy, "Fuck!" as I start to thrust. It's hot, hard and fast sex, each thrust rougher and more pleasure inducing than the one before.

"Fuck. Ariel. Darling. You. Feel. So. Good," I say, thrusting in and out with each word.

"Harder, Brae, harder, please," Ariel begs, wrapping her legs around my arse and pulling me in so there isn't an inch of space between our bodies as we seek out the high.

"Fuck, Ariel, I'm gonna come," I call out, letting go as she starts to go over the edge with me.

We come together, in panting breaths, and she kisses me to silence the scream of my release.

Her hands grip my neck again, pulling me down with her as she arches her back to lay back on the counter with the final aftershocks making us both tremble.

Caz May

With my dick still inside her pussy I kiss her again, and she grips my hair, yanking me back to gaze at me with lust in her eyes. "You came in me, Brae," she says as though she doesn't care.

"Shit, I did. I'm sorry, darling," I reply worriedly.

"I didn't stop you Braeden."

"True. I could clean you up," I suggest, winking at her. Her eyes go wide, almost begging me.

"You don't have to do that."

"Never done it, but for you I'm down, darling," I taunt, giving her a quick kiss before I start trailing kisses down her body.

She shivers, as my tongue laves over her scars, all the way down to her pussy that has my cum dripping out of it.

Gripping the edge of the counter to steady myself, I lick her sweet pussy from the bottom up to her clit. Her moan is loud, and lascivious. Tasting our release mixed together makes my head spin. It's oddly arousing and I lap it up, biting down on her clit as I delve my tongue inside her pussy, fucking her with it. Her hands find my hair, shoving my face against her pussy as she fucks my tongue.

"Fuck! Braeden, fuck!" she calls out, trembling again as I suck her swollen pussy, kissing her clit as another orgasm rocks through her.

Still with shivering aftershocks shaking her body, she yanks me back to a standing position, and sitting up she kisses me. Her tongue licks my lips, making the kiss urgent, and breaking it I smile at her.

"I love watching you come, darling."

"Yeah, what else do you love?" she taunts.

Tamed Hearts

"Hmm, making Briston come, fucking you, fucking him."

"Yeah, what's it like?" she asks, her cheeks colouring with her question.

"What? Fucking a guy, or anal?" I ask to clarify.

"Anal," she says, stammering the word out like it's the most dirty word known to man.

"It's amazing. But I don't know from a girl's perspective. You telling me you wanna try it?"

"I don't know, maybe," she confesses, again blushing. "I trust you and Bris to make me feel amazing, and not hurt me." The last words are soft, laced with unspoken emotion. I know I've hurt her. But now I'm hoping I'm closer to her forgiveness.

"I know, darling. I'm never going to hurt you again."

"Promise?"

"Promise. I love you Ariel, my darling."

Her mouth opens, as though she's going to say the words back, but she only smiles, giving me a quick kiss before sliding off the counter.

"Thanks again for the flowers and chocolates. That was really sweet," she tells me as I bend down to pull up my daks. "But I loved fucking you more. That shows you love me more than any flowers and chocolates ever could."

"Is that so?" I ask, tilting her face to gaze up at me with a finger under her chin.

"Yeah," she replies against my lips as I kiss her again. "But right now, even though I want to ride your dick, on the couch maybe, right now, you need to go."

And just like that my dick is aching for her, but I hear her words.

Caz May

"Daddy coming home soon huh?"

"Yeah, and I'll never hear the end of it if he finds you here. He'll be expecting me to be tucked up in bed, reading."

"Yeah, not in your underwear, fucking one of your boyfriends on the couch." The moment I say the words I regret them. I don't even know how she feels about me, and I'm calling myself—and Briston—her boyfriend.

"You said it. I was actually about to take a shower when you arrived on my doorstep, hence the underwear."

"Oh," I mutter, thinking dirty thoughts again. She's killing me, without even meaning to.

"So you don't normally answer the door wearing sexy underwear?"

Playfully she slaps my chest.

"No, dufus. And I thought it was my dad at the door. He always forgets his house keys."

"Right, well, honestly I probably should go. Think of me when you're touching yourself in the shower."

She stretches up on her tiptoes to kiss me, whispering against my lips, "Never."

Laughing our lips part, and I give her a kiss on the forehead.

"I'll see you at school, darling. I love you." She smiles at me, as I walk out, blowing me kisses that make my heart flutter.

Desperately I want to hear her say she 'loves me' again. The words are there—on the tip of her tongue—I can feel them, but for whatever reason she's not ready.

Tamed Hearts

I can only tell her myself, and heading out of her house with my heart beating for her I'm thinking of another way to tell her my words are true, that my heart is being tamed by her.

Caz May

Chapter Thirty

BRAEDEN

Sitting under a tree by the bleachers at lunch, I'm surrounded by friends, including my girl and Briston.

We're all sitting cross-legged, munching on our lunch and chatting. It feels nice, as though they're being accepted into my world, and everything is right with that world.

It's good to feel like something is right in my life, because things at home have been absolute hell. It doesn't even feel like home anymore. Hasn't felt like home since dad and Edwin died all those years ago, and the house we'd lived in for six years of my life was pulled from under us.

Now Carson thinks his goal, or purpose in life is to parade around playing with dirty money. He's been raking a lot in these past couple of weeks, counting it on the pull out table in the caravan cackling like a maniac.

I'd not gone home after seeing Ariel last night, except to sneak in this morning to grab my uniform. Carson was thankfully asleep, so it was easy enough. But my head is a world away, and I'm only just listening to what Briston is saying.

"So, Ar's, are you doing anything for your birthday tonight?"

I turn to look at Ariel, watching her face fall into a frown.

"What? It's your birthday, darling?" I ask, brushing my thumb across her cheek.

She gazes at me, giving me a sweet lopsided smile.

"Yeah, it's my eighteenth," she tells me, turning her gaze back to Briston to respond to him, "And no I'm not doing anything. I think dad's completely forgotten with mum's death and stuff at the hospital being so crazy lately."

"Yeah but Ar's, baby. It's your eighteenth. We should be partying."

"Nah, I'm not up for that, Bris. I'd rather just have a quiet one."

My heart breaks for her, but I get it.

My last birthday a few months ago came and went, completely under the radar. Carson tried to give me money,

Caz May

which I refused. And his other present was a set of gold knuckle dusters that he told me were to fuck anyone up who dared to cross me. I'd wanted to put them on straight away, and fuck up his face with them. But I didn't. I thanked him, gave him a platonic hug showing no affection for him, and shoved them under my bunk when he wasn't looking.

Ariel has tears in her eyes when she looks back at me.

"I get it darling. But you should've told me, regardless."

"I know. I'm sorry, but I didn't want you getting me a present you can't afford." Those words sting, but she means well.

"Aww, darling, that's sweet. Come here," I say, tapping my knee.

She climbs into my lap, not caring that we're surrounded by our friends who have no clue about us being together. I don't care one bit.

Caressing her cheeks with my thumb, I wipe her tears away and kiss her, wrapping my arms around her waist to pull her closer. She melts against me, the kiss becoming hot and urgent with our tongues teasing each others in a dirty dance. My dick strains against my slacks and hearing Briston scoff next to us, I pull back.

"You should probably go find a deserted classroom or something," he taunts, suggestively, giving me a wink.

"Oh yeah, you wanna join us? Give our girl a birthday present together?" I question him, tentatively reaching out to brush my thumb over his plump lips. He licks it, taking it between those lips that drive me wild with lust.

"Mmm, yeah. I need to give Ar's her other present in private anyway."

Ariel's eyes light up, and Briston stands, extending his hand to her so she can get up off my lap. I stand then, following them both inside the school building, with Ariel's hand in mine.

The corridors are empty at lunch time, and passing by Briston's locker he grabs out a small wrapped present, clutching it to his chest as we head into one of the classrooms at the very back of the school.

It's not used much—a spare one—so it only has a few long desks and chairs stacked at the back. Yanking the cord of the blind on the door I close it, stalking back to Ariel and Briston who have started kissing.

Ariel is sitting on the edge of a desk, with Briston between her legs. Stepping up behind him, he breaks the kiss with her, and turns back to kiss me. His kiss tastes like chocolate milkshake thanks to his lipgloss, and murmuring he turns around, cupping my erection as he kisses me harder.

Ariel pants behind us, and my dick groans in my slacks when I break the kiss with Briston to find Ariel touching herself with her skirt hitched up her thighs.

"Darling, that's hot," I tell her, watching her slipping her fingers in and out of her pussy, her eyes darting between Briston and I. "But we should be touching you on your birthday."

"I'd love that," she drawls as Briston and I stalk back towards her on the desk.

Briston kisses her lips, and with a hand on her tits I push her softly to lay down on the desk. Kneeling down on the floor—on one knee—with my hands on her thighs I pry her

177   Caz May

legs open. Sliding the lace of her knickers to one side I slip a finger into her pussy, watching her still kissing Briston, and moaning into the kiss.

Briston breaks the kiss with Ariel, kissing me as I pull out my finger of Ariel's pussy, putting it to her lips and coating them with her arousal. It's so fucking hot, hearing her moaning, knowing she's watching as I kiss Briston.

Breaking my kiss with Briston, my lips find Ariel's pussy, delving deep inside her to lap up all she has to offer me. Her hips raise from the desk, as she starts to fuck my face, letting out sexy, loud moans that have Briston covering her mouth with his palm to silence her.

Her hips are bucking up and down, as I continue licking her pussy. Biting her clit makes her tremble, her pussy spasming and sending her over the edge in an explosive climax. A squirting climax that soaks her knickers and drips down between her thighs onto the desk and floor.

"Damn, darling. That was some orgasm. You should probably take off those soaked knickers for me to hang on to," I coerce indecently. She lets out a giggle, sitting up on the edge of the desk to kiss me, licking my lips to taste her pussy on them.

"Damn, Ariel. You're so dirty, darling."

"Only for my B-boys," she teases with a sexy smirk, turning to kiss Briston as she stands up from the table.

She starts to palm his dick over the front of his slacks, and he moans into the kiss.

"Damn, baby. Suck me, please," he murmurs to her. Her eyes find mine and she uses her other hand to palm my aching dick as well.

Tamed Hearts

With another cheeky giggle, she commands of both Briston and I, "Take out your dicks." I love her demanding sexy tone, and so does Briston clearly as he stares at me whilst we both undo our slacks, pushing them to our knees and flipping our hard dicks out of our jocks.

Groaning I look at Briston's dick, fighting with the urge to suck him off myself. He grips my neck, yanking me closer to him, and kissing me so hard my breath is stolen. Our dicks collide together as we kiss, and Ariel whimpers next to us. The sounds she makes watching us together always turn me on.

Briston's breaks the kiss and Ariel smiles at us, hooking her fingers into the sides of her soaked knickers under her skirt. She pulls them down to her knees and crouches down, grabbing both my dick and Briston's dick in her hands. I can see her pussy under the skirt, smell her cum. It's making my dick she's stroking with Briston's at the same time even harder.

"Damn, baby, that feels so good," Briston murmurs. "Think you could suck both our dicks at the same time?"

Ariel lets out an exasperated breath, smirking when she leans forward and licks the tips of our dicks, her tongue darting in the slit and over the flesh, tasting the pre cum that's pearling.

I want to encourage her, but my words are caught in my throat with only a groan escaping when her mouth is over my dick, and Briston's too. Her lips are so wide, slowly and cautiously taking our hard lengths into her mouth.

Pausing she pulls back, standing and taking off her knickers. She hands them to me, and I kiss her, my hands

Caz May

untucking her shirt, fumbling with the buttons to open the white dress shirt so her black lace bra is exposed.

She gives us both that sexy dick hardening smirk.

"I want you to cum on me," she tells us both, dropping to a crouch again.

She sucks us both then, taking our dicks into her mouth in turn, then together, until we're both panting and on the edge.

Again she takes our dicks in her hand, pumping our shafts at the same time. Her back is arched, pushing her tits up and together Briston and I shoot ropes of cum all over her tits and stomach.

"Fuck Ariel, darling, you look beautiful with your skin painted with our cum," I tell her stepping closer to her.

"Lay down on the table, baby, so we can clean you up," Briston says from next to me with a wink.

Ariel follows his direction, desire flashing in her eyes.

Briston and I lick our come off together, our tongues brushing each others as we lave them over Ariel's stomach and tits.

Once her skin is clean, Briston kisses me.

"Mmm, Bris. You taste fucking delicious, man."

"Back at you. Should probably give our girl her actual present."

We all dress quickly, hearing the pre bell music starting to play through the speakers.

From the table next to him, Briston grabs the wrapped box. Handing it to Ariel, he says, "Happy birthday, Ar's baby."

Tamed Hearts

Carefully she rips the paper, to find a plain white box. Opening the tab, the box is filled with white shredded paper, and in the middle is a small butt plug with a pink, sparkly stopper.

"Oh my god, Briston!" Ariel calls out, eyeing it and looking at him with a wide grin.

"Do you like it?"

"I love it, Bris. Thank you for making this birthday so dirty, my B-boys."

We each give her a kiss, just as the bell goes. I tuck Ariel's knickers I'm still clutching in a fist into my slacks pocket, and take her hand with mine, following Briston out of the classroom.

I'm feeling giddy, not believing that we just got away with our little tryst at school.

At her locker, after seeing Briston off to class and once she's put her naughty present inside I shove Ariel against the lockers kissing her, squeezing her bare arse.

"I'm going to be thinking about you wearing no knickers all arvo, darling."

"Mmm, Brae," she murmurs. "I'm still wet, and it's dripping down my thighs."

"Fuck, darling, don't tell me that or I'll be fucking you against the lockers."

She gives me another kiss, panicking when the second bell goes.

Breaking apart, we both rush to class. I watch her running—not caring I'll be incredibly late for English—when her skirt is flipping up and showing me her arse.

Caz May

She might have said to Briston that she wants to be alone for her birthday, but I don't believe her.

My present isn't near as dirty as Briston's, but it means a lot to me, and heading to class my mind is spinning with sharing it with her, and then playing with Briston's dirty present as well.

❤

CLUTCHING MY GUITAR CASE, I climb into Ariel's window awkwardly. She doesn't even move when I fall into the room, but her eyes catch mine.

Instantly—seeing what she's doing on her bed—my dick hardens. Her pj shorts are around her ankles, and her legs open with the butt plug in her hand. As I cross the room towards her bed, she's trying to insert it, but flinches every time the pointy tip is near the unexplored hole.

"Brae..." she murmurs my name.

"Hey, darling. Looks like you need some help with that."

"I...can't...do...it," she stammers, almost crying. "I want to, but I can't."

I let out a laugh, sitting on the edge of her bed, and yanking off her pj shorts.

"You need to be really wet, darling."

"Oh, " she mutters, sitting up and kissing me without warning. "Kissing you makes me wet, Brae."

"Does it now?" I tease, sliding a hand down to her pussy and slipping two fingers inside her.

I kiss her lips again, finger fucking her, and loving the moans she can't help but let out.

Tamed Hearts

Ariel is always so responsive when it comes to anything sexual, and it's so hot.

Breaking the kiss, I ask her, "Are you ready, darling?"

"For what?"

"To come harder than you ever have before."

"Ok, I'm ready," she tells me, handing me the butt plug. Rubbing it over her pussy makes her murmur in pleasure. Once it's wet I press it against her arse.

"Relax, darling."

"Ok, Brae," she murmurs, as I slowly edge the plug into the unexplored territory.

"Oh my god, oh...fuck," she moans arching her hips up, her breath hitching as I slide three fingers inside her pussy to fuck her with them.

Her moans grow louder as I fuck her with my fingers faster, and harder, making her writhe in pleasure on the bed.

"Oh my god, Braeden! Fuck!" she calls out. "That feels so good. I'm going to come, fuck I'm going to come."

I withdraw my fingers from her pussy, making her gasp, as I rub her clit and pussy in a blur of my fingers passing over her flesh.

"Brae, fuck!" she calls out, making another pleasure filled gasp as I slide the three fingers back inside her, thrusting them in and out whilst I watch her face.

Her whole body is writhing with the pleasure, her legs trembling as she gets closer to the edge and she loudly moans, letting go in a rush that forces my fingers out of her pussy, her squirt so intense it hits me in the face.

Caz May

She's still trembling, aftershocks pulsing through her body when I lick my fingers clean, and kiss her, zealously. She moans against my mouth, laving her tongue over my lips in a kiss so intense my heart races, about to burst out of my chest.

Breaking the kiss, I smile at her.

"Darling, that was so fucking hot. Watching you come is fucking beautiful."

"I've never come that hard. And I...can't believe I squirted again."

Her cheeks colour.

"It's so hot, darling. It turns me on, so bad."

"Show me," she taunts, sitting up and pulling her top off, so her beautiful perky tits are bare and pebbled to attention.

"Fuck, darling. You're so beautiful. I love you," I tell her, my eyes on hers as I yank my own t-shirt off and lean over her to kiss her again.

We're pashing now, enjoying just kissing each other.

Her hands find my waistband, reaching inside my trackies to stroke my already hard dick.

I want more, but I haven't even done what I crawled into her bedroom window for yet. And after that climax she needs a break before I fuck her again.

Smiling at me, she asks, "Why did you bring your guitar?"

"For your birthday present," I tell her with a wicked smirk that makes her giggle. "But you distracted me darling."

"Oh, well I'd love to have it now...but..."

Tamed Hearts

"But what?" I ask intrigued.

"I want you naked," she says suggestively as I stand from the bed.

Dakking myself I step out of my trackies, crawling across her bedroom floor to get my guitar out of the case.

Moving back across the floor, I sit cross-legged with my back against the bed, my guitar in my lap.

Taking in a deep breath, I start to strum the simple melody, humming to prepare myself to sing.

I can tell Ariel is looking at me intently, but I'll break down and not get the words out if I turn to face her.

Closing my eyes, after taking in a deep breath, I start to sing,

"EVERY NIGHT, DARLING
I DREAM OF YOUR SWEET FACE
I DREAM OF YOUR INEXPLAINABLE EYES

GAZING AT ME, LOVINGLY

AND I SING
TO YOU
LOVE YOU BEAUTIFUL
YOU KNOW YOU'RE THE ONE

YOU'RE THE ONE
YOU'RE EVERYTHING I WANT
I NEED
I WANT
I NEED YOU
CAUSE' I

LOVE YOU BEAUTIFUL
YOU KNOW YOU'RE THE ONE

WHEN I FOUND YOU
I KNEW
YOU'RE PERFECT IN MY EYES

Caz May

YOU'RE THE WORLD TO ME
AND ALL I REALLY WANT IN LIFE IS YOU
CAUSE' I

LOVE YOU BEAUTIFUL

AND I SING
TO YOU
LOVE YOU BEAUTIFUL
YOU KNOW YOU'RE THE ONE
LOVE YOU BEAUTIFUL
YOU KNOW YOUR THE ONE."

I stop singing, strumming the final note, and letting my voice linger on the final word.

"Oh my gosh, Brae. That was amazing," she affirms, jumping off the bed and climbing into my lap after I throw my guitar aside.

"Did you write that?" she asks.

"Yeah, I did for you, darling. Happy birthday." She doesn't reply, just kisses me, cupping my cheeks in her soft dainty hands to pull me closer. This kiss is intense in that heart hammering way.

Breaking it she's looking right into my eyes, right into my soul, my heart that belongs to her.

"Brae, I...I love you," she confesses, taking ahold of my heart with the hand she puts on my chest.

I kiss her again, murmuring against her lips, "I love you too, darling."

My words are sweet, but I then tease her pulling back and questioning her, "You wanna know what it feels like to fuck with the butt plug in?"

Tamed Hearts

Her eyes light up with desire, as I push my aching dick up towards her pussy that's dripping all over my lap.

"Mmm, yeah," she murmurs, standing up and sauntering over to her desk.

Opening the drawer she throws me a silver foil packet that I catch effortlessly as I stand.

The butt plug is still firmly inside her arse, and it's glistening in the moonlight streaming in from her window.

I'd love to take her arse, to fuck her there or have Briston fucking her there whilst I take her pussy. Just thinking that has my dick that's already hard throbbing and desperate to fuck my girl until she's screaming.

Ripping the packet open, I slide the condom down over my dick as I stalk across the room to the desk.

We don't exchange any words. I can tell exactly what she wants, because it's exactly what I want as well.

Gripping her hips, her torso falls over the edge of the desk, so her butt is out towards me.

"Damn, darling. You look so fucking sexy right now," I tell her, making her moan as I spear inside her. I start thrusting in and out—hard—gripping her hips as my dick disappears inside her and I pull all the way back out, only to go back inside her even harder.

Fucking her with her bent over her desk is raw and hot, causing sweat to pearl our skin.

"How does it feel, darling?" I question her, stilling inside her and leaning over her back a moment to kiss her.

"Incredible, Brae. Harder, please. I want to come."

I follow her request, grasping her arse cheeks in my hands as I pound inside her pussy furiously.

Caz May

"Brae, fuck, so good. Yeah!" Ariel calls out, trembling again as she comes. Her release makes my dick pulse, ready for release.

Pulling out, I yank the condom off and cum all over her back, ropes of hot cum painting her flesh.

She stands up facing me with a wide grin, that makes me panic.

"Darling we weren't quiet," I say under my breath. She laughs and says, "I told you earlier today dad is at work."

"Oh right, cool, but shit."

"Yeah, I would've said something if I had to. Trust me."

"Of course, darling."

She gives me a kiss, and takes my hand.

"We should get clean," she suggests, biting down on her lower lip.

"If you want shower sex, I might need a moment."

"No sex, just need to get clean. I've got cum all over me," she jeers, touching her tits and stomach that have dried come on them from earlier today.

I laugh, because it's true, and getting her clean is the least I can do.

With our hands in each others, I follow her into a bathroom across the hall from her room.

It's strange being in a different part of her house.

Once in the bathroom, she drops my hand to turn on the shower, which is an open shower with a huge rain shower-head.

With a sexy smirk she steps under the water, beckoning me to follow her with a curl of her finger.

It takes me a moment, as I'm so mesmerised by her, with the water cascading over every curve of her body.

Stepping into the shower with her I envelope her in my arms, kissing her.

"You're so beautiful, darling. I hope you had a great birthday."

"Best birthday ever," she replies kissing me again.

Reaching down to her arse I slowly pull out the butt plug, and she shivers from the release, an aftershock of pleasure.

Dropping it on the tiles, it clanks but I don't focus on that. I'm staring at Ariel. There's so much love in her eyes, that mirrors the love I have back for her.

"Can you wash me?" she asks with a smirk.

"Sure darling," I reply, taking the bar of soap she hands me. I lather it over her tits, and stomach, loving the sweet murmurs she lets out.

This is so intimate, and makes my heart beat thud in my chest.

We continue the shower just washing each other and kissing for what feels like forever. The water temperature changes to tepid, and turning it off we get out, wrapping ourselves in fluffy white towels, and hobbling back to her room, still kissing each other.

Getting to the door of her bedroom, we hear a crash from downstairs.

Ariel stifles a giggle, shutting her bedroom door behind us.

"Shit, dad is home early. You have to go."

Caz May

Laughing, I quickly get dressed, shoving my guitar back in the case.

Climbing out of her window, I give her a kiss as she leans out. I'm finding it hard to stay on the ledge, and not fall to my death.

"I love you Braeden. Thank you for tonight."

"Anytime, darling. I love you too," I tell her starting to climb back down to the ground.

I can't stop smiling, looking up at one of the loves of my life standing at her window smiling at me.

Walking away though, I curse myself, because I let myself get caught up in being with her, and I still didn't tell her about my fuck up.

My fuck up that's going to break her heart when she finds out.

Chapter Thirty-One

Ariel

*A*ll night I couldn't stop thinking about Braeden. His amazing song and the amazing sex we shared. I'm still smiling now, sitting with Ava and some other friends at lunch by the bleachers. Braeden looks undeniably gorgeous kicking a soccer ball around with the team, and I can't stop staring, and smiling.

Caz May

"You're more smiley than usual," Ava says with a laugh, breaking my Braeden trance.

"Yeah, had a great night," I tell her blushing.

She laughs, poking me. "What kinda great night? Like a dirty one?"

"Yeah, I had the hottest sex with Braeden last night."

"I knew it! You've got that post sex giddy smile."

"You have no idea," I tell her, blushing. "I've never had sex like that, nor come like that."

"Sounds fun," Ava replies, giddily. "I'm guessing he told you then?"

I give her a confused look. "Told me what?"

"You don't know about Chasity?" Ava asks, looking down at the run in her tights.

"No. What're you talking about?"

"Shit, I'm sorry Ariel."

"Sorry about what. Tell me Ava, please. You're scaring me."

"I...he really hasn't told you?"

Her constant questions, and dodging my responses is annoying and making me angry and extremely anxious.

"Seriously Ava, hasn't told me what?" I probe, biting down on my lip to curb my anger.

"I really shouldn't be telling you."

My anger is now at boiling point. Ava's been such a great friend to me, and I hate that she's hiding something from me, just as much as I'm feeling anger at Braeden because from what Ava is dodging in telling me involves him.

"Please, Ava, just tell me," I beg, taking in a deep breath to brace myself for what she's going to say, as I'm sure it's going to break my heart.

"He slept with Chasity."

"What? You're shitting me yeah," I question, even though her expression tells me the truth. I can feel the tears stinging my eyes, but I don't want to cry.

"I wish I was. I'm sorry you had to find out this way, from me, and not Brae himself."

"Yeah, I...shit...I...love him...and he..." I mutter out between sudden hiccups.

"I know you love him. And he loves you too. He made a mistake, Ariel."

"Big mistake. He slept with another girl."

"Yeah, but you should talk to him about it. Don't let this break you guys."

I nod, not meeting her eyes, even when she touches my arm to offer some comfort.

My eyes find Braeden on the soccer pitch. He stops mid kick, turning his gaze to me, and smiling at me.

I can't smile back.

My heart is completely shattered.

I got played, taken into the fire by the devil himself, believing his sob stories when all he wanted was to fuck me, and discard me. I knew he had a reputation, but he'd never shown me that, fooling me.

I want to race up to him, and beat my fists into his chest, to scream at him, but making a scene at school is social suicide. And I need to calm down anyway, so I'm not a sobbing mess when I confront him.

Caz May

Standing up, Ava follows me to the bathroom, where I grab a wad of toilet paper. Blowing my nose into it, I throw it in the toilet and wipe my eyes with my sleeve.

"I can't believe I was so stupid to fall for him."

"We can't help who we fall in love with, Ariel. Just talk to him, when you're ready of course."

"Yeah," I say softly with a smile. The music starts playing from the speakers, signalling our summoning to class.

"You gonna be ok?" Ava asks, as we head out of the bathroom to our lockers.

"Yeah, I've got history with Bris."

"Oh cool, where was he today anyway?"

"Detention. Something to do with his English essay."

"Oh right, cool. Well, text me if you need me. And speak to Brae," she affirms, waving at me as she heads to her locker.

Waving back I nod, going to my locker to get my books.

I wonder if Briston knew and didn't tell me. So many thoughts about why Braeden would do that, and when it happened and why he told Ava are swirling in my head.

I'm not crying anymore, but I'm angry, and even though I really don't want to go anywhere near the hell hole where Braeden lives I'm going to confront him tonight, to find out the truth.

So much for no secrets between us.

Chapter Thirty-Two

Ariel

My emotions are still running high. I'm fuming, barely able to hold back the tears from cascading down my cheeks. I'd snapped at Briston when he asked me what was wrong, and recoiled from his embrace when he tried to comfort me. As usual he'd tried to get me to talk by throwing in some humour to cheer me up, but I couldn't even crack a smile.

Caz May

I'd hung back in the library after school, so that I could follow Braeden home after practice. It gives me a strange sense of déjà vu, from the day I followed him the first time.

Finding out he lived in the caravan park squeezed my heart, made me fall for the broken side of him, his wild heart. But now I know, despite his words that he doesn't have a heart.

ONCE AT THE CARAVAN PARK, I hang back watching Braeden stalk inside the caravan as though the weight of the world is going to hit him square in the shoulders the moment the door of the caravan closes behind him.

I wonder for a moment if his brother is home, but there's no car by the caravan.

Pulling up my big girl knickers, I take slow steps towards his caravan, not sure if I'm ready to confront him about it.

Reaching the caravan, I knock on the rickety door. I hear Braeden curse from inside before the door swings open, almost hitting me in the face.

"Oh shit, darling. I'm sorry," he says frowning and reaching out to hug me. I recoil, pushing past him as I shove inside the caravan. It's now or never. If I don't say what I need to now, I won't ever say it.

"Don't act all coy," I roar at him. His face falls, and he gives me a what the fuck look.

"What's wrong, darling?"

"You. You slept with another girl, Braeden!" I bellow at him, balling my fists to contain my anger. I want to beat them against his chest, and scream at him.

"Fuck!" he curses, balling his own fists. "Who told you?"

"That doesn't fucking matter! You should have told me, Braeden!" I seethe at him, stepping more into his personal space. He grabs my hand, but I snatch it back.

"Don't touch me!" I shriek at him, fighting the tears again.

"Fuck, Ariel! I'm sorry, ok? I should've told you, right after it fucking happened...but..."

"But what? You felt too guilty for cheating on me?"

"I didn't fucking cheat on you!"

"Really? Sleeping with Chasity *'had every guy in school'* isn't cheating on me?"

"I didn't cheat, because we weren't together."

"Fuck you, Braeden! We never broke up," I say through gritted teeth, my own lies hitting me hard.

"You pushed me away, Ariel. So the way I saw it, we'd broken up. It was a mistake, and I wish I could take it back."

"Too late now," I inform him, still with the same angry tone.

"Can you forgive me? It won't happen again."

I want to say yes, that I'd forgiven him even before I stepped inside the van and started hurling angry words at him, but I don't get to say another word because the caravan door slams open again.

Carson comes stomping inside, giving Braeden a cocky smirk.

"Well, well, what's happening here," he taunts, the smell of whiskey permeating the air from his mouth.

"Nothing, Carson. We were just talking," Braeden says to his brother.

Caz May

"Right, looks to me as though you didn't heed my warning about bringing your slut here."

Braeden seethes, raising his fist about to hit his brother, but Carson catches it in his grip before Braeden can make the punch.

"I wouldn't be doing that brother. You don't want your girl here to see me take you down for putting your hands on me."

My breath hitches in my chest. Carson's threats scare me.

I can see the fear in Braeden's eyes, and I hate it.

I'm still upset with him about Chasity, but I don't want to see him like this.

I don't want to see him get hurt. And I honestly don't know what makes me reach out to grab Braeden's hand, adrenaline maybe. But the moment my hand grips his, I regret it.

Carson's eyes rake me, dark raven completely dilated pupils staring at me.

"Aww, little slut is trying to protect him."

"Yes. Please. Don't. Hurt. Him," I stammer, gripping Braeden's hand tighter, whilst staring into Carson's soulless eyes.

"Begging isn't going to help, little slut. My brother here knows better than to bring sluts around here. And bringing you for the second time, he clearly hasn't learnt from the last time."

Taking a deep breath in, I stomp on his foot.

"Fuck! Little slut!" he bellows, launching at me and grabbing me around the waist.

My hand is wrenched from Braeden's.

Time stands still as I'm shoved against the wall.

"You can't win against me, but props for trying," he says right in my face, his alcohol tainted breath so close I can taste it.

His hand finds my throat, gripping it so tight I gasp for air. He turns to glare back at Braeden behind him.

"Watch your little slut, brother. Watch her taking her last breaths."

Again time ceases to exist, with Carson's cold stare back on me, as he squeezes my neck harder. I can already feel my skin bruising, and I try to fight back. To do anything to get free, but I'm close to passing out.

My eyes close. And I'm fading.

TAKING A GASPING BREATH, I inhale air into my lungs realising that Braeden has pulled his brother off me.

Opening my eyes I watch the scene before me, Braeden fighting his brother, laying into him with clenched fists. Blow after blow hitting his brother in the face, the chest, the stomach.

Carson still has the cocky grin on his face, taunting Braeden to hit him again, whilst barely fighting back. Something is amiss with that. And I'm honestly scared shitless, glued to the floor, but desperate to run out of the caravan for help.

Whilst I'm contemplating how to do that, with Carson able to see my escape I again gasp—this time in shock—when Carson pulls out a gun from his back pocket.

Caz May

"Braeden," I rasp, my voice hoarse and barely a whisper. He hears me though, stopping the pounding of his fists into his lowlife brother to look back at me. And big mistake.

Carson shifts the gun, raising it up as Braeden takes a step back towards me. He has the gun pointing it at the side of Braeden's head.

Carson lets out a maniacal laugh, demonic even.

"It's like Romeo and Juliet. The lovers dying."

"Only one dying today will be you, brother," Braeden threatens, making my heart beat catch in my chest. He wouldn't do that, would he?

I don't want to know, but I can't tear my eyes away from them, especially when Braeden grabs his brother's arm, wrenching it down so the gun is between them.

He shoves Carson to the floor, wrestling him and trying to turn the gun towards Carson.

I let out a scream. I'm so scared that I'm about to watch Braeden die, right before my eyes.

My heart is beating a thousand miles a minute and when Braeden yells, "Go darling, go get help!"

I run out gulping in air so hard I cough.

And that's when I hear it.

The most heart shattering sound.

Chapter Thirty-Three

Ariel

The gun went off, the shattering sound of a bullet ringing through the air.

No, no, no! Please no!

Panicking I run back inside to find Braeden standing over Carson's body in a panic.

Thank fuck, but holy shit!

Caz May

He's staring down at him, his breathing heavy and laboured. He turns to look at me, fear in his eyes that scares me as well.

Inhaling a deep breath, I tell my racing heart to calm a moment.

"Brae, what happened?" I ask softly, stepping up beside him. "Are you ok?"

His stare cuts right through me, his panic becoming my own when he curses, "Fuck, fuck he...fuck...he's dead. He... he..." His words are panicked, and he grips his hair so hard he could pull it out.

"Fuck!" he bellows again, so wrought with emotion it feels as though he's ripping my heart out. I'm torn with my own emotions, with worry that he's done the unthinkable.

Still I reach out, hugging him. He starts to cry, his tears falling on my hair.

Looking up at him, I softly tell him, "It's ok."

He pulls back from the hug, angry with my words.

Staring me down he screams, "It's not fucking ok Ariel."

I bite my lip, not sure what I can even say. He won't hear my words. And being honest every word I say to calm him feels like lies.

"Fuck...people are going to think I killed him," he says, balling his fists again before he punches the wall.

Seeing him like this is breaking me. I don't want to know, but I need to know.

"But did you?"

"What do you fucking think?" he screams at me, staring me down again.

Tamed Hearts

I'm stupefied with his dark eyes locked on me, expectantly. I'm completely tongue tied, opening my mouth for only a gasp to come out. My lack of words makes him angry.

"Ariel, come on," he says, a little calmer. "Do you really think I'd kill him?"

"I don't know Braeden," I reply, panicking and knowing the moment I say those words they're the wrong ones.

I see Braeden's heart break, hear the sirens, and panic again, rushing out without even looking at him. The police get out of the car's, and I watch them heading to the caravan. I should say something but I can't.

This feels like goodbye. The second time my heart is shattering into a million pieces here, right in this very spot.

I love Braeden, but he's so broken—to the point that he's possibly killed his brother—and I don't know what to believe, what to feel.

Surely it was an accident whilst they were fighting, but I honestly don't know. I stand still then, watching the police surveying the scene, and I let the tears fall.

Caz May

Chapter Thirty-Four

BRAEDEN

I'm still standing over Carson's body, watching the blood coat the floor around him when the police barge in with their guns cocked at me.

"Step aside son, hands behind your back," the officer says authoritatively.

My breathing is ragged, shaky, full of panic.

I'm going to be pinned for a crime I didn't commit. I can't see how this won't be on me, with no one witnessing what actually went down inside the van.

The officer cuffs me. The cold metal bites my wrists and I bite my lip to stop from cursing.

They're so calm, and my heart is racing.

I'm being arrested.

Everything, every facet of my life is going up in flames, completely going to shit.

Leading me out in the handcuffs I glance around the park, spotting Ariel standing stiff near the cop cars.

Fighting the restraint of the cuffs, and the officer leading me away from her I scream, "Ariel! Tell them! I didn't do it!"

She looks at me, but doesn't say anything. I can see she's in tears, wretched tears that are breaking my heart. I can't get to her. And I don't even know if I actually screamed the words or if they were silent screams of the fear that's rushing through me.

Our eyes are on each other, not daring to glance away as I'm slid inside the back of the cop car. It feels surreal, as though I'm dreaming.

God I hope I'm fucking dreaming.

But I know I'm not when the door of the cop car is slammed shut and I'm being taken away, only able to watch Ariel through the window.

The tears have started to fall down my own cheeks, my heart shattering as we drive away to take me to hell.

Caz May

AT THE POLICE STATION I'm lead into an interview room. It's dark, except for the swinging overhead light that casts an eerie glow over the table I'm sitting at in a metal chair that's cold under my arse.

The door creaks open, and a familiar faced man walks in, holding an iPad. He has a calm demeanour, but seems authoritative as well. I can't place where I know him from.

He sits in the chair opposite me, and puts the iPad down, resting his elbows on the table.

"Hi son. Name's detective Alessio. You want to tell me what happened?"

Right, detective Alessio. Ezekiel Alessio's dad.

Makes sense, but doesn't mean I'm going to speak to him. Zeke's not a friend, and I'm not going to play nice by speaking to his dad.

"Off the record if you need to get some stuff off your chest."

"Nope," I spit out.

"You look familiar. Were you friends with my boys?"

"No, detective. I know who Ezekiel is, but we're not friends, and I'm not going to speak to you about today."

"That's ok. You're in shock. Anyone you want to call?" he asks me, his eyes not able to meet mine, as though he knows more than he's letting on.

"No one who's going to care," I tell him, wishing I could wipe the tears away from my cheeks.

"Well, son, holler if you need anything. A sergeant will be by in a jiffy to get you settled for the night. We'll chat tomorrow."

Tamed Hearts

I huff angrily. There's nothing to say. If I say anything I'm most likely to implicate myself. Detective Alessio seems nice enough, but he's a cop and my name is tainted around town because of Carson.

When he stands from the chair, grabbing his iPad, he gives me a warning glare, and says, "You might not think it's best to talk, but trust me son, not talking is far worse."

And with those parting words, he leaves the room as quick as he came into it.

Barely a minute passes before a sergeant comes in to take me to a holding cell. Un-cuffing me, I'm pushed against the wall, patted down and told to strip to my boxers so I can put on the ugly orange jumpsuit he's holding up to me. It's so invasive. I can't help but wonder if saying something would've got me out of here, but then I have nowhere to go anyway.

Putting on the jumpsuit, I'm handed the mugshot board thing, and instructed by the sergeant to stand against the wall to be photographed. He then takes my fingerprints, and leads me to the cell, locking it behind me after I enter.

Taking in the tiny space, a rickety bed with threadbare blankets against one wall and a metal toilet and basin on the other side makes me feel like utter shit.

This is hell on earth.

I fucking hate myself.

Hate my dead fucker of a brother for putting me here.

I always knew he'd land me in hot water—hell—but I didn't expect this.

Sitting down on the edge of the bed, I let the tears fall, the sobbing wretched, fuck my fucked up life tears.

Caz May

I'm wondering—scared as shit—about if anyone would believe me if I told the truth. It seemed as though Ariel didn't believe me and she was there, moments before it went down.

I wanna talk to Briston or Ava. But I don't know their numbers, and my chance to call someone who cares passed when Detective Alessio left.

Fuck! I should've fucking said something.

Because right now, I'm being seen as murderer in a jail cell like my birth giver. And I can't believe that's what become of my life.

Lilith should've killed me then too.

It would've been better than growing up in hell, and having my heart ripped out when I gave it away.

Maybe I should end it all, and say goodbye.

Chapter Thirty-Five

Ariel

P olice are still milling about the scene after Braeden is taken away in the police car. A female officer I don't know taps me on the shoulder.

Caz May

"You alright, hun?" she asks, her face showing concern. I don't reply. My heart is still racing a hundred miles a minute. And I'm angry with myself for not saying anything when Braeden called out to me. I've probably broken his already ruined heart. My own heart is crushed, and I only have myself to blame. When he needed me I cast him aside.

Focusing my attention on the officer I try to speak, but only a raspy gasp comes out. She sees this as a cue to ask more questions, "Did you know the deceased?"

"Yes, I..." I stammer, not sure what to say about Carson.

"And the accused?"

"He's my boyfriend," I again stammer, biting my lip to stop myself from again breaking down into tears.

I can't look the officer in the eyes. I'm still shocked if I'm being truthful. And I honestly don't want to be here—being questioned like a criminal too—for a second longer.

Without another word I run—my Mary Janes' slipping off my heels and clomping hard on the gravel. The tears start falling down my cheeks again, and I don't stop running until I'm at Briston's front door. Knocking I try to calm down, to let air into my lungs and curb the panic I'm still feeling. When the door swings open, and my best friend—and other boyfriend—is standing in front of me, the tears become wretched.

He takes one look at me before grabbing my arm and pulling me inside, into a tight hug.

"Ar's, baby? What's wrong?"

"Braeden," I stammer, glancing up at Briston through glassy eyes.

"What about him?"

Tamed Hearts

"He did something bad."

"You know? About him and Chasity?"

I nod. "Yes, but that isn't what I'm talking about."

"Then what's wrong? Did he hurt you?" he asks, giving me a worried look when his dad waltzes into the room whistling.

"Hello, Ariel. Nice to see you. Everything alright?"

"No, I...um...Braeden...might have shot his brother. They got into a fight and his brother drew a gun."

"Oh gosh. Did you see this happen?" Mr Nicholls asks me, glancing between Briston and I with a questioning gaze.

"The fight yes, but I ran out to get help and that's when the gunshot was fired."

"Right...and is everyone ok?"

"No, his brother is dead," I reply monotonously, hating how the word dead sounds coming from my mouth, even though I'm talking about Carson who deserves to rot in hell.

"Have you spoken to the police?"

"Sorta. They arrested Braeden, but I couldn't speak to the officer. She was asking me too many questions, and I panicked."

Mr Nicholls pulls me into a side hug.

"That's understandable dear. I'll come with you to the station now. And you can fill Detective Alessio in on what you know."

"Ok," I reply, sniffing back the tears that are still stinging my eyes.

EVEN WITH MR NICHOLLS following me inside the station, I'm nervous. I know I've done nothing wrong, but going into a

Caz May

police station fills me with trepidation as though I'm a criminal. I can't begin to know how Braeden is feeling, most likely locked up in a jail cell; alone.

At the desk Mr Nicholls speaks to the officer, "Hi, we're here to make a statement regarding the young man who was brought in earlier this evening."

"No problems. I'll inform Detective Alessio you're here. Take a seat, won't be long."

I sit on the hard chairs to wait, and true to her word it's barely ten minutes before Detective Alessio comes out to greet me.

He nods at us both.

"Ariel, nice to see you. Come through and we can have a chat." He's informal, but direct. It calms my nerves. Mr Nicholls nods at me, squeezing my hand, telling me he'll be waiting for me.

Following Detective Alessio into the station I'm taken into a dingy office. He sits on one side of the desk, and I sit opposite.

"So, what can you tell me about the events this evening?" he asks getting straight to point, his eyes on me even as he starts tapping on the iPad in front of him on the desk.

"I went to Braeden's van to speak to him about something and we had a fight. His brother came home, and he was drunk and acting aggressively."

"To you or Braeden?" he asks, pausing his typing to glance up at me.

"Towards me, but it made Braeden upset and he started to fight Carson."

"Is this the first time they've had a disagreement resulting in a physical altercation?"

"No, it's happened before. Probably more times than I'm aware of," I tell him, sniffing back a sob.

"Right, and then what happened? Do you know who had the gun?"

"Yes, Carson pulled it on Braeden. He had it in his back pocket. And he put it to Braeden's head and threatened him."

"Hmm. And did you see who fired the gun? Was it in Braeden's possession at any point?"

"I don't know. I ran out to get help, and that's when the gun went off."

"Ok, and did you go back inside before police were on the scene?"

"Yes, and Braeden was standing over Carson's body, panicking."

"Was he holding the gun?"

"No, it was on the floor next to Carson's body."

"Ok, is that all you have to tell us?"

"Yes," I reply with a nod. "That's all I saw."

"Thank you, Ariel. You've been a great help."

"That's ok," I reply, thinking my words are stupid. "Could I see him?"

"Of course."

He stands from the desk, leading me out to another room with tables—like picnic type ones—in the middle.

"Wait here, and I'll have Braeden out in a moment."

Detective Alessio heads down a corridor, disappearing and leaving me in the cold room.

Caz May

It seems like ages when I feel the air shift with Braeden and a guard entering the room. He's sat down opposite me, his cuffed hands resting on the table.

With panic in his voice he says, "Ariel, darling. You know I didn't do it. You know me."

I gulp back a sob, clutching his cuffed hands.

"I know Braeden. I just panicked. I'm sorry."

His eyes are focused on me, but he doesn't say anything. Seeing him so torn up—speechless—and scared is breaking me.

"I told them, Detective Alessio. I told him. And they're going to look at all the evidence. It's going to be ok Brae, I promise."

I hope everything I'm saying is true, and I'm hoping he's hearing my words, knowing it's going to be ok.

His lips upturn in a slight smile.

"I love you, Ariel," he tells me, sincerely. "But you need to move on from me if I get this pinned on me. Promise me that?"

"I promise," I affirm, squeezing his hands. "But that's not going to happen, Brae. You didn't do it."

My words light up his face, and leaning across the table I kiss him, cupping his jaw with my hands. The kiss is hard, a kiss to tell him that I don't want to say goodbye, for this kiss to be our last.

The guard huffs from behind me, and I giggle when breaking the kiss, as it was clearly against the rules. The guard pulls Braeden up to his feet, and as he's taken back to his cell I call out, "I love you."

Tamed Hearts

It makes him smile, just a slight one and I hope knowing I love him will help him get through being in this hell hole. Heading back out into the waiting room, Mr Nicholls is still waiting for me.

"How'd it go?" he asks, following me outside.

"I told detective Alessio what happened. And I saw Braeden. He's ok, but scared."

"Yes, I'm sure. Let's get you home."

"Thank you, Mr Nicholls," I say, getting in his SUV.

"Anytime, dear," he replies as he starts the engine, taking me home in silence.

💔

HEADING INTO SCHOOL the next day after Braeden went to jail, the news—fake news—is all anyone can talk about. The corridors are buzzing with everyone chatting about it, and ambling in it feels as though everyone's eyes are on me.

At my locker, Briston is leaning against it. Seeing him makes the tears fall down my cheeks again, and rushing to him I wrap my arms around him, crying into his shoulder. He rubs my hair and my back.

"It's ok, baby," he says softly, squeezing me tighter. We only break the hug when the announcement comes through the speakers, "All students need to report to the gym immediately on the bell for a whole school assembly."

"Hmmf," I grunt, following the hoards of students to the gym when the bell goes immediately after Principal's Reading's voice cuts out. Briston takes my hand, practically dragging me into the hell we're about to endure. Right now

Caz May

I'd honestly rather be in bed, than about to face this hell. The chatter hasn't died down. Everyone knows what this assembly is about.

It's barely been ten minutes when principal Reading takes the stage, stepping up to the podium.

"If you could take your seats quickly, and quieten down, thank you." Voices quieten at his request, and only the squeak of the fold down seats fills the room. The hush that's taken over the gym is eerie, like the quiet at the caravan park before the gunshot pierced the air.

Mr Reading clears his throat and starts to speak monotone, "Students, as you may have heard in the news, a member of our student body is currently in custody for…" I know he's still speaking, but I can't focus on the words.

I hear him say, 'murder' and I sob, almost screaming as I rush out of the gym, breaking down into tears as I shove the double doors open, running out into the corridor. My breathing is rushed, panicked, and I'm crying so hard I can barely see.

A voice calls out to me, "Ariel, are you ok?"

I stop running, and turn to find Miss Canning heading towards me. Reaching me she stops me from running with her hands on my shoulders.

"I…had…to…get out of there," I pant through my sobs, my breathing still shaky.

"Take a deep breath, and speak to me about it," she tells me, calmly. I inhale, filling my lungs with air before exhaling, and wiping my tears away with the back of my hand.

"I was there, Miss C."

Tamed Hearts

She doesn't say a word, just looks at me encouragingly, nodding for me to continue.

"I didn't see him actually shoot him, but I heard the gunshot when I ran out to get help. And I'm so scared that he did it."

"We can only hope he didn't, but we just don't know anything else yet. Mr Reading wanted to make sure students were not spreading rumours and the like."

"I know. But I can't deal with everyone talking about Braeden like that, when he's not here to defend himself."

"That's understandable. It will be sorted out by the police. And Mr Reading will ensure talk of it at school is toned down. Are you going to be ok?"

"Yeah, I will be. I just love him so much. I can't…" I cut my words short, rephrasing, "I don't want to believe he did this. I don't want him to be a murderer."

"None of us do. Let's hope for the best, whilst preparing ourselves for the worse," she says wisely with a soft smile.

"Yeah, I guess I can do that," I reply with a nod. "Can I be excused from the rest of assembly?"

"Of course. Head to the library, and I'll see you in Art second period." She squeezes my hand, leaving me standing in the corridor as she goes back into the gym. I head to the library, still feeling a little teary.

I want to believe Braeden isn't a murderer, but a part of me wonders if he honestly did just snap—and take the gun —to shoot his tormentor dead. I couldn't blame him for wanting to be free of his vile brother, but rotting in jail for the crime of murder seems like a fate worse than death to me.

Caz May

Chapter Thirty-Six

BRAEDEN

Once more I'm led into the interrogation room, in my orange jumpsuit with my hands cuffed. If the cops wanted to make me feel like I'd committed the crime I'm being accused of this is sure as hell making me feel that way.

I'm barely in the room a minute on my own when Detective Alessio comes in, this time with not only his iPad, but a shabby seen better days box with a label on the side that has 'Chappell case' on it.

"We meet again," Detective Alessio says as he takes his seat on the other side of the table, after putting the box to the side of the table so he can still see me. His glare makes my pulse race.

All I can do is nod, and mutter a soft, "Yep."

"I'll start with some facts. One, Ariel came in the other night and gave a statement, which didn't give us much."

"Right, um, so I'm screwed?" I ask, cursing myself for speaking so informally to a cop.

"No, son. Not at all," he says standing and taking some things out of the box.

Firstly is the gun, and some polaroid pictures of my brothers' lifeless body on the floor of the caravan. I didn't need to see those images again, they've been in my mind since the night it happened. Every time I've closed my eyes I've seen Carson falling to the floor over and over again.

The last thing Detective Alessio gets out of the box is a rather large stash of drugs.

"Can you tell me anything about these or the incident now?" he asks me, tapping the clear white bags of powder on the table in front of me.

Taking in a deep breath, I swallow down my nervousness.

"They're all Carson's...were his and we got in an argument when he came home, wasted."

"What was the argument about?"

"He called Ariel a slut...and tried to hurt her."

"How? Did he threaten her with the gun as well?"

"No, he was just physical with her. Tried to touch her, so I shoved him off and we got into a physical fight."

Detective Alessio nods, telling me with a murmur to continue. I'm still nervous, hoping my story lines up with Ariel's.

"Carson pulled the gun on me and as I was trying to push him away Carson shot himself," I admit, feeling a weight lift off my shoulders from having that out in the open.

"Right, and this?" Detective Alessio asks, presenting the money from my stash to me, as well as my soccer ball money box. He asks with an odd gaze, "Where's that all from?"

"It's mine," I confess, wishing I had use of my hands to run them through my hair to calm myself. "But it's from working at Quiksilver. I was saving it for when I could get out of Lockgrove Bay."

Detective Alessio shakes his head, sighing. "It doesn't look good Braeden. Your fingerprints aren't on the murder weapon but having that amount of cash around when your brother and yourself have been involved in the drug trade doesn't seem innocent."

Grunting I reply with nervousness in my voice, "I know, but I'm clean. I've never done drugs and I…"

Panic hits me, not sure if I should admit selling them that one time. Probably a stupid thing to admit when I'm already in the firing line for a far bigger crime, regardless of my innocence.

"What Braeden? You need to tell me the whole truth."

Tamed Hearts

"Carson asked me once a few months back...but I never sold any drugs," I lie, biting down on my lip so hard I draw blood, and lick it away quickly to soothe the sting.

"Well, son, I hope you're telling me the truth," he says, an authoritative but caring tone in his voice. I like that he calls me son. It's been so long since I've heard any male call me that with a voice that shows they care about me. I know he's just doing his job, and has to believe i'm guilty but I get the sense that Detective Alessio believes I'm innocent.

"I am," I tell him, before adding quickly, "What's my chances of getting bail?" I want out of here. I want to see Ariel, and Briston.

"I can't answer that yet," he tells me, gathering the evidence back up into the box. "The crime scene and the autopsy is still being processed."

"So I have to stay in custody?" I ask, forlorn and frustrated. "What about work and school?"

"They've been informed of the circumstances."

Of course they have. I'm probably the talk of Lockgrove Preparatory. The sexy soccer player falls from grace, murders his brother.

"Ok. So...um...do you think I'm going to get off or am I... am I looking at a murder charge?" I stammer out the words, again worrying my lip between my teeth.

Murder.

Murder means I'll likely spend the rest of my life in jail. In literal hell on earth, without the two people I love the most in this fucked up world. I'd rather be dead myself than have to live through that.

Picking up the box, he gives me a smile.

Caz May

"If you're telling me the truth Braeden then you'll be fine. You seem like a good kid."

"Ah ok, thanks," I reply, smiling slightly back when he adds, "If Ariel Findley thinks so highly of you then I'm going to give you the benefit of the doubt and go with that sign of your character. But we have to go by the law and the process of investigation."

"Ok," I reply with a nod, not sure what else there is to say in reply to that statement. Ariel must have talked me up, said she loves me. The very thought makes me giddy.

Fuck I miss her—and Briston—so much it hurts. I really hope I get out of here soon.

Detective Alessio leaves the room, giving me a curt nod as he passes through the door and a guard comes in to escort me back to my cell. The moment he takes the cuffs off I run my hands through my hair, grunting in frustration.

"Hey guard, dude. Think you could get me a guitar? And some paper and a pen?"

"Probably not," he grunts back, making me feel like an idiot for asking.

"Ok. You don't have to be a dick about it."

"Watch your language. I'll see what I can do, but privileges like that are earnt," he cajoles at me like a right tosser. "And calling me guard dude isn't going to earn you any damn privileges."

He turns and walks away and I flip him off.

Tosser.

I'm just going to have to sing songs to myself, and hope for some sleep that isn't nightmare filled.

Tamed Hearts

When I think about the last few months—the last year, actually—the only time I've slept a decent nights sleep is when I've been in Ariel's arms. She's my remedy.

Caz May

Chapter Thirty-Seven

Ariel

Getting home from school my eyes are bleary, from barely stopping crying all day.

The moment I walk inside I drop my backpack at the door, about to head to straight into my bedroom to wail into my pillow when I hear dad's voice from the kitchen,

"Ariel, get in here now." He's angry, and I really don't want to face him right now.

There's a knot in my stomach, worry that won't let up or let me breathe deep. And I not only want to cry until I fall asleep, but I want to cut, so bad my thighs are throbbing.

Plodding into the kitchen, I try to sound a little happier when I greet dad, "Hi dad, what's up?"

"Your teacher called."

He's definitely angry, veins in his forehead popping as he tries to curb his wrath.

"Oh, really? What about?" I ask with a croaky voice, trying to hide the worry I'm feeling.

"About you running out of assembly, over something about that Braeden boy."

"Oh, um...I did, but I couldn't stay when..."

"When what, Ariel?"

"Mr Reading was talking about him. And what he did, which he didn't do."

"You're not making sense, Ariel Jane. Have you been seeing this Braeden again? Outside of school?"

I gulp, telling my guilty conscience to shut the hell up, and stop the nausea bubbling in my stomach. Desperately I want to lie to dad, tell him no, and that the last place and time I saw Braeden was at mum's funeral but lying to my father always gets me nowhere.

"Yes," I falter on the one syllable. "At mum's funeral, and after as well. I...love him."

"Don't give me that rot Ariel! That boy is not worthy of you."

Caz May

I grunt, wanting to protest but all that escapes my mouth is a raspy gasp.

"You're not to see that boy again outside of school. I strictly forbid any contact with him, Ariel Jane."

His threat is shown in his dark eyes that are glaring at me, forcing me to relent. But I'm not going to.

Not seeing Braeden will hurt too much. The hold he has on my heart is tight, and with him in jail right now I need to see the other person who has a grip on my heart, my Briston. He's the only person who will get how I'm feeling. Provoked from dad's warning to me, I roar, "Fuck you, dad! You're an arsehole!"

I storm out, not waiting for his response.

I've never cursed out towards my father before, and the very thought of what he might do to me has me out the door—after picking up my backpack—in seconds.

Dad's wrath is not something I want to experience tonight when my emotions are still on edge.

Running to Briston's I let the tears fall down my cheeks again, let the emotions out, the anger and the pain of having my heart torn to shreds.

Chapter Thirty-Eight

Briston

*O*pening the front door, I'm not expecting to find my best friend standing there, rocking on her heels, in tears. She'd been all over the place at school—all day—in tears one minute, smiling the next.

Caz May

"Hey, Ar's baby," I greet her cheerfully.

"Hey Bris. Can I come in?"

"Of course baby. You still upset about Brae?" I ask as she crosses the threshold into my house.

I take her hand, then, leading her to my bedroom so we don't have to face questioning from mum.

She shakes her head, and nods at the same time, her confusion clear when she utters a quivering, "Yeah, no."

I hate seeing her crying, especially when it's something to do with Braeden. But tonight it seems like more than what's happening to Braeden is upsetting her.

Sitting down on the bed together, I put out, "Talk to me Ar's."

Through her teary eyes she glances at me, sniffing.

"Dad. He...found out about assembly."

"About Brae?"

"Yeah, I guess, but about me running out."

"Oh, was he pissed?" I question her, gripping her hand and squeezing it comfortingly.

"Yeah he's forbidden me to see Brae."

"Oh that's shit."

"Yeah, I'm missing Brae so much. And I'm so confused."

"About what happened?"

"Yeah, I don't think he killed him but honestly Bris, I don't know what to believe."

"Yeah me either," I admit.

"Do you still love him? Do you think he could have done it?"

"Of course I fucking love him. But honestly I don't know...he does have a temper but it still seems out of character for him."

Again Ariel sniffs back her tears. "Yeah, but you don't know everything about his past that I do." Those words make me irate.

I don't know about Braeden's past—his home life—because he won't let me in. He hasn't shared anything with me that's not physical. And even though I love being with him, fucking him I deserve more from him.

"Right," I snap, feeling so many things I don't even know how to verbalise them without upsetting Ariel more.

"Don't be angry, Bris. I can't help how Brae and I feel about each other."

Now I'm even more angry. I need to tamp it down.

"So you're telling me you love him more?" I question her, adding muffled under my breath, *'even though he could be a murderer.'*

"Don't Briston! He's not a murderer!" she bellows at me, shoving me away. "And no I don't love him more. I love him different," she confesses, confusing me.

"Different, how?"

"I don't know how to explain it, Briston," she snaps at me. "Can we just forget all this shit for a bit?"

"Yeah, you wanna stay the night?"

"Would that be ok?" she asks eagerly.

"Of course, dufus," I tease with a laugh, adding, "You want first dibs on the shower?"

A smirk teases me then, her eyes hinting something dirty in them.

"We could save water," she says suggestively, quirking her eyebrows up at me and winking. The suggestion makes my dick jolt.

"Oh yeah, baby," I jeer standing up from the bed and grabbing her hand to pull her up with me. I kiss her, already impatient and ready to get her naked. Breaking the kiss she laughs, cupping my semi in my trackies.

"Someone's keen," Ariel teases with a cheeky smirk.

"Always with you, baby," I tease back, clasping her other hand and dragging her out of my room towards the bathroom.

Shutting the door behind us, I flick the lock closed and shove Ariel against the door kissing her firmly. Her hands roam my body, plunging my trackies to the floor so I'm naked. She palms my aching dick, kissing me deeper as I explore under her uniform, desperate to get her out of it.

"Ar's baby, you need to get naked for a shower," I tease her gripping her shirt in my fist, and kissing her cheekily.

She bats her fists against my chest, playfully laughing.

"I know that dufus, but you didn't give me a chance to get naked."

She starts to strip then, torturing me as she slowly— really slowly—unbuttons her dress shirt, letting it fall to the floor down her arms. My eyes boggle at the sexy lace bra she has on underneath. It cups her tits perfectly, and I groan leaning down to kiss each perfect mound of porcelain flesh.

Pushing me back, she unzips her skirt, sliding it over her hips with her eyes locked on me the entire time. My dick is enjoying this show, bouncing up and down eagerly. I'm rock hard, no other foreplay required.

Once her skirt is off, she's only in her bra and knickers, and I step back, turning the taps on in the open shower still with my gaze on my best friend. Fuck I love her. And fuck does she look sexy in black underwear.

Steam starts rising into the room, and I slide back across the tiles into the shower, closing my eyes a moment as I let the water cascade over my body and wet my hair.

Opening them Ariel is now naked, standing by the shower, gawking at me and nervously biting her lip. Reaching out I grab her hand, pulling her into the shower with me, wasting no time with semantics before I'm kissing her. Against my lips she giggles, her tongue dancing over my lips, and fuck it turns me on more.

Shoving her against the wall, I grip her hips, thrusting my dick inside her pussy so hard she breaks the kiss and moans so loudly I'm sure Mum will hear her from down the hallway, even over the sound of the shower running.

"Shhh, baby," I murmur, kissing her to silence her moaning, thrusting into her even harder.

I'm so on edge, loving every damn minute of this fuck in the shower, of just feeling and forgetting all the other shit going on in our lives. Ariel's pussy is pulsing around my dick, and I need to come.

"Come Ar's. Come for me baby," I tease, thrusting hard to hit her g-spot with the tip of my dick.

She lets out a loud moan, her whole body shaking with her release.

Caz May

Without warning she kisses me, and whispers against my lips, "Fuck, Bris. I love you."

"I love you, too, Ar's," I whisper back, pulling out of her pussy and stroking my dick roughly, painting her tits and stomach with ropes of hot cum.

Ariel rubs it all over her body with her fingers, her eyes on me. "Damn, Ar's, watching you do that is so sexy," I jeer, bending down to lick my cum off her body, as she puts her fingers in her mouth, tasting my cum from her fingertips.

"Mmm, Bris," she murmurs, her fingers then lacing through my hair as she pulls me to my feet, kissing me causing me to stumble back under the spray of water.

We continue kissing as the water runs all over our bodies.

Being with Ariel is always sweet, beautiful and dirty.

I break the kiss, and whisper, "I love you, Ariel Jane Findley," as I turn off the water, and grab a towel as I step out of the shower.

"I love you too, Briston Elijah Nicholls," she replies, taking the towel from me and kissing me again. "Thank you for helping me forget for awhile."

"Anytime, baby. I won't ever say no to fucking you," I tease, waddling out of the bathroom with her following and laughing.

Hearing her laugh after today, and every crazy thing that's happened this past week is the best sound on this damn planet.

Chapter Thirty-Nine

Ariel

*B*reakfast at Briston's house is always amazing. No matter what day of the week it is his mum cooks up a storm of pancakes, french toast, bacon and eggs.

You name a breakfast food, and she's probably cooked it.

Caz May

Briston oughta be as big as a house with his dad being a chef, and his mum also being an incredible cook.

I'd always loved coming to his house to eat something home cooked—that I didn't cook myself—as it's always delicious.

Sitting down at the breakfast bar, with Briston next to me, his mum piles a couple of plates with food and pushes them towards us both.

Briston doesn't even say a word before he starts shovelling food into his mouth, groaning like he's having an orgasm. His mum is grinning at us, her eyes darting between us. It's clear she loves seeing us together.

As I start to eat, she says sweetly, "Always knew you two loved each other."

Briston grunts, scoffing at her, whilst I smile at her when she asks her son, "Briston, dear what about that Braeden boy?"

He gazes at her, his eyebrows raised. "Haven't you heard mum?" he questions.

"Heard what, dear?"

"That he's in jail right now," Briston replies in a monotone that is like a punch in the chest to me. "He might have killed his brother."

Fuck me, that hurts. I burst into tears, not loving how my best friend is talking about Brae, someone he supposedly cares about; loves.

His mum shakes her head, shock painting her face.

"Oh no, I haven't heard that. You know I don't watch the news."

Briston nods in response.

Tamed Hearts

"Yeah, we don't think it's true but," he declares, making my heart feel a little better.

"I hope not," his mum replies, turning her gaze to me, and asking, "Ariel, dear, are you ok?"

I sniff back my tears, sobbing, "No...I...um..." The tears fall harder. And I stand up from the stool, about to rush out of the room when Briston's mum pulls me into a hug. She rubs my back, cooing, "Aww sweetie, I know it all hurts."

Her hug is comforting, especially now with my own mum gone. I've missed comfort like this and I only step back from the comforting embrace because Briston gets up from his stool, screeching it along the tiled floor. The sound is jarring, and I give him a glare.

"I'm going to go get ready for school," Briston says, leaving me with his mum.

She squares her hands on my shoulders, looking at me with concern that makes my heart race.

"I didn't want to say around Briston, but your dad called me last night to check up on you."

Of course he did. Dad knows me. Knows that Briston's house is my second home, and honestly more of a home than my own sometimes.

"Oh..." I stammer, sniffing back more of my tears that refuse to quit.

"He said I can't see Braeden," I tell Mrs Nicholls. Hearing myself say those words is like a knife to the heart. I miss him so much, my whole body hurts.

Just when things were getting back on track with us, and I'd admitted how much I love him again, he's been snatched away. And I don't know if i'm ever going to get

Caz May

him back this time. If he stays in jail--gets convicted of murder, regardless of his innocence--I know I'll never get to see him again. And that shatters my heart, into a million pieces.

"He didn't tell me that," Mrs Nicholls tells me taking a step back. "But he's worried about you and wanted us to have a girls chat."

Again I sniff back my tears, giving her a smile. "I'd like that, Mrs Nicholls. I could never talk to mum about those things, nor dad either."

She gives me a nod, telling me she understands, before she asks, "So have you been safe?"

I gulp, not able to meet her eyes that are also asking me the question.

"I always tell Briston to protect himself."

Still looking at the floor, I mutter my reply, "Um, most of the time yeah." I hear her intake of a shaky breath, and I'm a little scared to admit the truth. "We've forgotten a few times, and I thought I was pregnant once but my period was just late."

Again she nods.

"Well, sweetie, protection is important," she tells me, in a caring tone.

"I know. We just get carried away sometimes," I confess, feeling a blush rise up my cheeks. I can't believe I'm openly having this conversation with Briston's mum, and she's not yelling at me for having sex with her son.

"Yes, dear, that happens," she replies with a laugh. "I'll ask your dad if I can take you to the gyno."

Tamed Hearts

I give her another smile, knowing my cheeks are still aflame.

"Thank you. And Mrs Nicholls?"

"Yes, sweetie?"

"I love Briston, so much."

Her smile is wide, face breaking wide when she replies, "I know sweetie. He loves you to," she tells me, pressing a kiss to my forehead. "And I'm sure things will work out with Braeden."

"I hope so," I reply, adding in a softer voice, "I love him too, but a lot has happened between us all and I don't know if I can be with him. It hurts a lot."

"You have to trust your heart will lead you in the right direction. He seemed like such a lovely boy."

Once more I smile at her, feeling as though a weight has lifted from my shoulders.

"Thank you for the chat and advice."

"Anytime Ariel," she voices, adding something that makes my heart swell, "I'm always here for the girl my Briston loves."

I give her another hug before rushing back to Briston's room to get ready for school.

Caz May

Chapter Forty

BRAEDEN

After what's seemed like weeks, not days I'm getting out of jail.

It felt a little weird to be led into the interrogation room this time without the handcuffs and ugly orange jumpsuit.

I don't actually know why I even have to come back into this space, why I can't just walk out the door, but when a

Sergeant comes in, pulling the opposite chair out and turning it around to sit on it backwards I sigh in relief.

Maybe I'll get some answers, but by the look on his face I get the feeling I'm going to have a whole lot of questions plaguing me when I walk out of this hell.

"So Braeden, I'll cut to the chase," the Sergeant starts. "The bullet wound to the chest could have only been self inflicted," he explains to me, his tone methodical, like he's said the same words on a different day to someone else. "That and your fingerprints were not the weapon but on Carson's clothes."

I'm speechless, only able to nod in response as I absorb his words. "And likewise Carson's were on your clothes which shows self defence, as you mentioned in your earlier statements."

"Yep," I stammer, not able to say anything else more coherent as I'm piecing it all together in my head, reliving it even though I don't want to ever honestly remember it ever again.

"We also dug up some other evidence about Carson's drug dealing. And that he'd been in contact with your mum in regard to some criminal dealings," he adds matter of factly with a cheerful look on his face.

"What happens to the money that was found?" I ask nervously, biting down on my lip.

Sergeant Booker's expression changes to one more authoritative.

"All proceeds of the crimes committed go back to the state," he divulges.

Caz May

Slamming my fist on the table I protest, "Some of that money was mine from work."

"It may well have been but as that can't be easily established without it being in a financial institution we have no choice in how we can deal with that money," Sergeant proclaims as though he's reading from a textbook, his response sounding rehearsed.

It makes me so fucking angry.

I'd worked hard for that money, and now it's going to be stripped away from me as dirty money.

"For fucks sake," I curse, barely resisting the urge to stand and throw the table at him in a fit of rage. "I've probably lost my job. Lost everything because of him. I'm fucking destitute!" I bellow, not giving one iota of care that I said fucking in front of a cop.

I've never understood why swearing is illegal. What cop —or Aussie—doesn't swear in public, and use fuck as a word for everything you can think of.

It's a universal word.

Sergeant Booker doesn't care. Barely bats an eyelid when he says, "I assure you, your job is still yours. And we can put you into contact with a social worker at Link to assist you with anything you need."

Yeah, fuck that shit.

"Thanks, but I'll pass. I don't want to talk to some shrink," I tell him, shaking my head violently. The only person I want to talk to now is my remedy, my Ariel.

"Suit yourself. The option is there."

"Yep, whatever," I snap hastily adding, "so I'm free to go?"

Tamed Hearts

I'm honestly over this conversation, getting antsy for a hit of fresh air.

"Yes, you've been acquitted of all charges," he declares, all jolly like Santa. "Just need to sign some paperwork at the desk."

I get up to walk out, and when the Sargent follows me out he stops me at the door.

"There's also a box of personal effects for you at the desk," he tells me with his matter of fact tone. I don't know if I like him, but thankfully I don't have to worry anymore about dealing with cops. I'm a free man.

Still I reply, "Thanks, Sargent Booker."

He walks away, whistling as I go to the front desk. I'm immediately handed a small stack of release paperwork, which I quickly sign with a scribble that barely looks like a signature.

The officer nods at me, plonking the case file box in front of me. She doesn't say anything as I grab the box and walk out the door clutching it to my chest.

It's full of photos, and old junk. I want to throw it out, because I don't want to see or deal with any memories—good or bad—about my fucker of a brother. He doesn't even deserve a funeral. And I don't have the money for that anyway. In my opinion the fucker should be cremated, whilst I pretend he's burning alive and going straight to the fiery pits of hell. Sounds like a hella of a plan. Will have to organise that but firstly this box of shit needs to be dealt with. I glance at the giant skip bin by the cop station, and stop in front of it about to tip it all in when a photo on the top catches my eye.

Caz May

It's got my dad in it. And others that I don't recall.

Taking in a deep breath, I turn away from the bin, deciding to take it back to van and look through it first, if only to think of the good memories of my family.

BACK AT THE VAN, I kick the door open and put the box down on Carson's bed.

Glancing around I'm shocked that it's fully cleaned, not a speck of blood anywhere.

No personal effects either. It's basically a shell, and I want to scream out in anguish.

My tosser of a brother has put me in hell. I've lost everything. My whole life has been shot to shreds with his death.

I've got nothing, no clothes, no bedding, and no food. And no money to consider getting any of that either. It would've been better if he'd shot me. I might have gone to actual hell for all I know, but I'm practically living it anyway.

Sitting cross legged on the mattress of Carson's old bed I start to look through the photos. Most of them are of us boys with dad, and a few of the birth giver holding us in the hospital. She has a permanent scowl on her face. Of course she'd not be happy when it came to anything to do with myself and Edwin.

Cautiously I pick up one that shocks me, completely taking my breath away.

It's me with dad, maybe when I'm a year or two old. He's holding me against his hip and standing next to him, clutching his hand is a blonde haired girl with pigtails.

She's little as well, probably the same age and looks vaguely familiar.

Caz May

Chapter Forty-One

BRAEDEN

Studying the photo I wrack my brain, trying to think back to happier times. I don't recall ever spending time with cousins or anything like that and I really don't have a clue who this girl is, despite her looking familiar. Like family, familiar.

Shuffling through more of them I find there's baby photos that are not my brothers. And a guy I'm sure I've seen before around town but I can't work out who he is either. My mind is in a spin.

Screaming out, I scrunch the photos in my fist, tempted to rip them and throw them out of the caravan to fly away in the wind.

As tempting as that is though, it won't take the memories away and I can't help but think of Carson's words about not knowing dad. I really hadn't taken those words to heart, but they're hitting me head on going through this box of shit.

It's bringing up memories, and most of them are the horrible ones.

The ones of my fucked up birth giver yelling at dad for again being home late. And her putting goldfish biscuits on Edwin's highchair straight from the box, completely ignoring me tugging on her pant leg and begging for something other than junk food to fill my grumbling stomach.

Fuck! I'm fucking starving, and I don't even have a fucking dollar to my name for a fucking hamburger from Macca's.

This is fucking hell, surely. I've got nothing, literally. No phone, no damn money...only my soccer uniform, and cleats.

Why the fuck couldn't the cops leave the van with my stuff in it?

They turned the whole place upside down in their drug bust and they've left me to be a homeless waste of space.

Shoving the box of photos aside I get up off the bed, panic hitting me as I wonder if they really did get rid of everything I owned.

Caz May

Rushing through the caravan to my bunk, I bend down, my bare knees crashing against the linoleum floor harshly. I inhale a shaky breath, peering under the bed, and feeling around with my hand.

Exhaling when my fingers brush my guitar case, I yank it out, thankful to still have it. The one thing that was dad's. The only connection I have to him now is this guitar, and the love of music he instilled in me. Those are the memories I want to keep. Him playing for me, teaching me how to strum chords, and exploring my voice with him until all hours of the night. Of course Lilith hated that I had that connection with dad, but those nights were the happiest times of my childhood. And curse Lilith Chappell for cutting short the happy childhood times by taking my dad away when I was six.

There's only one thing to do now, to get answers about those photos, and answers about why she took dad and my little brother away from me. It's last thing I want to do. I'd rather be back in jail, but if I want the truth, I need to go to see Lilith herself, my she devil of a mother.

Pfff, even thinking of her as my mother makes my stomach churn in disgust. She's fucking poison.

And I'm fucking terrified to face her, even though I need to. I need to face hell to get to heaven.

Chapter Forty-Two

BRAEDEN

It feels damn surreal heading back into school.

The fucking cops had tossed my uniform out, so I'm freezing my arse off in my soccer uniform. I'm probably going to get in the shit for wearing it, and most likely be suspended on my first day back because of it.

Caz May

Like I need that, when I'm already so behind and probably going to end up failing year twelve because my stupid dyslexic brain will be so overwhelmed.

I fucking hate myself right now. I'm living in hell, and have entered the part of hell that's my own personal nightmare.

The corridors are full of students, and they're all staring at me—whispering—all sorts of rumours flying around that are turning my gut.

I want to bite back, yell at them. Like I'd seriously be back at school if I'd murdered my brother.

Fucking dickheads.

Edging down the corridor, I try to keep my head high, ignoring the whispers as I head to her locker. I need to see her.

I want to talk to her. And touch her. Kiss her, to warm my shivering arse up. I'm hoping to ask her to come with me to see Lilith.

Stalking closer to her locker, my heart race thrums harder. Even in her school uniform, she takes my breath away. Her chestnut locks are down her back in a long braid, her skirt barely covering her arse cheeks.

Fuck! Just looking at my girl from afar is giving me a hard on.

I step up behind her, wrapping my arms around her waist. She gasps when my breath fans against her ear.

"Hey darling. I've missed you."

I'm hoping she's turning around to kiss me, but she brushes me off, shoving her hands against my chest so I stumble backwards, flabbergasted.

Tamed Hearts

"Leave me alone, Braeden," she stammers, worrying her lip between her teeth. I don't have a word to say. She might as well stab me in the fucking heart.

Her eyes are hooded and she's staring at me as though she's hurting as much as I am.

Our hearts are breaking whilst we stare at each other with unsaid words.

"Why darling?"

She sniffs.

"I'm hurt by how you pushed me away that night I saw you in jail."

"I had to Ariel. I had no idea if I'd get out. I didn't want you to wait for me."

"Yeah, well it doesn't matter now," she spits out. "I can't see you anymore. Dad has prohibited me from seeing you... so."

She can't be serious.

I can't breathe.

My remedy, the one good thing in my shitty life is being torn from me.

Please, someone, just kill me now.

"I need you Ariel," I plead, taking her hands with mine. "Please." I hate how pathetic I sound, begging the girl I love with my whole damn heart to hear me, and not push me away when I'm falling apart right in front of her. Fuck my fucked up life.

"I can't be around you, Braeden," she tells me, yanking her hands from mine as she steps aside.

Caz May

The bell cajoles, and as she starts to walk away, she breaks my heart, completely shatters it with her called out request, "Leave me alone. Please."

Fuck! I slam my fist into the lockers, so hard it bleeds, the red liquid dripping down my knuckles that are now throbbing.

Sucking on them to make it stop, I curse myself whilst also thinking about bleeding out.

It would be better than being in this hell. And honestly I don't want to be here, curse school, fuck life.

I run out of the school building when the second bell goes. Skipping is probably an idiotic idea but who fucking cares. My life is going to shit anyway.

I run to the park, sit on one of the park benches and light up my cigarette.

Thank fuck for having some smokes that I bummed off another inmate still in my possession, and thank fuck for remembering to tuck a few in my pocket today.

I let the smoke out slowly, letting it calm my anger. Might as well pluck up the courage to go to see Lilith, now or never or some shit.

Chapter Forty-Three

Briston

*R*unning late for school, after staying in the surf too long I'm dashing in the gates after the second bell.

251   *Caz May*

I'm like the damn white rabbit from Alice in Wonderland, barely glancing up, afraid that will slow me down.

My backpack slips down my shoulder, crashing to the ground at my feet at the very same moment someone rushes out of the gates.

Bending down to pick it up I notice it's Braeden, and even though I'm likely facing detention I pause to watch him rush out of school.

He looks distraught, as though his heart has been ripped out. I'm tempted to go after him, because fuck, I'm missing him so much, but I'm still upset and hurt about how he's treated Ariel. And she'd probably be pissed with me seeing him when she can't.

Getting to my locker, hurriedly I shove my bag inside and skid down the corridor to English class, barely keeping a hold on my books.

Opening the door of the classroom, it's full of students chatting with thankfully no teacher in sight yet. Probably means we've got a substitute and my arse won't be getting a detention today.

Sighing in relief, I spot Ariel at the back of the room, a sad but sexy pout on her lips.

Scooting into the chair next to her, elbowing her in the side I ask, "Ar's what's up baby?"

She turns to glare at me, still with the pout, so I give her a kiss on the cheek.

She sighs, deeply, and says softly, "Brae is back."

I know this, but I act nonchalant.

"Yeah, did he speak to you?"

Tamed Hearts

"Yeah. Kinda. I didn't really let him speak."

"Oh right," I snap, a little confused about why she wouldn't let him speak. Yes, he's not treated her the best lately, but I'd at least thought she'd want to hear him tell her about what happened.

"He said he needed me. And that hurts," she confesses, her head down. "I don't want to love him anymore."

"I know Ar's. I get it, but he's easy to love," I say, kicking myself in the guts because my words seem stupid. I hate the fact that I still love Braeden.

"Yeah," Ariel replies shakily, sniffing back tears. There's nothing more to say, and we turn our focus to the teacher who has finally made an entrance and is glaring at us so she can start the lesson.

I honestly can't focus though, as I'm thinking about whether I should talk to Braeden.

After out last encounter he's been distant, connecting with Ariel more. And honestly I think it will hurt to much.

Caz May

Chapter Forty-Four

BRAEDEN

Last time I saw Lilith Chappell I was ten, four years almost to the day of when she shattered my whole existence with her selfish actions.

Carson—not rest in peace, not so dear brother—had dragged me to the jail to see her, telling me that, *'mummy'* wanted to see me for my special double digit birthday. And that she had a special present for me.

I'd never been so scared in my life—other than the day she murdered Dad and Edwin—as I was walking into the jail, knowing I was going to face her again, and have those tainted memories come crashing back.

And now another eight years later those same feelings are plaguing me whilst I'm sitting on the bus, heading to the jail on the outskirts of town.

Lockgrove Bay Prison houses some of the most notorious criminals from all over the state, and it's said to be haunted by ghosts past of when the death penalty was actually a thing in Australia, and all manner of prisoners were hung for their crimes.

Lilith—she devil—Chappell should have been hung for her crime, murdering two people and almost murdering a third.

Thinking about her coming after me later that night—knife in hand—and slicing down my back through my threadbare pyjama top causes me to choke on my coffee, spitting the liquid out over the back of the seat in front.

The scar on my back—covered by my whole back tattoo—throbs as well and rubbing it as I stand up, I'm thankful the bus has stopped, but not glad to be at my destination.

DEBARKING THE BUS, I gaze up at the prison gates, my heart racing. I want to get back on the bus—come back another day—but it's already driven off, and I either stand here for another twenty minutes in the cold waiting for a bus back, or I have to go inside and face her.

Caz May

Pushing the foreboding gate open, it creaks and groans as though it's letting out all the prisoners feelings and thoughts.

I seriously can't believe I'm here doing this, but each unhurried step I'm taking is leading me inside to face her, and to hopefully get the answers I want—need.

Pushing the double doors of the prison open I exhale, realising I was holding my breath. Cliched I know, but I was doing it.

Sighing I throw my coffee cup in the bin at the entrance and take the final steps to the front desk. It's got bars and perspex to not let the inside horrors out I'm guessing.

The guard at the front desk greets me, "Hello, how can we help you today, young man?"

"Hi, I'm here to see Lilith Chappell, if that's possible."

"Possible, yes, depending on your relationship to the prisoner and your reasons for today's visit."

"She's my mother," I choke out, hating calling her that.

"Lovely, you're the other son I take it?"

"Yeah, and I...ar...need to see her to inform her of some unforeseen circumstances." I can't believe the words I'm saying, my voice not even sounding like my own.

"No worries. Just sign in on the iPad, and we'll get things rolling."

"Great, thanks," I reply, tapping the iPad screen and typing in my name, and who I'm visiting. Pressing enter, a little printer spits out a slip of paper with the details on it.

"Bring that through with you, Braeden," the guard instructs, standing and pressing a button under the desk that unlocks the metal door to the right of the desk. "Come on through, I'll meet you inside."

Pushing the door it creaks and I trudge inside, to find the guard waiting for me. She hands me a lanyard to put the slip of paper in, and ushers me to a room to check me over. It's like déjà vu from being in custody myself, but not quite as invasive.

After I've been searched, I'm led into another room, with the seats, perspex and phones on either side to speak to the inmates.

Since I'm not actually going to be able to close enough for Lilith to touch me my nerves settle a little. Not completely, but some of the tension has eased.

I TAKE A SEAT, and the guard leaves me be. No one else is here right now, and it's deathly quiet, so quiet I can hear my heartbeat hammering in my chest.

I gasp when Lilith sits on the other side of the perspex and we both pick up the phone receivers to talk.

"Braeden, dear. How nice of you to come see me," she says over sweetly, each word measured and slow.

"Hello Lilith," I draw out, scowling.

"No mum for me?" she asks, with a chuckle.

"You lost the privilege to be called that twelve years ago, Lilith," I tell her, already annoyed at her, but I need answers and I don't know how long I have.

GRABBING THE PHOTO out of my pocket I hold it up to show her, demanding, "Tell me who the girl is in this photo?"

257   Caz May

Lilith chuckles again, a cocky smirk on her face when she answers, nonchalant, "That's your sister."

"My fucking what?" I bark, completely flabbergasted and confused.

Lilith laughs again.

"Well, your half sister. Your daddy couldn't help but stick his dick elsewhere."

Clenching my fists under the table to quell my anger, I ask more, "What's her name?"

Lilith scoffs, as though she doesn't want to tell me.

"Lilith, what is her damn name? I deserve to know who my sister is."

"Dakota."

"As in Neelson?" I question, raising my eyebrows at her.

"Yes, stupid floozy of a girl she was, even as a kid." Her words, and the disdain on her face disgust me.

"Right, anything else you want to tell me?"

"Nope, nothing, except it was lovely to see you." Her tone isn't sincere, which gives me great pleasure.

"Well, it wasn't lovely to see you, but before I go I guess you should know that Carson is dead."

Her mouth falls open, a pained whimper escaping her chapped lips.

"How? Did you do something to him? Bad deal?"

I laugh then, taunting her as she waits with bated breath for me to tell her of her golden child's demise.

"He shot himself whilst he was trying to shoot me," I inform her, watching tears spring to her eyes that shock me. The she-devil has feelings, but only for him. She's never cared about anyone but her beloved Carson and herself.

Tamed Hearts

I HANG UP THE PHONE, standing and see her mouth *'it should have been you'* as I walk away. Of course she'd say that—think that—I should've been the one to die. But it doesn't even matter now.

I head out of the prison then, signing out at the desk and ambling out to the bus.

It seems as though both of my parents made bad choices that affected my life, and the very thought of how different my life could've been makes anger bubble in my guts, and chest. Anger at my dad for his actions, that pushed Lilith over the edge into madness. His choices cost not only his life, but changed mine after his death. And my opinion of my parents is now tainted.

Caz May

Chapter Forty-Five

BRAEDEN

The entire trip back into town—on the bus—the news about Dakota is troubling me, so much so, I'm fuming.

It's clear I've been fed lies all my life, by everyone who supposedly cared about me. It makes me question everything, whether Edwin was my little brother and whether I'm even related to Lilith or not, if I'm her son or another of dad's illegitimate children.

So many questions are racing through my mind, and the moment I get back to the van, still seething with anger I shove through the door, not giving a shit that the door slams so hard its hinges groan.

Grabbing the box of photos and things off the bed I expel them across the van, watching each and every photo float to the floor.

The calmness grates on my frayed nerves, watching pictures of the happy times with dad fall to the floor. He was a liar, not the man I thought he was, and Carson's words rush back to the forefront of my mind.

I only shared one special bond with my father and with this news even that seems tarnished by this new revelation about the man I looked up to, admired for his musical ability. And I need to get rid of everything, every memory of him; good or bad. I can't pinpoint why, but they all have to go. I don't want to think, feel, or play a song ever again.

Picking up his—my—guitar by the neck I hoist it above my head, screaming as I smash it against the counter. It shatters, a shrill chord ringing out as the strings snap. Letting all the rage out, I smash it until it's in pieces before falling to the floor in tears.

Crazy emotions and thoughts are rushing through my mind. I'm wondering if Dakota knows. It gets to me because surely she would have said something, knowing she has a brother the same age. That thought brings up questions too. I don't know when her birthday is, and it makes me curious about whether we're twins, and whether Lilith is actually my 'mother' or if my parentage is a complete bullshit lie as well.

Caz May

Gripping my hair in my fist, I scream. I need to—want to —talk to her, my sister. I need to find out everything, whether she knows anything, and if we're twins. I need to know all of it, no matter how much it hurts I need to know.

Also, I want to talk to Ariel and Briston, to confide in them both and explain everything. Because fuck I miss them, and everything we've shared together.

The only way I can describe how I'm feeling now is wretched, wrecked, and heartbroken.

My wild heart is crying out to be tamed.

Chapter Forty-Six

Dakota

Guys don't talk to me, and I'm ok with that. Even guys in my friendship group—that are more courtesy of my best friend Ava being popular—don't talk to me. But this morning as I'm heading out to the bleachers at recess to sit with Ava, I can hear Braeden calling out my name, "Dakota!"

I pick up my pace, turning back to him and shrugging my shoulders at him. Why he's trying to talk to me at school is

Caz May

puzzling. We might hang out with the same friends, but I don't really know him and I definitely don't talk to him.

"Dakota, please," he calls out, begging me, "Wait up a minute."

I stop running, and he catches up to me, breathing in deep to catch his breath. I want to snap at him, annoyed but I'm all tongue-tied. I've never really been able to talk to guys. My shyness always gets the better of me.

Braeden glares at me then, his expression odd and unreadable.

"I have to talk to you...it's important," he tells me, yanking a folded piece of paper out of his pocket.

He hands it to me.

"Here, look at this."

Unfolding it I gasp as I glance over the words on the paper. It's a copy of my birth certificate.

"Why?" I stammer, annoyed that my voice is so shaky. "Why do you have this?" I question, waving it in his face.

"Because I'm your brother Dakota," he informs, his voice not wavering.

My eyes nearly fall out of my head. This cannot be true.

"What? How?"

"My dad slept with your mum around the same time Lilith was pregnant with me," he informs me with a tone that tells me he knows what he's talking about.

"Who's Lilith?" I ask, smacking myself in the head for being an idiot.

"My mum," he chokes out, like he hates the word. "She's in jail...for um..."

Ok, Braeden has gone to crazy town.

Tamed Hearts

"What? You sound crazy, Braeden."

He shakes his head, glaring at me and sighing out a raspy breath before explaining, "She killed my dad, Dakota, because of you for fucks sake. And my little brother as well."

Well, colour me shocked.

"Seriously! Are you heartless?"

What he's saying can't be true, surely. But why in the hell would he make up something like that. Still I'm not sure if I should believe him.

"No, I...I...just...I don't know," he stammers, showing me he's upset and maybe didn't mean his words to sound so cruel.

"Would my parents know?" I ask, pondering all of the things he's saying as I hand him back the birth certificate I'm still holding.

"I guess so," he replies, shrugging his shoulders.

"Fine," I snap, a little harsher than I intended. "Can you come home with me after school?" I ask, feeling suddenly shy because I'm asking a boy over, and he's not the type of boy my parents would approve of me bringing home to meet them.

"Um...yeah...why though?" Braeden questions me, confusion in his voice.

"So we can speak to my parents. Make sure."

"Ok," he replies, about to walk away.

"Meet me at the front gate after the last bell," I request as I walk off, completely overwhelmed.

Caz May

I want to tell Ava, to confide in my best friend but sitting down beside her, even when she gives me a quizzical look I don't say a word. I'm still sceptical.

"What did Brae want?" she questions me. I can't look her in the eye and lie, so pulling out my muesli bar from my pocket I unwrap it and take a bite.

I study the chocolate chips on the oat goodness, and mutter through my mouthful, "Oh nothing. He um thought I dropped something. But it wasn't mine."

I'm blown away that I got the blatant, elaborate lie out of my mouth. I give myself a mental pat on the back, shoving the rest of my muesli bar in my mouth.

"Oh right, fair enough," Ava replies, sipping her chocolate milk.

"What are you buzzing about?" I question her. "Something to do with Zeke?"

"Yeah, but I can't tell you Miss Prude," she replies with a laugh. Little does my best friend know that my little miss prude status is a distant memory. I haven't told her a lot of things lately, and that upsets me, but I definitely like my privacy, and in my life any form of privacy is a blessing.

Chapter Forty-Seven

BRAEDEN

After school, sitting on the bus next to Dakota my pulse is racing. I'm so nervous about the news I'm most likely going to hear. Part of me doesn't even want to know—to stay in the dark—but the lies would likely bury me in anguish if I don't find out the truth.

Dakota won't even look at me, staring out the window and scooting so far across the seat so we don't have to

Caz May

touch—even a little bit—and it kinda hurts. She's supposedly family, and can't even look at me, or say anything to me. I know she's shy, and doesn't talk to guys, but this shutting me out feels personal and cruel.

"Dakota, are you ok?" I ask, touching her thigh. Immediately I draw it back, her look of horror at the meant to be comforting touch cutting right through me.

"Yes, but I'm not talking to you."

"Um, ok," I stammer, still hurt. "Did I do something wrong?"

She looks at me then, her eyes puffy as though she's been crying.

"You know what you said, Braeden. Just leave me alone until we get to my house."

I don't reply, just wait until the bus stops at the final stop and Dakota rises from the seat shoving me in the back as I stand as well. We disembark the bus, and she kicks the dirt as she walks to a farm gate. I knew Dakota lived out of town, but I was not expecting this--an actual farm. It seems like another world—kilometres away from Lockgrove Bay— even though it's only a twenty minute drive from the middle of town.

The gate screeches as she opens it and I follow her to the other side, waiting for her to close it before we head down the driveway towards the farmhouse at the end that seems like a mirage in the distance.

Once at the house, she drops her bag at the door and kicks off her shoes into a pile at the door, so I do the same, gulping when she opens the front door, calling out, "Mum, I'm home."

Tamed Hearts

I follow her inside into an old, homely and huge kitchen. The dining table in the middle easily seats twelve people and it's set for sixth people with cutlery and plates.

A blonde, short and petite woman turns to face us, as Dakota sashays into the room to hug her. Her mum's eyes catch mine, as she hugs her daughter and my heart falls to the floor with the look in her eyes.

"Oh, and you've bought a boy home," she states not as a question.

Dakota nods at her.

"Yes, this is Braeden…"

"Braeden Chappell," her mum finishes for her, and I nod whilst Dakota looks shocked that her mum knows my name. Before I can even reply, to greet her or anything she crosses the vast room, hugging me and bursting into tears.

Her hug is warm, inviting and how a mother's hug should feel. I don't want her to let go, so when she pulls back, squaring her hands on my shoulders I whimper from the loss of contact, of comfort that her hug gave me.

Her next words shock me, breaking my heart even more than it already is.

"I'm so sorry Braeden. So sorry for everything."

"It's ok. I um…actually don't know much."

"Sit down," she says, looking to Dakota to add, "sweetie, could you add another place to the table?"

I take a seat at the end of the table and her mum sits down, sighing and brushing off her hands on her apron.

"Ok, so tell me what you know about your family? My family?"

Caz May

"Well, not much," I tell her, grabbing the birth certificate out to show her. I put it on the table as I continue speaking, "Basically, my dad and my little brother were killed by Lilith when I was six."

She nods, telling me to continue without words. "And I'd been living with my older brother Carson since then. We got into a fight a couple weeks ago, and he shot himself."

"Oh my, Braeden. I'm sorry to hear that."

"Don't be. Carson wasn't a good brother. He was involved in all manner of crimes, and he abused me physically for years."

"We should've done something. Honestly I had no idea about Carson."

"Yeah, it's ok, Mrs Neelson. You didn't know."

She smiles at me.

"Call me Matilda, and honestly I should've done more for Dillon's son."

It's been so long since I've heard someone say my father's name. It hurts and I gulp, sniffing back tears.

"So, can you tell me what happened?

"Of course," she says, sincerely. "We knew this day would come eventually. Dakota, sit down please. You need to hear this too."

Dakota sits on the opposite side of the table, putting her elbows on the table.

Matilda unfolds the birth certificate, glancing over it quickly.

"Ok, so I'll start by letting you know that your father loved you both," she tells us, glancing at her daughter for a moment, "but because of the fact that both Lilith and I got pregnant only months apart, we decided to keep it from you and raise you separately. I loved Dillon, but Martin didn't want any controversy so we kept it quiet."

I don't know what to say, so keep quiet and don't even dare glance at Dakota. I can hear her sobbing, and sniffing back the tears.

"It broke my heart to not see you after you were born, Braeden. I really wanted to be a part of your life too, but Dillon wouldn't have it. And he pushed me away, not even wanting to see Dakota either.

"He said it hurt too much to look at her, because she looked so much like me. And we couldn't be together."

"So, do you know what happened with Lilith after?"

"Not much. You probably know more than I do about those six years before Dillon's death."

I nod, but know I don't need to explain everything to her.

"Yeah, did you come to his funeral?"

"Yes, but only the church service. It was quite confronting. And I feel horrible that I didn't support you more."

"I appreciate you telling me now."

Dakota pipes up from the other side of the table, "So, dad isn't my dad?"

Matilda looks across at her, her expression sad.

"No dear, not by blood, but in every other way."

"Great," Dakota snaps. "Just fucking great." I've never heard her swear. It seems so out of character for her.

"Language Dakota Abigail. Be thankful you were raised in a loving family."

Caz May

"Whatever, mum."

"Mind yourself, young lady. I will not stand for this behaviour in this house, with company who will be a part of your life."

Matilda stands, heading over to the oven that is beeping a symphony.

"Braeden, dear, will you be staying for dinner?"

"I'd love that," I tell her with a smile. "Can I help with anything?"

"No thanks, dear, go with Dakota to wash up and dinner will be served when Martin comes in."

Dakota huffs as she stands up, nodding at me and then down the hallway.

Hastily getting up I follow her, taking in each room with open doors. Her younger siblings are playing in one bedroom, and she smiles at them as we head down the long hallway to a bathroom.

Quickly I wash my hands, glancing at her as she does the same. Her behaviour is odd. I've never known her to be so mean.

"Dakota, do we still have a problem? Your mum has confirmed you're my sister. I'd honestly like to get to know you and your family more."

"I don't need another brother," she snaps at me, shoving past me to head to what i'm presuming is her room. I stop in the open doorway, hesitant to enter her space, because it's clear she doesn't want me too. I feel lost, out of place, not welcome.

She's sitting cross legged on her bed, staring down at her fingers.

"Dakota?"

She huffs, gazing up at me.

"What Braeden? Why don't you just fuck off, like you basically told me to."

She's angry, and I'm honestly not sure why.

"Well, um...I..." I have no idea what I'm even saying. Dakota cocks her head to the side, again huffing like a bratty toddler.

"Why are you so upset with me about this?" I ask, finally getting my brain to cooperate with my mouth.

"Because you blamed me for your dad and brother's death," she yells standing up and stalking towards me.

Oh shit, right, I did say that. Idiot.

"Oh right, I did, and I'm sorry for saying that."

"You should be," she sasses, hand on her hip.

"I was just upset, and looking for someone to blame other than Lilith. I didn't know the truth."

"And now that you do?"

I let out a laugh, smiling at her.

"I take it back. Lilith is the only one to blame for those actions. I just want to get to know you, my sister," I say, elbowing her in the side.

"Fine, I'll get to know you, but only because you're my brother," she jeers with a cheeky smile.

We both laugh then, and I pull her into a hug that she doesn't refuse.

"Thanks, Dakota. I've always wanted a family who cares about me."

She laughs and smiles.

Caz May

"Yeah, no shortage of love in this house. Let's head back to the kitchen. Sounds like dad is home."

I follow her back out into the kitchen, to find the rest of her family—my family—seated at the dining table. I take a seat next to Dakota, and we enjoy a lavish dinner of Roast beef, and vegetables with gravy. It's been a long time since I've eaten anything like it, and it's absolutely delicious.

As we eat, everyone chats, and I can't help but smile, feeling happier than I have in a long time. It's amazing being part of a family.

AFTER DINNER, Matilda takes me home, back to the van which honestly doesn't feel like home anymore. It never did. I've been homeless essentially with a roof over my head that never felt like home. The only place that has felt like home recently—since I was a kid—has been in Ariel's arms, or Briston's bed.

I give Matilda directions, and her expression is sad the whole drive. I'm getting the impression that she'd do anything to make up for lost time, to make things better for me, as she feels like she failed my dad.

Pulling up at the van, she cuts the engine, about to get out. But I shake my head at her, and say, "Thanks for the ride, Matilda. No need to get out. I'm good."

Her hand reaches out for mine, her eyes locking on me when she asks, "Are you happy staying in the van?"

I nod, even though I'm not happy being in the van at all. I hate it. But I don't say that, instead telling her, "It's fine. I'm still working, and I like the space."

Lies, well two lies, and a truth. I don't tell her I've never felt more lonely, missing the two people I love more than anyone.

"If you're sure. My household might be a bit over the top, but you're always welcome Braeden. You're family."

I give her a smile.

"Thanks, Matilda. I appreciate it," I tell her, my hand on the door handle to get out of the car. She leans over to give me a kiss on the cheek, a motherly gesture that warms my heart.

"Take care of yourself Braeden, dear," she says softly, as I jump out.

"I will, thank you again for the amazing dinner and the ride."

"Anytime. Goodnight, dear," she says with a wide smile, as I close the door and head to the caravan as she drives off. She honks the horn and we wave at each other.

Things have definitely been a complete whirlwind lately. It feels as though I'm at a crossroad in my life, and hopefully heading towards the path of good things ahead. And I hope those good things are getting the two loves of my life back, to heal and tame my heart.

Caz May

Chapter Forty-Eight

BRAEDEN

Over the past week, I'd focused on cleaning up the van whilst trying not to cry buckets.

The hardest thing was throwing out my guitar. I regretted smashing it now that I know the truth.

Yeah, dad cheated on mum, but he fell in love with someone else. It's kinda fucked up but I get it, since I'm hopelessly in love with two people myself.

Granted my Ariel and Briston aren't speaking to me, for their own reasons which in my opinion are bullshit.

Ariel has shown me the last few months that she doesn't take anyone's shit, but she's taking her Dad forbidding of seeing me to a whole new level, pushing me away when I can tell that's not what my girl wants.

And I love Briston, his demanding sexual side, but he's a pussy—pussy whipped—when it comes to Ariel. No matter what he'll always side with her, without hearing the full story most of the time. It cuts me deep.

I need to get everything out in the open and get back into their daks, because when we're together—as a threesome—everything feels right.

The three of us together completes my heart.

HEADING INTO SCHOOL, once again I feel like every damn person is staring me down. Eyes on me as though I'm a pariah and not welcome to grace the halls of Lockgrove Prep anymore.

My dirty laundry—Carson's actually—including his demise at his own hand had been plastered all over the news, so people were aware I was innocent, but still I was the social outcast of school. The soccer team captain from the wrong side of town couldn't walk into school like he owned the place anymore, according to my peers—but I still did it—my head held high as I meandered in a little to close to the second bell to make a quiet entrance.

I'd wanted to speak to Ava before school, but the trill of the second bell has me skidding to my locker to shove my backpack inside and grab my books in a mad dash before first period.

I'll have to dwell on my question to her until break. And getting to class that very thought makes nervousness bubble in my guts. I don't think she'll say no, considering Zeke isn't here, but it's still a possibility.

I could also ask Dakota, but she's not always one to attend school events like the ball. That hadn't really crossed my mind before knowing she was my sister, but it intrigues me now. I really want to get to know her more.

THE FIRST TWO PERIODS DRAG, and by the recess break I'm antsy for some fresh air, and a ciggie. Smoking at school isn't really a good idea, but if I go to behind the bleachers the prying eyes of teachers won't find me, and being honest they wouldn't dare say anything to me after everything that's happened lately. Plus being the soccer team captain, teachers tend to turn a blind eye to any of my —or my teammates—reckless behaviours at school.

Quickly I dash past my locker, grabbing out a ciggie from my stash before chasing after Ava as she heads out the doors.

"Av's wait up!" I holler with my heart thumping as I head out behind her.

"Hey, Brae," she beamed, excitedly adding, "What's up?"

"I...um...wanted to ask you something," I mumbled apprehensively.

"Yeah, cool," she chirped, smiling at me as we headed towards the bleachers. The nervousness sends chills up and down my spine, and reaching the bleachers I stand back, leaning against the cold metal frame to calm myself.

Anyone would think I'd never asked a girl out before. Cautiously, I slide my cigarette from my pocket, along with my lighter that I flick to light up my death stick. Slipping the lighter back in my pocket I take a slow drag, heading the smoke for the buzz before exhaling it steadily.

With the cigarette between my fingers, I hold it up to Ava.

"Want a drag?"

"No thanks," she mutters disgustedly.

I take another drag, quickly puffing out the smoke this time.

"So," I begin, feebly. "I was...um...wondering if you'd go to the ball with me?"

"As a date?" she asks, uneasiness in her tone. Great. She's going to shoot me down. No doubt about to tell me no, and that Zeke can come home after all. My plans to get to talk to Bris and Ariel are about to go down like the last dregs of my cigarette.

"Well, nah, as friends," I splutter, choking on the drag I take. "Like if you're not going with someone else."

Her eyes affix on me, with a smile lighting them up.

"I'd love to!" she beams excitedly, almost jumping out of her skin.

"Ripper," I jeer, throwing my cigarette butt on the ground and stubbing it with my toe.

My gaze is on the grass when I apprehensively ask, "Could you pick me up?"

"Of course, I'll organise a ride," she assures me, giving me a cheeky smirk when she adds, "Can't wait to see you in a suit."

I chortle then, laughing so hard my sides hurt.

"I scrub up alright. Bet you do to."

"You'll have to wait and see," she teases me with a wink. It's fun flirting with her, knowing it's just harmless fun.

Poking her in the side with my elbow, I question her, "How's Ezekiel these days?"

Her face falls as her eyes rise to meet mine again.

"I miss him, but we're good most of the time."

"Sweet," say, turning away to hide my crestfallen expression from her. I'm clearly not hiding anything though, wearing my emotions on my sleeve, as she lightly touches my arm comfortingly.

"I don't know what happened Brae, but they'll be there," she tells me warmly.

"Yeah, long story, but I'm hoping it will be a night to remember."

She laughs, giving another one of her cheeky, friendly flirtatious smiles.

"It will be! It's our year twelve ball."

"Yeah, anyway I gotta go catch coach about something at training yesterday. I'll see you later," I tell her, giving her a kiss on the cheek. "Thanks again Ava. You're a great friend."

She returns the gesture of the cheek kiss.

"Anytime, Brae. And back at you," she coos sweetly, as I run towards coach on the other side of the field.

Tamed Hearts

Part one of get the loves of my life back went off without a hitch.

I'm so grateful to have someone like Ava in my life, and now my plan to win Ariel and Briston back is in motion I'm feeling a lot more chipper than I have in weeks.

I only hope my world doesn't completely crumble, as I can't stand to even think about anymore heartbreak.

Caz May

Chapter Forty-Nine

Ariel

The entire year has been such a rollercoaster, and it's insane that we're so close to graduation and the year twelve ball is right around the corner. I'd taken dad's Amex, ready to give it a workout.

Excitedly I'm being dragged towards 'Florentina Bridal' on Main Street by Ava who's giggly. It's the only shop in town that sells formal wear, most clothing shops being every surf brand under the sun.

Before now I'd also been a wallflower when it came to school dances, either not going or wearing the same dress I wear to every formal thing.

Getting to the dress shop, Ava pushes the door open and the assistant glares at us, rolling her eyes at yet another couple of giggling school girls entering the shop. I take in the racks of gowns, awestruck at all the colours.

Ava drags me closer to the bridesmaid type ones, tugging on my hand so hard I stumble in my thongs, nearly tripping up.

"Ava, slow down," I chastise, laughing. "I'm about to fall on my butt!"

"Sorry," she apologises, stopping in front of the purple dresses. "I'm just really excited to help you find a dress."

Her face falls with those words and I have to ask, "Aren't you excited about getting a dress too?"

She starts pushing the dresses aside, thumbing through them and not looking at me when she mumbles, "Kinda, but I'm upset that Zeke couldn't come home."

Touching her arm, I get her to look at me.

"That sucks, but you'll still have fun."

"Yeah, I will, but I wanted to share the experience with Zeke. I didn't get to go with him to his year twelve ball, because we weren't together then."

"Makes sense, sucky though," I reply, nodding as she pulls out a strapless dress, holding it up against me.

I run my hands up and down my arms self consciously.

"I can't wear that, Ava."

Caz May

She scoffs, telling me, "No one will be looking at your arms, Ariel."

"I know, but I can't. Not to something like the ball."

"Ok, we'll find something else, with sleeves."

We start scanning through the dresses in silence. It doesn't appear as though I'm going to find anything I'll be comfortable wearing when Ava pulls out a velvet bodied long-sleeved dress with a silk bottom that flows down from the waist.

"It's perfect," I shriek excitedly, taking it from her when she gestures towards the change rooms.

"Go try it on!" Ava instructs, rushing over with me and sliding the curtain across as I step inside the small space.

As I undress, I speak loudly, "Is Zeke coming home for grad?"

"Yeah, I'm excited to see him then."

"Cool, I'll bet."

"How're things with your boys?" she questions, something odd in her tone as though she knows something she's not telling me.

Stepping out of the change room, I smooth down the skirt of the dress as I turn to admire it in the mirror. Ava's eyes catch mine and I reply to her question, "Things are good with Briston, but not really with Braeden."

"Oh really? Haven't you seen him since he got out of jail?"

"Barely. Dad prohibited me from seeing him, but I still love him," I tell her, forlorn.

"Oh that sucks balls," she replies crassly.

"Yep, and I miss being with him too."

Ava laughs then, and I turn to glare at her annoyed.

"What's funny about that?" I question her, baffled by how rude she's being.

"He's my date," she informs me, with a soft smile. "But I get the feeling he only asked me so he could see you and Briston."

"Oh right, and probably."

She nods, laughing again but a little more cautiously. "So is this your ball dress?"

"Yeah, I think so. I love how the neckline shows a hint of cleavage to tease my boys."

"They won't know what's hit them."

"Definitely," I affirm, heading back into the change room.

Ava calls out boomingly, "I can't wait to see Braeden in a suit. He's going to look so hot!"

After getting redressed, I slide the curtain open, holding the dress over my arm, I smile at her feeling a blush rise up my cheeks.

"He'll look delectable in a suit, as will Briston, but I'm looking forward to the after party."

"Oh yeah, sexy boys in only their birthday suits, huh?" Ava teases, as though she knows exactly the dirty thoughts I'm thinking.

We laugh together, striding to the counter to pay for my dress. It costs five hundred dollars, but it's perfect.

I don't honestly know what Braeden is thinking, but curse my dad for prohibiting me from seeing him.

Caz May

I'm in love with Braeden—that hasn't changed—and I'm going to do everything I can to show him, to tame his wild heart that I'm sure beats for mine.

Chapter Fifty

Ariel

*S*lipping my knickers up my legs I watch Briston from where he's sitting on his bed in only boxer shorts.

He licks his lips, moaning. "Damn, Ar's baby. You look sexy in lacy underwear."

I laugh at him, giggles that I can't stop.

"I might, but you need to stop staring and get ready, or you'll be going to the ball in your underwear."

Caz May

He laughs then, a deep chuckle that makes his chest vibrate as he stands and stalks towards me.

Without warning, he kisses me with a sensual meeting of our lips that makes me gasp.

Jerking me closer with a hand around my waist, his fingers on the bare skin of my hips sends tingles pulsing through me, and his tongue starts to play with mine as he deepens the kiss.

Naughty Briston is out to play tonight, and that has me excited, and him as well given the bulge in his boxers that's pressing into my lower belly.

Breathless, I pull away from his kiss, taking a slight step back from him.

"Bris, please. We have to get ready."

He again lets out the deep chuckle, the one that stirs up lust for him in my belly and between my thighs.

"I know that Ar's, but you can't make me go to the ball with blue balls. Doesn't seem right."

"Fine," I snap at him, smirking as I step towards him, and slide my hand inside his boxers to palm his growing erection.

Starting to stroke his dick, he murmurs out words through his clenched teeth, "Damn, Ar's. That feels so good," he tells me with a deep groan, as he shoves his boxers to the floor, causing his hardness to jut forward in my grip.

"Briston, stop, what are you doing? You need to get dressed," I protest, dropping my hand from his length.

"Come on Ar's. Touch my dick, please," he begs, again stalking towards me. "I'm so hard for you baby."

Tamed Hearts

"Fine, but we have to be quick," I say in a rush, adding, "And quiet, in case your mum comes to check if you're ready."

Briston chuckles again. And I grab his dick, stroking his length and making him moan. He cups my sex through my lacy knickers, the brush of his fingers teasing my clit. Just that light brush of his callous fingers through the lace sends a shiver through me. Without warning he slips a finger inside my knickers, flicking my clit before touching me as well with teasing strokes of his finger inside me. His dick is starting to throb in my grip and kissing him, I cup the tip of his dick so it's covered with my palm. He lets go, biting down on my lip as he rides the wave of his release, covering my hand with his cum. My release hits, making me tremble, my knees going weak as he pulls his finger out.

His eyes are on mine when he puts his finger to my lip, and I lick it clean.

"Damn, Ar's baby. That was hot."

I laugh, lifting my hand covered with his cum and smearing it all over his chest, painting his body with it until I reach his lips. He laves his tongue over my palm, lapping up his cum with a smirk on his sexy face.

"You got me all dirty, Ariel," he taunts, gripping my chin and bringing my lips to his for a kiss. It's a hot dirty, fast kiss, that I break and drop to my knees in front of my best friend.

Smirking at him, I lick his dick clean, and slowly as I get to to my feet I lick all over his stomach, cleaning the cum from his skin. When reaching his mouth once more I kiss him, whispering against his lips, "All clean, Bris."

He breaks the kiss this time.

Caz May

"Thanks for that, baby."

As Briston pulls his boxers back on I watch him a moment, feeling a blush rise up my cheeks thinking about our quick little tryst. He breaks my thoughts.

"Ar's, baby. You need to get your pretty purple dress on," he tells me with a snide laugh.

"Funny, Briston," I jeer back, rushing to his wardrobe to grab my dress from the hanger. Slipping it on, I step out into his room again to find he's put on a navy suit, and crisp white shirt unbuttoned to show a sexy glimpse of his pecs. He's holding the suit jacket, and throws it on the bed when I cross the room towards him asking, "Can you do up the zip for me?"

Reaching him, I grab my hair to hold it over my shoulder as Briston slides up the short zip of the dress. His hand lingers on the small of my back, heating my skin again. Turning to face him, he wolf whistles.

"You scrub up sexy, Ariel."

"So do you, Briston. The blue of the suit makes your eyes pop and your skin glow."

He chuckles. "And that dress was made for your body Ariel. It fits you perfect and I love how it shows just a hint of your perfect tits."

I give him a quick kiss in reply.

"You ready to get our ball on?" he asks, suggestively, giving me a wink.

"Ready as I'll ever be," I reply, taking his hand as he picks up his jacket and drapes it over his elbow as we head out of his room.

Tamed Hearts

IN THE LOUNGE ROOM we're bombarded by Briston's parents oohing and arhing about how good Briston looks and how beautiful I look.

His mum pulls me into a hug, whispering in my ear, "You look so beautiful Ariel. I'm so sorry your mum can't be here to see you."

Pulling back from the hug I smile.

"Thanks Mrs Nicholls. She would've loved tonight, and seeing me going with Briston would've made her so happy."

"It would've. It's a pity your dad had to work as well tonight."

I laugh and give her another smile.

"He said to take lots of photos for him."

"Oh, definitely. And we better get to that, as the limo will be here any minute."

Shuffling up next to Briston, he snakes an arm around my side, pulling me close as his mum starts snapping photo after photo. She takes ones of us smiling, a couple of us with goofy faces and one of us kissing, which is my favourite.

"Don't send that one to my dad," I instruct her with a wary smile.

"Oh," she stammers, concerned. "Is he not ok with you and Briston together?"

"He wouldn't be happy seeing me with any boy."

"That's just because you're his innocent baby girl. He loves you, and I'm sure he'll come around."

She's about to say more when a horn honks outside, signalling the arrival of the limo. Briston takes my hand again and we head out to the white limo, both smiling wide as we run down the footpath and slide inside together.

I can't stop smiling, thinking about dancing the night away and feeling like a belle of the ball with one of the loves of my life by my side.

I'm nervous to see Braeden, but just the thought of seeing him makes my whole body tingle.

Maybe it's time to stand up to my dad, to make him see that I'm not his innocent—far from it honestly—little girl anymore.

Tamed Hearts

Chapter Fifty-One

BRAEDEN

Scanning the ballroom I'm antsy whilst looking for Ariel. Ava elbows me in the side. "Looking for someone?" she asks me with a smile.

Turning to look at her, I can't return the smile. I'm too nervous about seeing Ariel, knowing she's going to look stunning from what Ava told me about her dress. I'm also

Caz May

excited to see Briston in a suit. He looks sexy in anything but I'm sure he's going to rock a suit better than most guys.

"You know I'm looking for Ariel. I'm so nervous about seeing her."

"It will be fine, Brae. Despite what happened, I don't think her feelings for you have changed."

"I hope not," I reply, letting out a sigh.

And my breath catches in my throat and chest, my heart stops a moment when I spot Ariel.

Stunning doesn't even being to describe how amazing she looks, how beautiful she is in her purple dress with her dark brown hair flowing in loose spiral curls. As she enters the ballroom, she brushes it back over her shoulders, taking Briston's hand with hers and pulling him onto the dance floor.

Hanging back I watch them together, dancing as though no one is watching. They both look so happy, and I wonder if I should even confront her when maybe she's moved on from me completely.

The song changes to a slower tempo one and Briston pulls away, whispering something in her ear before he leaves the room. Ariel glances around, perplexed about what to do with her date gone.

I take that as my chance, striding across the dance floor and capturing her in my arms, one around her waist, the other on her shoulder.

Starting to sway our bodies together to the slow beat of the music I'm expecting her to pull away but she doesn't.

Leaning in as we dance I steal a kiss from her without thinking. She returns the kiss, open-mouthed and when the song ends I take her hand with mine and lead her out into the quiet of the hallway.

Again I drop a kiss against her lips, an intensely passionate kiss that has my heart racing.

A little breathless, I pull back, my forehead against hers when I murmur, "I miss you little bitch." It's been ages since I've called her that, but it comes out of my mouth with a hint of teasing.

She doesn't seem to mind, moving back a little so her back is pressed against the wall. And her eyes on mine are shining with desire when she replies, "I miss you too, Brae, so much it hurts."

Her hand goes to her heart and I capture it with mine, feeling her heartbeat against it when she continues softly, "I still love you."

Gazing into her eyes, still with my hand on hers over her heart I tell her what's in my heart, "I never stopped loving you either but I had to let you go."

"I know Braeden, but even though dad forbade me from seeing you I never stopped loving you."

"Yeah, but I couldn't have you around as much with Carson so out of control. And then when I went to jail, I didn't want you to have to deal with that."

"I know...but I just wanted to help. I care about you," she tells me, catching my other hand with hers and lacing our fingers together.

Squeezing it I beg her, "Just love me, Ariel, please."

"I do and so does Bris." Those words stab at my heart. I still love Briston too, and knowing I haven't cut my losses with him by hurting Ariel means the world.

Caz May

"I didn't mean to hurt either of you," I admit, feeling the weight of my actions hit me hard in the chest.

"Well, you did, Brae but I don't want to talk about that now," she tells me, shaking her head. "I just want to get out of here and be with you."

I chuckle softly.

"You read my mind," I tell her with a smirk, before asking, "Where's Bris?"

"He went to the bathroom," she tells me, nodding down the long hallway to the left.

"Cool, let's go find him and head out."

I again take her hand, as we step away from the wall and stalk down the hallway towards the men's room at the very end.

STALKING INTO THE MEN'S ROOM, I find Briston at the sinks, washing his hands and smoothing back his hair.

Stepping up behind him, his gaze rises to meet mine in the mirror. And he gasps, biting down on his lip ring to possibly stop himself from saying something hastily.

"Hey, Bris. You look hot in a suit, man," I tell him, stepping closer to him so our bodies are almost touching.

He shifts, pressing his crotch against the metal sink frame. He groans at the contact of the cold metal, and my stepping even closer to cage him in. I'm aching for him, desperate for him.

Without warning, his gaze drops and he turns to face me, causing me to stumble back a little.

"So do you," he admits, again biting his lip ring, this time muttering, "But I can't Braeden. You hurt Ariel. And seeing you dancing with her before I came in here, tore my heart out."

He looks right at me, tears in the corner of his mesmerising eyes. He's tearing my heart out right now, at arms reach, but so far away.

"We talked about everything," I confess, raking a hand through my hair, and taking a deep breath to continue, "Things are shit man, but I need you both. You feel like home, Briston."

God I want to fucking kiss him, and so much more. Being so close to him and not being able to touch him is absolute fucking torture.

"I have missed you," he admits with a wicked smirk that makes my stomach flip with lust. "But you have to be serious Braeden. I can't deal with any more heartbreak. Ariel's or mine."

"I get that Bris. I still fucking love you both."

"I'm still in love with you too, even with you stomping on my fucking heart and hurting Ariel."

This time I don't say anything, instead I shove him against the wall, and just kiss him, a hard, raw and possessive kiss.

Panting for breath after, I ask brazenly, "Can we go back to yours?"

It's probably not even an option, but I need him naked and in my arms, making me feel good, making all the pain and heartbreak of these past months a distant memory.

"Just us?" he enquires, winking at me and adding, "Or Ar's as well?"

"All three of us, yeah," I reply with a nod, smirking.

Caz May

"Yeah, sweet. My parents have skipped out for the night."

"So you're down to fuck me again, and Ariel?"

"Yeah, that kiss has already made me hard, so I'm down for sure."

I take his hand with mine, intertwining our fingers, loving how our large hands complement each others.

We walk out holding hands, and spot Ariel leaning against the wall at the end of the hallway. I wrap my arm around Ariel, kissing her temple softly.

"You boys made up too?"

"Yeah, darling," I murmur, smiling at her. "And if you're down, we were going to head back to Bris' for a dirty end to our night."

"Sounds great. I've missed getting dirty with my B-boys," she replies with a teasing tone, giving me a kiss that is just a teasing peck—and a lavish lick of my lips—but a promise of what's ahead for the rest of the night.

Chapter Fifty-Two

Ariel

*H*eading out of the building with Braeden's arm wrapped around me, his hand in Briston's I call the limo back to collect us.

Waiting curb side for it, I'm giddy with anticipation of a dirty night with both of my B-boys. It's been so long since we've been together as a threesome, and my whole body is

Caz May

becoming tingly and warm right down into my knickers just thinking about being with them both again.

The limo pulls up in front of us, and I open the door, the boys shuffling in before I do. They drop hands, and Briston slides up the partition so the driver can't see us.

Barely a moment after he does so—and the car starts driving away—we start pashing each other, firstly Braeden and I before Briston sets a kiss upon Braeden's lips after he breaks the kiss with me. And I watch them, my knickers becoming increasingly wetter with my desire. My clit is throbbing and I let out a moan that causes the boys to break their kiss and glare at me laughing.

"You turned on baby?" Briston questions with a delicious smirk on his gorgeous face.

"Oh, yeah. Very, very wet for my B-boys."

"Mmm, I love the sound of that, darling," Braeden teases, his hand on my thigh. Even through the fabric of my dress, I can feel his touch heating my skin.

He chuckles, sliding down to his knees on the floor of the limo and grabbing the hem of my dress to hitch it up my thighs.

Briston is staring at me, watching as pleasure starts to take over my face, with Braeden kissing up my thigh towards my centre that's pulsing with desire, knowing what's about to happen.

When Braeden's kisses reach my lacy knickers, his tongue licking my clit I gasp, a breathy raspy, "Fuck, Brae," escaping my lips. I'm already on edge, and turn to kiss Briston who is sitting beside me, smirking like a sexy devil.

I can barely concentrate on kissing him though, as Braeden's teeth find the elastic of my knickers and his slick tongue makes contact with my arousal. His kiss against my clit makes my whole body throb, and he slides one, then two fingers inside me, still kissing and licking my flesh and moaning.

My gaze turns back to Briston to find he's sitting back on the seat, his slacks undone and his hard dick flipped out of his boxers. One hand is behind his head, the other stroking his length whilst he watches Braeden going down on me.

Fisting Braeden's hair, I push his face closer, moaning loudly when he sucks my clit and inserts another finger inside me. He pumps the three fingers in and out, harder, and faster, and licks and kisses every drop of my arousal. I'm so close, my core is throbbing and when his fingers curl up to caress my g-spot I shiver, my thighs shaking as I come.

Tugging Braeden up towards me, I kiss him passionately, murmuring from tasting my climax on his lips and tongue as he deepens the kiss. His fingers brush against my knickers, and aftershocks ricochet through me.

He breaks the kiss, smirking at me.

"You're so fucking beautiful, Ariel. And when you come, darling, you're fucking stunning."

I don't have words of reply, instead I reach down to palm his erection through the front of his black slacks. He groans, and starts to undo his belt, his greedy, needy eyes darting between Briston and me.

Flipping his dick out, he again groans when I shift on the seat and push him down so he's sitting on the opposite side of me than Briston is. Leaning over Braeden, I take his dick into my mouth, licking his precum as my tongue starts to slide down his shaft as I take him deeper. His hand grabs my hair, pushing my head down and holding me still as I pleasure him more.

"Damn, darling. You know how to suck a dick."

I moan against his dick, feeling his tip hit the back of my throat. He starts to pulse in my mouth, and pulling back a little I feel his hot salty load coat my throat.

Swallowing hard, I sit up, smile at him and give him a quick kiss before I turn towards Briston, and kiss him. He groans against my lips, suddenly spreading ropes of come all over the seat beside him.

"Shit Bris," I jeer with a laugh, as the limo grinds to a halt with us now back at Briston's house.

"Shh, Ar's," he whispers, hiding his snigger as he tucks himself back into his boxers. Braeden does the same and opening the door of the limo we climb out, rushing inside to the rumpus room.

His parents are away for the night, and the very thought of something else happening makes my stomach flip with desire.

I love my B-boys, and tonight I'm ready to go to the heights of pleasure with them.

Chapter Fifty-Three

BRAEDEN

Following Briston into the rumpus room, the tension between us is on high gear, radiating between us.

It's a cool night, and he turns on the fireplace before turning to Ariel and yanking her into his arms, kissing her fiercely.

Watching them kissing, I shrug off my jacket, and shirt, tossing them to the floor. Briston breaks his kiss with Ariel,

Caz May

his gaze shifting to me for a moment. With our eyes locked on each other's, he dares me to get naked, taunting me with his wickedly sexy smirk.

Sliding off my slacks and then my boxers, I don't look away from him for a moment. Licking his lips, he breaks our gaze, focusing back on Ariel as he helps her out of her dress.

With the firelight illuminating us in the darkness, Ariel looks stunning in her sexy underwear, almost as though she's an angel. Stalking towards her I kiss her as Briston gets naked. Still kissing Ariel, I tug off her knickers, palming her arse as I slide them off her. She breaks the kiss, looking between Briston and me, as she undoes her bra, and drops it to the floor. Touching each other, our hands over every inch of skin we fall to the floor, our bodies colliding and my dick stirs with lust. Briston is kneeling beside Ariel, stroking his hard dick. It's a fucking glorious sight, seeing him turned on by seeing our girl and me naked.

"Ariel, darling, do you trust me?"

"Yes, Brae, I trust you," she murmurs raspy as I brush my thumb over her clit whilst slowly slipping three fingers into her dripping pussy.

Starting to thrust those fingers in and out of Ariel's pussy, I stretch up to kiss Briston on the lips, hard and lustfully as he strokes his dick.

When I break our kiss he leans down and kisses Ariel, gazing at her with so much love in his eyes, but also with pleasure dancing in them. My dick is aching, painfully hard but I want to make Ariel come again. She looks undeniably beautiful when she comes.

Tamed Hearts

"You wanna come, darling?" I question her, leaning over her body to kiss her perfect tits, laving my tongue over them.

"Oh yes, please," she rasps, as I pull my fingers out of her pussy before slipping my whole fist inside her.

She moans loudly, screaming out, "Oh shit, fuck! Braeden!"

I push my fist further inside her pussy, up to my wrist, and start to pump it in and out, raking my fingers over her sensitive insides. She's writhing on the floor, and throws her arms above her head as the pleasure takes over her body. Briston is still, just watching me pleasuring Ariel.

I'm about to say something when Ariel again screams out a moan of pleasure, her pussy squirting in an explosive pulsating climax. Pulling my fist out, I put it up to Briston's lips and he licks it clean.

"Our girl tastes good, huh, man?"

"So good," he murmurs back, grabbing my neck and yanking my face to his for a kiss. I can taste Ariel on his lips and tongue, and fuck it's so damn arousing my already hard dick throbs even more.

Breaking the kiss, I glance at Ariel a moment, before looking at Briston.

"You wanna fuck me, stud?" I tease him.

"Of course, sexy, but only if you fuck our girl whilst I fuck you."

I lean down again over Ariel, kissing her gently, sweetly and lovingly.

"You want that darling?"

Caz May

"Yes, please Braeden, fuck me," she says as a whisper against my lips.

"Lay on your side darling," I instruct her, watching her follow my request as I grab out a condom from my slacks pocket.

Sheathing my dick quickly I lay down behind her, rubbing my hard dick along her wet pussy. She murmurs turning back to kiss me, as Briston gets into position laying down on his side behind me. I push inside Ariel's pussy, and she moans, a moan I swallow with a kiss as Briston plunges raw inside my arse.

Tearing my mouth from Ariel's, I groan starting to thrust my dick into her pussy, whilst Briston rocks inside my arse. This is new heights of pleasure. Pleasure that I've never felt before. Pure ecstasy.

Ariel's leg is in the air, and holding it I thrust harder, stilling a moment as Briston's pelvis stills as well.

"Holy fuck, this feels good," Briston bellows. "I'm so close."

I turn back to kiss him, hard and raw, still pumping my dick into Ariel.

"Come inside me, stud," I request, my eyes on his. Glancing between them both, with last final deep thrusts we all come together, screaming and moaning our release as we let go trembling.

Briston pulls out first and turning to face him first I tell him, "I love you, Briston. I fucking love you." I seal my words against his lips with a tender kiss, before pulling out of Ariel's still trembling pussy and angling myself so I'm facing her.

"You ok darling?"

"Yeah, Brae, better than ok."

"I love you Ariel, darling, so fucking much."

She kisses me, whispering against my lips, "I love you, more, my Braeden."

We don't exchange anymore words, or kisses. Briston stands, extending a hand to help me get up off the floor. I take it, pulling myself up so our chests collide.

"Let's take our girl to bed?" I suggest, glancing down at Ariel still seated on the floor. Her eyes are droopy, and she's practically falling asleep.

Bending down I scoop her up into my arms, carrying her to Briston's room. He walks ahead, yanking back the covers of the bed so I can drop Ariel's tired body on the sheets.

She murmurs softly, stretching her arms above her head as she gets comfy. Briston walks around to the opposite side of the bed, sliding in next to Ariel, as I do the same. Ariel again murmurs, kissing Briston, and then me before her eyes start to fall shut. I give Briston a deep kiss, and laying down properly we both drape an arm over Ariel, falling asleep with our arms around our girl.

It's bliss.

The perfect end to a perfect night of pleasure, and love. I have them back, and my heart feels tame, and I'm beyond happy.

❤

THE SUN STREAMING IN the window wakes me, and I find Ariel and Briston are already awake and kissing each other.

Caz May

A pang of jealousy hits me, until Ariel rolls over and looks straight into my eyes, brushing the flop of my hair out of my face.

"Morning, Brae," she purrs at me, her voice still raspy from sleep.

"Morning, darling. Do I get a good morning kiss as well?"

"Of course," she taunts, cupping my jaw and kissing me hard, her tongue teasing mine. Breaking the kiss, I'd love to take our morning pashing session further, but I need to talk to both of them. My world has been turned upside down of late and I need to confide in the people who love me the most.

Sitting up in bed, I sigh running a hand through my hair.

"I...um...need to tell you guys something."

They both sit up then as well, glaring at me, but not saying a word.

"Something big," I continue, rubbing my sweaty hands together.

"You can tell us anything Brae," Ariel tells me, then asks, "Is it about your mum?"

I give her an angry glare.

"Don't ever call her that," I roar, adding a calmer, "But no, it's not about her."

"Then what is it, Brae? You do something bad?" Briston asks, taking my hand and squeezing it reassuringly.

"So, um...after Carson died I got given some stuff, like photos and documents."

Briston squeezes my hand again, and Ariel takes my other hand, holding it with hers and rubbing her thumb over my palm. It's both distracting and comforting.

"And I found a picture of me, my dad and a girl my age who I didn't know. But she looked sorta familiar if that makes sense."

They nod, and Ariel says, "Definitely. Did you find out who it was?"

"Yeah, it was Dakota."

"Oh, um shit, but cool," Briston says eyeing me worriedly when I can't look at him.

"So what does that mean?" Ariel asks me, a hand against my cheek to turn my gaze to her.

I gulp, taking in a deep breath.

"She's my sister," I admit, feeling the weight of telling someone lifting off my shoulders.

"Shit, Braeden, that's wow," Ariel shrieks in shock.

"Yeah, man. Never would've thought that, but yeah, cool."

"I know. I was super shocked, but some things Carson said makes sense now."

"Nice, so are you like actual twins?" Briston asks intrigued.

"No, my dad slept with her mum and mine, super close together so we were born only like a month or so apart.

"And then Dakota's non birth dad didn't want a scandal so they hid the truth."

"That's a lot to take in, but I'm glad it's all out in the open now for you," Briston says, giving me a smile.

Caz May

"Yeah, we're shocked but happy for you. You deserve the love of a family Brae," Ariel says sweetly, leaning forward to kiss me tenderly. "You should get to know her more and spend time with her family."

"I will. Thanks for being so amazing, you guys. I love you so much."

They don't reply, but lean forward and both kiss me at the same time, showing me how much they both love me. And that's all I ever wanted, to be truly loved.

Chapter Fifty-Four

Ariel

*W*earing a T-shirt of Briston's as a dress, and carrying my shoes in my hand by the straps I'm casually strolling home.

The sun is warming my skin, and thoughts of last night are warming my insides. I'd never felt so much pleasure in all my life, never had an orgasm that rocked my body so hard I couldn't stop trembling, and then to have yet

Caz May

another soul shattering orgasm after that. I'm still tingling all over, still trembling.

Something changed with my B-boys last night. We'd had sex before, but last night felt life changing. Like they took ownership of me completely, and now own my heart, my body and soul.

My B-boys have tamed my wild heart and I've tamed theirs.

My heart is now pounding as I get closer to home. It's time to tell him—my dad—that I'm not his innocent little girl anymore, and that I'm in love with two guys. He may not be upset about Briston, as he's always thought of Briston as a second child, but I can't see him being even remotely happy about my being in love with Braeden; at all. He's never liked him, since he found him half naked in my bed, and with everything that's happened Braeden is probably on dad's list of non liked people. But I know Braeden, and most people get the wrong impression of him, not knowing his past and the trauma he's gone through.

Getting home, just past eight am I find the front door unlocked. That's unusual, but I'm glad as I didn't take keys last night.

Opening it I'm greeted by Windy, miaowing his hello loudly and circling around my bare legs. I've been neglecting him a little since Mum died. He was more her cat than mine, always curled up with her in bed and all I'd really done was make sure he had his fill of lucky cat biscuits and treats. It'd been to painful to be around him, but he'd started to show me more affection in the last month or so

Tamed Hearts

and that was comforting. Picking him up, I stroke his silky soft fur as I head into the kitchen where I can hear dad making breakfast.

"Morning, dad," I greet him, sitting down on the breakfast bar stool with Windy in my lap, still stroking his fur to give myself some courage to actually talk to dad.

"Good morning, dear," dad replies, turning towards me and putting a plate of buttered strawberry jam toast in front of me.

I'm a little concerned—nervous—that he doesn't appear to be angry at my not coming home the night before.

"I trust you had a good night with Briston," he states, almost question like with a raise of his eyebrow at me.

"I'm sorry I stayed at Briston's last night. We were just so tired after the ball."

"It's fine, Ariel. I trust you, and Briston is a good boy," he tells me, the tone in his voice very fatherly, reminding me of when we were kids and Briston would come over to play. Dad always called him a 'good boy' when he used manners and wasn't cheeky.

"Yeah, and um…" I start, grabbing a piece of toast and taking a bite out of it, chewing loudly with my mouth open.

"What dear?" dad asks, really not seeming his usual angry self.

"I'm in love with Briston," I tell him, gulping as I swallow the remnants of the last bite of toast down.

"I know that Ariel. He's your best friend."

"No, dad, not as my best friend. I love him…and I…" I take another bite of toast to swallow my words down. I'm

Caz May

not sure if I'm ready to tell him the truth, to tell him I'm actually in love with two boys over breakfast like it's something you do every day.

"Well, I'm not exactly thrilled Ariel, but you could be with a worse boy than Briston."

"Um, about that," I stammer, telling my heart to stop pounding so hard.

"What are you getting at? Why do I get the feeling you're hiding something from me Ariel Jane?"

"Because I am," I again stammer, biting down on my final piece of toast, nervously watching dad eating some as he glares at me with fury.

"I...um...I've slept with him, and I'm also in love with Braeden," I admit, feeling a weight lift off my shoulders.

He's not happy about my confession, balling his fists to calm himself.

"I told you to stay away from that boy. He's not worthy of you, Ariel."

Standing up, I let Windy jump down off my lap, shoving the stool aside.

"You don't know him like I do dad. I love him and Briston. And I will not stop seeing or being with either one of them."

Standing my ground feels great.

He appears to calm, but doesn't say anything in reply.

About to head to my room, I tell him, "I'm going with the boys to the beach to scatter mum's ashes today."

He nods, shoving another piece of toast in his mouth, and mumbling, "Ok, dear. Have a good day. I'll see you when I get home from work tonight."

Tamed Hearts

I don't say anything then, just head to the bathroom to shower before getting dressed to meet the boys and head to the beach.

❤

Standing on the foreshore—with my B-boys on either side, arms around my waist—I'm clutching the small urn with the ashes of mum's belongings inside.

Tears are streaking my cheeks, my heart constricting in my chest.

This is really goodbye—the final goodbye—and setting mum free to truly be at peace. It hurts like hell, and I choke back a sob, feeling Braeden kiss my temple softly.

"You ok, darling?" he asks as a hushed whisper into the wind whipping around us.

"Yeah, I will be," I mutter, stepping out of the boys embrace and further into the water lapping our toes.

A wave rolls in, and opening the urn I hold it out in front of me, and close my eyes. Taking in a deep breath I tip it upside down, letting the ashes catch on the wave that splashes my knees. The wind whips around me, and I open my eyes, watching all the ashes flow into the sea and some whirl around me in the wind. I spin around, holding the urn out for a moment longer. It makes me feel calm, wrapped in love and I know mum is looking down on me, telling me to continue taking chances with my heart.

Heading back over to my B-boys, I wipe the tears from my cheeks and clutch the now empty urn to my chest.

Caz May

I take their hands with mine, intertwining our fingers together and without saying anything we amble back up the beach to Briston's jeep.

They give me smiles, making me feel at peace and happier than I have been in months.

Chapter Fifty-Five

BRAEDEN

Dropping Ariel home I follow her to the door, whilst Briston waits in the car.

Pulling her into an embrace she sighs against my chest, and my heart soars with love for her.

Lifting her chin up to view her scarlet cheeks, stained from crying and her sweet natural flush I kiss her, zealously, taking her tongue with mine.

Caz May

"I love you, darling," I whisper to her, breaking the contact of our locked lips, but still close enough with my forehead against hers that her lips feel my words. "You gonna be ok?"

I brush my thumb across her cheeks, caressing her porcelain skin.

"Yeah, Brae," she tells me sweetly, adding, "I love you too."

There's a beat of silence between us, with us just holding each other tightly, and gazing at each other.

"You going to be ok?" she asks me, her dark brown eyes boring into mine with the loaded question.

I give her a smile.

"Now I've got you and Bris back, yeah I will be."

I kiss her again, not wanting to let go of her, now or ever again. Having her in my arms, her lips against mine is heaven on earth.

She'd told me on the way to the beach about telling her dad about us, and he hadn't hit the roof but I'm still wary. I need to tread carefully where Dr Findley is concerned if I want to show him I'm a decent guy who loves his daughter and deserves her love in return. It's all I want, other than being with Bris as well.

Pulling back from the kiss and hug, I kiss her forehead and smile at her as I stumble back to the car.

Getting in Briston's jeep, I watch Ariel head inside her house, once again feeling as though she has my heart with her.

Tamed Hearts

GETTING BACK TO BRISTON'S, his parents are home when he drags me into the kitchen. His dad is cooking something that smells like heaven, and super fancy.

A pang of jealously hits me thinking about all the amazing food Briston has probably eaten growing up, and he acts as though he has no idea how good his life was and clearly still is. I love the guy, but I'm jealous of how perfect his life is. His mum is hovering around the kitchen, tasting whatever is cooking by dipping her finger into the bubbling pan. His dad grabs a tea towel, playfully slapping her on the butt with it.

"Don't spoil the food, honey," he teases her with a cheeky wink. It's so nice seeing a couple still in love so openly.

"Just checking its decent, since you're such a bad chef," She taunts him back, before pouring herself a coffee, and turning her attention to Briston and I in the room. Briston scoffs.

"Seriously, mum. You make me lose my appetite sometimes."

"Oh Briston my baby," she teases her son, grabbing his cheeks in her thumbs and pinching them. "You love that we still love each other. You've got it good, my baby boy," she practically chastises him, her gaze on me with the final words.

"How're you doing, Braeden?" She asks me, a soft smile on her lips before she takes a sip of her coffee.

I gulp, wondering if I should tell her the truth or if Briston has told her anything about what's happened

Caz May

recently with my brothers death, and my going to jail and then finding out that Dakota is my sister.

She answers my questions without me replying. "Briston has told me thing's have been pretty traumatic with your brothers death and your stint in jail." Her tone is soft and calm, which stops my hammering heart, calming my own nervousness. She makes me feel welcome in her home, as though she genuinely cares.

"It's been hard. I don't like being in the van anymore but I have nowhere else to go."

A caring smile lights up her face and she looks to Briston when she suggests, "You're more than welcome to stay here. We'd love to have you."

Her offer has me excited, even more so than when Mrs Neelson offered support.

Mrs Nicholls has always shown her acceptance of me, and has been open to Briston and I together from the first time she met me. I love that. It makes me feel like I deserve love from a parent.

"Thanks, Mrs Nicholls. I'd love that and i appreciate you offering for me to live with you so much."

She again smiles, wider than before.

"No problems dear. We'll organise things in the coming week."

I nod at her, and smile at Briston who has a cheeky smirk on his face that tells me his dirty mind is on overdrive with thoughts of us living together. It will be like the holidays I spent here, waking up with him, kissing for days on end and fooling around together until our dicks ached from multiple orgasms.

Tamed Hearts

With my hand in his, and not another word Briston drags me away to his room. We're barely in the room, after he slammed the door shut behind him before we start pashing, wildly as though we're starving for a taste of each other.

As we pash our hands are all over each other and we stumble together across the room to his bed. He pushes me down, falling on top of me, and grinding his hips into mine so our dicks brush against each other in our daks.

"Missed you so much, stud," I admit, licking my lips and fisting his hair, tugging on the tousled strands to bring his lips back down to mine.

He murmurs, breaking the kiss with a groan.

"Back at you sexy," he teases. "You down to fuck?"

"With your parents home?" I question, glaring up at him whilst biting my lip apprehensively.

He chuckles, giving me a teasing peck of a kiss that makes me groan for more.

"You know they don't care," he declares, still with the chuckle in his voice. "And if you're moving in, we'll be roomies and there's no way I'm keeping my hands off you," he admits, pressing his body down on mine harder.

That feels so good. His dick is already hard, as is mine, and fuck I need him, right fucking now.

It's so different being with Briston than with Ariel. They both turn me on, and make me feel but with Briston its a different type of pleasure. He knows exactly how it feels to be pleasured by a guy, knows what turns me on.

Caz May

"Mmm...yeah...being with you feels too good," I admit, again tugging on his hair to bring his lips back to mine for a raw, illicit kiss.

We only break the kiss a moment, both stripping of our T-shirt's and throwing them aside before we'e frantically kissing again, grinding our pelvises together and making our dicks harder.

When I break the kiss, panting, and breathless he laughs at my eager words, "Get fucking naked, now stud. I need to fuck you." He sits up and yanks his trackies down, then his boxers, exposing his glorious dick to my gaze. He already has pre cum on the tip. And I dip my finger in, putting it to my lips and smearing it over them.

"Fuck, Brae," he curses out, kissing me again and licking his pre cum off my lips, moaning into the dirty pash.

As he keeps pashing me, his tongue licking my lips and battling with my mine , his hands are touching me everywhere and he yanks my trackies down, cursing a 'fuck' against my lips when his hands find my dick bare and ready for him. We break he kiss, shifting so we can discard the clothes completely.

He gives me another kiss, and asks against my lips, "You wanna top?"

"Don't care stud. I just need to fuck."

He lets out a loud groan, the tip of his dick teasing my tight hole when he leans over to capture my lips again.

Chapter Fifty-Six

Briston

Breaking another hot raw kiss with Braeden, I lean over to yank out some lube from the bedside drawer.

Flipping the tube open, I squeeze some out onto my fingertip, rubbing it over Braeden's arse. He groans, his tight

Caz May

hole pulsing and ready to take my dick. Leaning back over his naked body, I slowly jab my aching dick inside Braeden's tight hole. He takes me all the way in, clenching around me, as I start to pump in and out watching him whilst he watches me fisting his hardness steadily.

"God, fuck you feel good around my dick, Brae," I bellow, grabbing his dick with my hand, and stroking him whilst I hold his hand with my other hand. Sparks course through my body, blood rushing to my dick so it throbs inside him as I thrust harder.

"Bris, fuck me harder. Fuck, man, I'm going to fucking come," he groans loudly, pressing his hips up to push my dick inside him more. We're both groaning, moaning and panting, our bodies slick with sweat. Braeden lets out a throaty groan spilling his load all over his stomach, panting as I squeeze every last drop of his cum out of his dick.

Rubbing it over his stomach with my fingers, I lick each finger as I lose myself, my dick pulsating inside him as I fill him with my load.

"Fuck Bris, you're so dirty man."

Pulling out, I lean down, and lick every inch of his cum covered skin, all the way up to his lips that I take in a heated kiss.

I collapse next to him after breaking the kiss, panting, and not able to stop smiling when Braeden turns to face me. His eyes search mine, and I can't stop staring at him, rendered speechless for a moment with the look in his eyes.

Tamed Hearts

"Bris man," he starts, taking my hand with his. "I fucking love you. I never thought I'd fall in love with a guy, and fall for two people as well. But you and Ar's own me, man."

I kiss him, a kiss that shows him he owns me too.

"I love you more than I ever thought I could love someone else," I confess, kissing him again, harder, but with a teasing sweetness, a kiss that we've never shared before. "I thought I loved you before we were together, but being with you and Ariel has made me feel whole," I tell him, loving that he's the one to kiss me this time.

I'll never get enough of his raw, passionate kisses. The way he bites my lips, softly yanking on my lip ring, and swirling his tongue into it and over my lips drives me wild. His kisses are raw, bruising and passionate.

He breaks the kiss, licking his lips and staring right into my eyes causing my heart to pound.

"You set me on fire, Bris," he declares zealously, a rasp in his voice. "I love that you know how to make me feel incredible with just a touch."

"Mmm...back at you, Brae," I murmur, licking my lips. "You set me on fire with just a look. No one gets me as hard as you," I tell him, nodding towards my again hard dick.

"I can see that," he teases, grabbing my dick in a tight grip. "You're insatiable."

"So are you," I jeer, kissing him again, as we dive under the covers pashing. He continues rubbing my dick, stroking it and his at the same time. We don't come up for air, until we're both on edge, on the precipice.

"Fuck!" I call out, coming again from our dicks rubbing against each others. He follows suit, covering his hand in

Caz May

come. I yank it up to my lips, and lick it clean, giving him another kiss, and whispering, "I love you Braeden."

"I love you too Briston."

We cuddle close, our skin touching everywhere it can. Randomly I blurt out a question, "Do you have a middle name?"

He nods.

"Yeah, it's Devon. Like d'von."

"Nice. I love it...Braeden Devon Chappell."

"Yeah, you got one?"

"Yeah, Elijah. People used to call me Ben because of my initials."

He laughs, smirking at me.

"I'd rather call you Bris, or stud," he teases me, giving me a kiss still with a smirk.

"I don't care what you call me, as long as you're mine."

"Yours, stud," he teases, palming my arse cheek.

"I'm yours too, sexy," I taunt back, taking his hand and squeezing it. "I love you, so damn much. Can't wait to have you in my bed forever."

"I love you too, and Ariel as well. I need you both like air."

I don't say anything else, just pull him closer with a hand in his luscious hair as I kiss him until we're breathless.

I hope he's my forever, because he's tamed my wild heart.

Chapter Fifty-Seven

BRAEDEN

Pulling up in the caravan park in Briston's jeep, my heart is thumping in my chest.

He hasn't been privy to this part of my life, and despite him telling me how much he loves me last night, I'm nervous to let him in on the hell of my life before Carson's death.

Caz May

I get out of the car before I can hear him say anything. He follows behind me, straight into the van that doesn't have much in worldly possessions left inside. I don't really even want to bring much to move into his place anyway. So much of the stuff in the van reminds me of Carson, and I want to leave all that behind.

Briston is standing at the door, glancing around and it's making me feel exposed, my whole shitty life laid out before his eyes.

"Fuck Brae, man, I'm shocked you were living here. You should've told me, man."

I shake my head, bending down to pull out the gym bag, and small suitcase tucked under my bunk bed.

Standing, holding them I say, "I didn't want you and Ar's involved in my shit. She saw enough as it was, and it broke my heart."

"Yeah, I get that Brae but we love you. All of you, no matter your home life or past."

"I know," I reply softly, opening the flimsy wardrobe on the wall of the van, and shoving the little clothes I've got left inside the gym bag. Briston doesn't stop watching my actions, his blue eyes almost stormy with his emotions. "And now Carson is gone I can move on."

"Yeah, you deserve that Brae," he tells me, taking the full gym bag from my grip and slinging it over his shoulder.

I unzip the suitcase, to check that my teddy bear, my music books, and school stuff is still in there. Thankfully it all is and I sigh, zipping it back up as I nod to Briston to head out. I snatch my pillow from the bed—with the dirty metal music lover pillowcase on it—and turn to Briston.

Tamed Hearts

"This all you're bringing?" he asks, concerned.

"Yeah, I don't need anything else. I want to leave all this behind, it's hard to truly let go but I'm happier knowing the truth."

"For sure," he says, heading out of the van.

Closing the door behind me, I swallow hard, taking in a deep breath as I descend the steps of the van for the last time. If it wasn't going to land me—most likely—back in jail, I'd set the fucking thing alight and watch it go down in flames. It would be therapeutic to watch, but I can't do it.

Briston's gaze turns to Carson's car parked in front of his.

"You got keys for that?" he questions me.

"Yeah, you think I should drive it? The cops cleared everything out."

"It's yours now, I guess. Drive it. It's a classic."

Again I swallow a gulp, wary about getting behind the wheel of a car, and my dead brothers car at that. But having my own car would give me some freedom that I've never had before, and that's exciting.

FOLLOWING BRISTON back to his house—driving Carson's car—I feel edgy, but exhilarated.

It's definitely strange to be behind the wheel of a car, for the first time since getting my license years ago.

Technically I can't drive on my own, but the police in Lockgrove Bay never care about that, as most kids around town drive well before they're supposed to. Small town pros.

Caz May

Pulling up on the street outside Briston's house I get out of the car, locking it with the key, and following him inside whilst dragging my suitcase behind me. He has my gym bag slung over his shoulder.

With a nod, he leads me down the hallway and I'm about to take my gym bag from him, to put my stuff in the spare room when Briston laughs, and jeers at me, "not a fucking chance. You're sleeping in my fucking room, forever."

We continue down the hall, past the bathroom to Briston's room. We're barely in the door of his room-- having dropped the bag and suitcase on the floor--before we're kissing.

I honestly can't get enough of him, he's so damn insatiable. And I'm already giddy thinking about nights spent in his arms naked.

His mum comes past then, laughing at the door to Bris' room.

"Ahem," she clears her throat, causing Briston and I to jump apart in shock. "Settling in I see," she jokes with an exuberant smile that has me a little wary. Sometimes I'm not sure how to read expressions, or people's emotions.

"Yeah sorry, Mrs Nicholls," I reply, warily. "I can sleep in the other room if you're not ok with us rooming together."

She laughs, giving me a warm smile.

"Don't be silly, dear. I trust my baby boy. And he loves you, so I'm not going to keep you apart."

I return the smile, glancing at Briston who is practically scoffing at his mum's words.

Tamed Hearts

"Thank you. I love him too," I tell Mrs Nicholls, snaking an arm around Briston's waist and pulling him closer.

"I know dear. It's good to see you happy together," she says as she turns to leave, closing the door behind her.

Briston groans, "Thank fuck for some alone time."

"You left the door open, dufus," I taunt him.

"Can you blame me for wanting to get my hands and lips on you, sexy?"

"No, stud, I feel the same about you. Can't wait to sleep naked in your arms every damn night."

"Starting right now," Briston teases, kissing me.

We stumble together—backwards towards the bed—and hitting the edge with our knees we fall to the bed kissing.

I could certainly get used to this bliss.

Caz May

Chapter Fifty-Eight

Ariel

*I*t's a warm night, perfect for stargazing which I haven't done—in months—since that night Braeden nearly kissed me for the first time. He's sitting next to me on the picnic blanket, his arm around my waist as I gaze into the telescope.

Kissing my temple, he murmurs softly into the darkness, "You're more beautiful than the stars, darling."

Tamed Hearts

I turn my gaze to him, feeling my cheeks heat with an intense blush. The words also make my insides flutter, butterflies in my stomach and knickers.

Playful I slap his bare, tattooed arm.

"Stop, Brae. You're making me blush."

"It's true darling," he tells me with a smirk that lights his eyes up with desire. He leans forward, kissing me intensely, taking my breath away.

Panting I break the kiss, softly whispering, "I love you, Braeden. Thanks for coming here with me tonight."

"I love you too, Ariel. I'm here for you anytime you need me."

"I know, and thanks for listening to me about dad being an arsehole."

"As I said, anytime. Have you thought about what you're going to do next year, more?"

"I know I want to do Arts, but he's still not having a bar of it. I'm sick of fighting with him about it."

"Yeah, that's fair enough. It'll all work out, I'm sure."

"I hope so. Right now I just want to forget about it."

"Yeah, and stargaze? Or something else?" he questions me with a wink.

I bite down on my lip, nervously gazing down at his crotch in his shorts.

"Here? Now? In the park?"

Moving closer, so our foreheads are touching he whispers, "Yes, darling. I want to fuck you, right here, right now under the stars."

Caz May

My heart stops, and then races. Just the thought of that is thrilling, so dirty, but also has me worriedly asking, "What if someone sees?"

Braeden laughs at my question, tucking my hair behind my ear, and kissing my neck.

"It's dark, except for the blanket of stars, and look around darling, we're the only ones here." I do glance around the park, and he's right. There is no one—not another soul—but for us in the park at ten pm on a Tuesday night.

Still, I'm not comfortable with getting naked in public. Not saying a word however I climb into Braeden's lap, and with a hand around his neck, I pull him closer to kiss him.

I can feel his hardness pressing against my vag, and breaking the kiss he teasingly asks, "Darling, are you wearing any damn knickers under that short as shit skirt?"

"Just a g-string," I reply smiling.

"You're a dirty girl, darling. I love it."

Grabbing my waist, he lifts me off his lap for a moment, requesting, "Pull my boardies down, darling. My cock is aching to fuck you."

He's never used the word 'cock' before, usually dick, and I like it. It sounds dirtier. Dirty like the sex we're about to have.

Reaching down—when he lifts his butt up a little—I pull his boardies over his butt, yanking them down to his knees, and his cock springs forward, slapping against my clit as he centres me back onto his lap.

Thanks to the barely there fabric of my g-string, with just a wiggle of my hips his cock slips inside me, and I moan loudly.

"Mmm, Ariel, darling, your pussy is so tight." I inwardly cringe at him saying the word pussy, but clearly my body didn't hate how he said that, as my 'pussy' is thrumming, pulsing with pleasure as I start to bounce my butt on his cock.

Cupping his jaw in my hands, I lock eyes with him, stilling my bouncing hips for a moment when I taunt, "I love your cock filling my pussy, Brae."

"God, fuck, Ariel," he growls, taking my lips hungrily in a burning hot kiss that makes his cock throb inside me as I fuck him harder and faster whilst our mouths devour each other with the same animalistic need.

This is hot, dirty, naughty sex, but it's more than that. Even with this kinda sex can feel the love between us, partly because my heart is galloping in my chest.

Tearing his mouth from mine, Braeden cries out, "Fuck, darling. I'm gonna come inside your pussy."

I'm riding his cock so fast and hard, I'm panting, and sweating to the point of being breathless.

"You gonna come for me, little bitch?" he taunts me, using his old nickname for me.

"Yes, Brae, yes," I pant, baring down on his throbbing cock inside me, as I fall over the edge with a shaking orgasm.

I'm still trembling, riding out the aftershocks when I feel his release explode inside me, and he moans, his mouth

Caz May

forming an 'o' before he stills, biting down on his lip and falling backwards onto the picnic blanket.

His cock is still inside me—softening—and I lean over his chest, kissing him.

"That was amazing Braeden. I love you."

His fingers brush over my cheek, caressing it gently.

"You're amazing, Ariel. You're my whole damn world, darling. And I can't believe you love me, as much as I love you."

I'm about to reply, when his phone beeps from beside him on the blanket, with a text message lighting up his screen.

I slide off his lap, and he shifts to yank up his board shorts, before picking up his phone.

A smile forms on his face, and he laughs holding up his phone for me to see the message.

Where are you?

It's Briston. And Braeden gives me a wink, before he types a message out. He'd gotten a new phone recently, after the whole Carson debacle, and not having to stress so much about what he did with his money. And this new iPhone 8 meant he could now use emoji's which he now had an obsession with.

After typing the message, he holds the phone up to me again for me to see he's sent—

IN THE PARK WITH ARIEL.

I slap his arm.

"Brae, that's dirty."

"Well, we did just fuck in the park, darling. And Bris is a dirty boy too."

"Yeah, true. And you love him."

He laughs, pulling me down for a hard kiss. "So do you, little bitch. But you love me more?"

I don't reply to that, because I honestly don't know the answer to that question.

I've loved Briston for so long, it feels natural to love him, but loving Braeden is different. It's more intense, passionate, and all consuming and I'll never get enough of him. To reply to the question, I kiss him to show him that I love him with my whole heart.

He must know my struggle for words, as he whispers against my lips, "I get you, darling. I love you, blue sky."

I glare at him, raising an eyebrow at that quirky declaration.

"Huh?"

"I love you, Ariel Jane Findley all the way to the blue sky, and back down to the ground. And I know you love me, blue sky, as well."

"I do, Braeden Devon Chappell, I love you blue sky."

I kiss him again, short lived as his phone vibrates again with a text message.

It says—

I'm coming

And Braeden laughs, "And I love this fucker too."

"Me too, Brae. You and Briston are my B-boys, the two boys who have my whole heart."

He gives me a kiss, sitting up.

Caz May

We quickly pack up my telescope and the blanket, heading back to his car.

Shoving it all in the boot, I'm slamming it shut when Briston pulls up in his jeep with the music blaring.

The smirk on his face as he gets out is cocky, and possessive. And I love it.

Braeden just fucked me, but right now seeing my sexy best friend getting out of his soft top jeep—shirtless—has me soaking my g-string, ready to fuck him, and Braeden all over again.

My B-boys make me a dirty, naughty girl.

Chapter Fifty-Nine

Briston

Getting out of the Jeep—that I reversed into the carpark—Ariel's gaze over my body makes my dick jolt in my boardies. She and Braeden are leaning against the bonnet

Caz May

of his car, and his arm is around her, possessively pulling her close.

The pang of jealousy—of them clearly having a late night tryst in the park without me—hits me hard in the feels.

They've definitely gotten closer these past few months, and even though I know they both love me, I get the feeling their connection is deeper.

When I'm alone with Brae, his sole focus is on me, and I feel the deep consuming love he has for me, but when I see him with Ariel I see that love in his eyes when he looks at her, and see it in the sweet little things he does; like kissing her temple and smiling at her, or taking her hand with his. He's doing that now—lacing his fingers with hers—as he greets me with a kiss.

"Missed us, huh, stud?" He questions teasingly.

"Nah, just missed your dick. And I couldn't resist the allure of some late night public indecency."

Ariel giggles, stepping away from Braeden's side and closer to me. She cups my aching dick in her hand.

"What did you have in mind, baby?"

Damn, I like this side of my girlfriend.

Looking her dead in the eyes with a smirk I inform her of my intentions with a teasing tone, "Fucking yours and Braeden's brains out in the back of my Jeep."

With desire flashing in her eyes, she taunts back, "You want me to ride your cock, Briston?"

Fuck, she said cock, with her voice all raspy and sexy.

Stumbling towards the tailgate of the Jeep, I stammer, "Oh fuck yes, baby." That makes her giggle, and the

Tamed Hearts

moment I open the tailgate, swinging it to the side, I shove my boardies to the ground and sit on the edge of the Jeep, my back against the seats.

Ariel stands between my open legs, and shimmies her skirt down, over her hips, before sitting in my lap and claiming my mouth in a kiss, starting to rock her hips over mine.

I hear Braeden grunt as he steps up behind Ariel, and I moan from the loss of her lips on mine as she turns her head back to kiss him.

Watching him get lost in kissing her makes my dick throb, and I stab inside Ariel's pussy, stilling my thrust once I'm fully inside her. She tears her mouth from Braeden's and we both watch as he plunges his boardies to the ground as well. I start to thrust in and out of Ariel's pussy, moaning and panting as my pace increases. Her gaze shifts between both Brae and me and her pupils dilate as her pleasure increases.

Braeden kisses her forehead.

"Darling, do you trust me?"

"You know I do, Brae."

She groans, a slight whimper escaping her lips before she bites down on them when Braeden asks huskily, "Can I take your arse, darling? I want to claim that hole as mine."

"I'm not ready for that, Brae," she stammers, her cheeks colouring, fear making her whimper.

He kisses her then, taking her fear away, and I feel Braeden's dick stretch my arse wide as he pushes inside me instead.

Caz May

"Oh fuck, Braeden!" I call out so loudly Ariel clamps her hand over my mouth.

"Shh, Bris. Someone might hear you."

Laughing I lick her palm before I pull it away from my mouth to reply, "I don't give a fuck, baby. I don't give a shit about anything when you're riding my dick, and Brae is fucking my arse. Feels too fucking good to care."

Leaning down she kisses me, hard and deep, lashing her tongue with mine as she bounces up and down on my dick, moaning her pleasure into the kiss.

Braeden grabs her hair, yanking her back for a kiss whilst she still impales me with her pussy, and he still slams into my arse. It's undeniable, animalistic pleasure, and I can't take it a second longer, screaming out, "I'm coming!", as I suddenly lose my load inside Ariel's pussy, throbbing as she clenches around my dick, letting go herself.

Mere moments later, I feel Braeden's hot come fill my arse, and drip down my balls as he pulls out and Ariel climbs off my lap.

We don't say anything to each other, just glare at each other as we tug our clothes back on.

I take Braeden's hand and pull him against me.

"Thanks for the ripper fuck, sexy. I love you."

"I love fucking your hot arse, stud. Love you, so hard, Briston."

He kisses me again, stealing my breath away, and making my heart race.

"I'll see you at home after I drop Ariel home."

"Sounds good," I reply turning to Ariel and kissing her sweetly, more gently than I kissed Braeden.

Tamed Hearts

"Thanks for riding my dick, baby. I love you, Ar's, baby," I tell her, adding with a smirk before she can reply, "and I love coming in you."

She playfully slaps my arm. "I love you too, Bris, baby, and you can come inside me anytime."

I give her another quick, sweet kiss before shutting the tailgate of the Jeep, watching her and Braeden get in his car. He honks the horn as they drive away.

I'm about to get in the Jeep when a highway patrol cop car drives into the carpark. It stops beside the Jeep, scaring the shit out of me when the window rolls down.

"Briston? Is that you, son?" The familiar cop asks.

"Yeah, constable Kent."

"What're you doing out here alone at this hour?"

"Just chilling and enjoying the view tonight," I tell him, hiding the snigger because my view was certainly not the stars.

"Your parents know?"

"Yeah, I'm heading home now, scouts honour."

He laughs, chuckles deeply.

"You never were a scout, Briston. Get on home now."

"On it constable Kent," I say cheekily, opening the door of the Jeep and getting in, starting the engine as he pulls away.

Sighing, combing my hands through my unruly, knotty hair I nearly hit my head on the steering wheel.

That was a close call.

A dirty tryst that could've landed us in jail, but damn it was perfect—a fuck from heaven—and the even better

Caz May

thing is I'm going home to have Braeden in my bed, in my arms—all night—and hopefully for longer.

I'm brutally, crazily and obsessively in love with Braeden Devon—mine—Chappell. So much so, I don't even mind sharing him with my best friend.

Chapter Sixty

Ariel

*T*hings had been such a whirlwind the last couple of months, finishing up with school, and hanging out with my B-boys and our friends.

Dad had let me be, and seemed to finally be on the side of being ok with my loving two boys, but he was still at me about finishing up school with good enough grades to follow in his footsteps. There's no way I'm going to be a

Caz May

doctor. And if I tell dad I want to pursue something art related at uni, he's sure to hit the roof, so I'm just biding my time, appeasing him by telling him I'll think about adding medicine to my uni preferences when I honestly won't be doing anything of the thought.

Being the English exam today I'm nervous. I love english but it's never been my strongest subject, and it's practically a prerequisite for any uni course and I want to do the best I can.

Standing outside the hall, waiting to go in Braeden has his arms wrapped around my waist, holding me close enough to feel the rapid beating of his heart.

Looking up at him, I ask, "You nervous?"

"Yeah, you know I am."

"You'll be fine. Ms Donato gave you the coloured glasses to help yeah?"

"Yeah," he says with a smile, reaching into his slacks pocket for the glasses our english teacher gave him to help with his dyslexia. He puts them on, smiling wider at me.

"Mmm, you look like a sexy nerd," I tease, standing up on my tip toes to adjust the glasses on his face.

He kisses me, full on and with tongue.

"Ahem," comes a voice that causes us to break the kiss and turn towards the noise to find Mr Daniels giving us a warning glare.

We laugh together, stepping apart but holding hands when the double doors are pushed open for us to go inside the exam room.

The small desks are set out a metre or so apart in rows. I let Braeden lead me up the front, looking around for

Briston, who slides into a seat at the very back. He slouches in the seat, clearly not caring much. He doesn't know what he wants to do at Uni either, and he'd probably surf his life away if his parents would let him.

Braeden drops my hand and slides into a seat a row from the front. I sit behind him, nervously touching the exam paper on the desk, reading the words on it, 'DO NOT turn over until commencement.'

It seems so foreboding, as though something horrible will happen if you disobey. Maybe a paper cut from hell—which honestly I'd welcome right now—because cutting would quell the nervousness I'm feeling.

Braeden turns around, giving me a grin.

"Good luck, darling."

"Good luck, sexy nerd," I tease him before he turns back around, and Ms Donato clears her throat at the front of the room, explaining that we have three hours to complete the exam, excluding the fifteen minute pre reading time. She announces that we may turn our papers over to begin.

I flip over the exam paper, carefully reading it and barely getting even halfway through reading the multiple choice questions before the reading time is done.

It doesn't matter though, as three hours is plenty of time to get it done. It is tricky though, as I'm finding it hard to concentrate, thinking about the plans I've arranged with my B-boys to go to the beach tomorrow to celebrate the end of exams. But it's also those thoughts that get me through the most boring, tedious three hours ever, whilst staring at the back of Braeden's head, and wondering what all his tattoos mean to him.

Caz May

I also decide in that moment that I'm going to get a rose tattoo on my wrist and forearm to cover the worse of my cutting scars.

It's time to change my life, to grow up and become the best version of myself with my B-boys by my side, curse what dad thinks.

Chapter Sixty-One

BRAEDEN

The sun is shining—high in the sky—for our day at the beach together.

It's so crazy that our life at high school is coming to an end, exams over and only graduation to go.

The beach is busy, lots of people around but my focus is only on my two favourite people.

Caz May

Near the cliffs, we drop our belongings, Briston and I admiring Ariel—our girl—as she strips down to her blue bikini. The cups of the top push her perfect tits together to show a hint of sexy cleavage, and the bottoms sit below her belly button, accentuating the curve of her hips. She holds her arms over her belly, clearly a bit self conscious.

I kiss her, grabbing her hands, and pulling them away from her body.

"Darling, don't hide your sexy body from me and Bris."

"Other people will see my scars. I've never worn a bikini in public before."

"Ar's, you look so stunning, no one will look at your scars baby."

"And if they do, we'll curse them out darling. You're so damn beautiful."

"Definitely, baby," Briston tells her when she gives him a shy, sweet smile.

She's more confident in her own skin now, our reassurance with our lustful gazes on her showing her that we mean our word.

"You ready to ride a wave?" Bris asks me, picking up a surfboard from the sand beside us.

"As ready as I'll ever be," I admit, getting a confidence boost from Ariel smiling at me.

"It's easy, Brae," she tells me, as we follow Briston to the waters edge. She sits on the sand and Briston and me head into the waves.

"So get on the board, sit on it and paddle out," Briston tells me.

Tamed Hearts

I wait a moment to watch Briston mounting his board and beginning to paddle out further into the waves, before I follow suit.

Awkwardly I mount the board, and paddle out myself, feeling nervous but energised.

Facing the shore, we're sitting on the boards that are bobbing in the surf as small waves roll in.

"So, when a decent wave is coming in, you need to lie forward, and start paddling before you slowly stand up, and ride the wave," Briston informs me, with hand gestures and modelling. "You can ride into shore or into another wave."

"I think I'll try and go into shore to keep our girl company," I say when Briston shifts on his board, eagerly.

"Get ready, this wave is ripper," Briston informs me.

Following his actions, I lay down on the board, paddling like mad, and shakily getting to my feet on the board. It's thrilling standing up and feeling the water pulsating under the board as I ride the wave into the shore, my arms out by my sides to keep my balance.

Reaching the sand, I jump off the board, stumbling and falling onto my butt next to Ariel who can't stop laughing.

"Have fun?" she asks through her laughter.

"Yeah, that was amazing," I tell her, scooting closer to her on the sand.

She nods towards the water, where Briston is surfing the waves like a professional. He catches a last wave, riding it into shore with us watching him.

At the shoreline he's a little more graceful in his exit out of the water, jumping off his board and picking it up as he stalks towards us.

Caz May

"He's so damn sexy," Ariel murmurs next to me, causing my gaze to shift to her.

"Yeah and so are you, darling," I tell her, giving her a kiss when Briston flicks water all over us to break us apart.

Stopping on the sand in front of us—looming over—he gives me a wink.

"We should take our girl to the spot," he suggests with a smirk.

Standing up, I help Ariel up too, with an outstretched hand, before cheekily brushing the sand off her pert arse. She giggles, slapping my hand away and Briston kisses her, dropping his surfboard on the sand.

Picking her up, he throws her over his shoulder with a grunt, and with me following we go to the alcove together. Ariel is shrieking the whole way across the sand, excitedly.

Once we're at the cliffy alcove, Briston puts her down, pushing her body against the rocks and kissing her hard.

We all strip naked, us boys watching Ariel take off her bikini.

"Damn, darling," I tease, eyeing her and then turning my attention to Briston for a moment. He's just as mesmerised by seeing our girl naked.

Briston kisses me then, his hands all over me as we devour each others mouths in a raw kiss that makes Ariel moan lustfully.

Breaking the kiss with Briston he steps aside as I kiss Ariel, pushing her chest against the rocks.

"Please, Brae," she begs, a whisper against my lips.

Gazing right into her eyes, her head still turned to mine I sink inside her pussy, gripping her wide fuckable hips to thrust harder as Briston steps up behind me. He slides his dick inside my arse, rocking his pelvis against my arse, as I rock into Ariel, pushing her against the cliff more.

"Fuck, fuck!" Briston calls out, his arms above his head as he thrusts harder.

Giving him a kiss my thoughts wander to about how much I love both of them.

Being with them both—in the heights of pleasure and in public—is euphoric.

And thrusting one last time, hearing Ariel scream out, "Oh fuck, Braeden, I'm coming!" I lose myself, my dick throbbing as I let go inside her pussy, at the same time Briston let's go, pumping his dick inside me and stilling for a moment as he fills my arse with his hot come.

He pulls out and I pull out of Ariel, turning to kiss him quickly, before I turn to Ariel and kiss her.

After Briston tugs his board shorts back on, as I tug mine on and we help Ariel back into her bikini, before each taking a hand of hers in ours to head back to where we left our stuff on the beach.

We don't exchange words, but no words need to be said.

Caz May

Chapter Sixty-Two

Ariel

The boys are sitting on my bed, already wearing slacks and crisp white shirts.

They share a kiss, before glancing back at me prancing around my room in my underwear whilst I try to locate my leopard print heels.

"Ar's baby, you're so on edge," Briston informs me with a cocky grin.

"I can't find my shoes," I tell him, dropping to my knees on the floor near the bed to check underneath.

I push Braeden's legs aside, and lift up the valance to peer under the bed and low and behold my shoes are there. Hooking them by the stiletto style heel, I pull them out with a triumphant, "Yes!"

The boys laugh, that deep sexy chuckle type laugh. And Braeden grips my hair, pulling me up and setting me in his lap.

"Loved seeing you on your knees, darling," he teases, giving me a sudden bruising kiss against my lips that sends a jolt of pleasure into my knickers.

After the kiss, I'm about to slide off his lap when he grabs me around the waist.

"Not so fast darling," he taunts, gazing across at Briston who has a wicked smirk on his face.

"We've got a grad present for you," Briston says teasingly, reaching into his pocket and pulling out a small purple device that looks like a tampon, with a loop on the end.

I gasp, my eyes darting between my B-boys who both have the sexy, wicked smirks.

"Is that what I think it is?" I question them, my heart racing.

I knew my B-boys were dirty, naughty boys from all of our last sexy times together. And Briston especially, buying me the butt plug for my birthday. But this is something else, and I'm nervous, but excited.

"Yeah, darling, it's a remote controlled vibrator," Braeden says, calmly. "And you're going to put it inside your pretty pussy, and let Bris and I tease you with it all night at Grad."

My cheeks colour, thinking about climaxing in public.

"But won't that make me come?" I ask.

They both laugh again.

"We fucking hope so Ar's,"Briston teases, holding it up to my lips.

"Lick it darling, get it nice and wet, and slide it inside your pussy for us," Braeden says suggestively.

I take the vibrator into my mouth, licking it as Briston rolls it around between my lips. And then he hands it to me —by the loop—as I get to my feet.

Braeden yanks my lacy white knickers to my knees, and brushes a finger over my already sensitive clit.

"Damn, you're already wet as fuck, darling," he teases suggestively licking his lips, and making me blush as I push the device inside me.

I tug my knickers back up, and Braeden stands, pulling me against his hard body, kissing me fiercely, and calming me, keeping me on my feet when my thighs shake with Briston pressing the remote to start torturing me slow, dirty and sweet.

Breaking free from Braeden I launch at Briston, still shaking a little from the pulses hitting my g-spot.

"Stop, Bris, stop!" I scream at him, my voice shaky, because it feels good and I don't honestly want him to stop.

He stands then, winking as he hands the remote to Braeden and he slips it into his pocket.

Tamed Hearts

"We're only just getting started, baby," Briston taunts, eyeing me and then Braeden who has his long fingers teetering on the side of his pocket containing the remote.

A pulse hits me, and I'm so close to the edge—already—that I want to scream out, and let go but I don't.

It feels so good, so dirty, and I actually kinda love it, giddy to see how the night plays out with these two dirty boys in control.

Braeden presses the button again, taunting me, "Go get dressed in that sexy maroon, wrap around dress, darling."

He winks at me, and I give him an up yours, with a smirk as I slip my feet into the heels beside my bed.

Deliberately I sway my hips from side to side as I saunter across the room to my wardrobe to put on my dress.

If my B-boys are going to torture me—even sweetly—I'll do the same back.

They'll be so damn horny by the end of the night, I'll have my B-boys by the balls.

When did I get so damn dirty?

And yes, I love it.

Ariel Jane Findley—me—is a dirty girl for my B-boys.

Caz May

Chapter Sixty-Three

BRAEDEN

Sliding into the car—with Briston on one side of me in the backseat—and Ariel in the middle I lean over to give her a kiss, my hand in my pocket.

Ariel's dad is driving us—he's locking the front door, not in the car yet—and we're meeting Briston's parents there.

It gives me a moment to begin the sweet torture of our girl.

Tamed Hearts

Whispering in her ear, "You ready, darling?" I groan, and press the top button for speed one.

Ariel bites down on her lip, clenching her thighs together. Briston's hand is on them, prying them apart a little, his long fingers slipping between them and closer to her pussy.

"Feel good, baby?" Briston asks her, a raspy tone to his voice as he kisses her.

"Yes, shit," Ariel murmurs, her legs falling open and inviting Briston's fingers to explore. They slide under the hem of her dress, and he groans when he reaches her pussy, no doubt already soaked pussy.

"Is she wet stud?" I ask him, locking eyes with him, and smirking.

"Wet as fuck, sexy," he jeers, licking his lips, and reaching over and grabbing me by the neck to crush our lips together for a kiss.

Whilst kissing Briston, I press the other button to increase the speed of the vibrator, making Ariel groan, and nearly curse out loud when the driver door opens and slams shut.

Briston and I pull apart suddenly when Mr Findley glares at us, clearing his throat.

"Guess I'm the chauffeur for the night," he says oddly, his stare icy, and angry. He doesn't know the half of it, most likely thinking that his little girl is still innocent.

Her standing up to him about us all being together was hot, but I don't think he has any idea of how naughty we are when we're together.

Caz May

Being with my girl, and my guy is the hottest, dirtiest sex I've ever had in my life. And I'm thinking tonight might take it up a notch.

Teasing Ariel all night is sure to have her on edge and ready for the next step in our sexual journey together. My dick is already throbbing in my slacks just thinking about the possibility of filling her, and sending her to the heights of pleasure.

Ariel bites down on her lip, before replying to her dad's statement, "Just drive, dad, please or we'll be late." Her tone is husky, and annoyed. It's damn sexy.

FOR THE DRIVE TO SCHOOL for the ceremony, I don't dare press the button for the vibrator. I'm sure Ariel would kill me if I submitted her to coming in her knickers with her dad right in front of us in the drivers seat. But all thoughts of that are gone when we get to school, and the car is parked.

Briston gets out first, and before Ariel can even undo the seatbelt I press the third button—the highest speed.

She bites down on her lip, mouthing *'fuck'* as she clenches her thighs together before she trembles, her thighs shaking as she comes on the backseat of her dad's landrover.

Smirking at her, I tease, "You come darling?"

"Yes," she pants, aftershocks making her shake, as I tilt her face to mine abruptly.

Crashing my lips to hers, I kiss her hard, and whisper against them as I pull back, "You're going to come so much tonight, darling, you won't be able to walk tomorrow."

She murmurs a soft 'mmm', unlatching her seatbelt, and smirking at me as she slides out of the car into Briston's arms.

Tucking the vibrator in my pocket, I press the number one button again as we head across the carpark towards the gym for the graduation ceremony. Ariel stumbles on her high heels, glaring at me with a warning glare that turns me on.

Briston snakes his arm around her side, dropping her hand he's holding.

"Careful, baby."

She looks at him, and then at her dad.

"You alright, honey?" he asks her, not taking his eyes of his daughter even though I'm sure he wants to stare me down until I'm six feet under.

Briston could probably fuck her in front of him, and he wouldn't bat an eyelid, but I can barely look her way without getting death stares. I'm exaggerating, I know. But he doesn't have it in for Briston like he does for me.

"Yeah, dad," Ariel replies, standing tall. "I'm just not used to walking in heels."

"Ok, honey," I'll see you after the ceremony," he says, kissing her forehead, as he shuffles into some seats where Briston, Ava, and Dakota's—mine now, kinda—parents are sitting. They all wave at us, as we head to towards the student seating at the front.

We stop at the end of the row of seats, and I grab Briston by the waist, yanking him against me for a kiss.

Whilst kissing him, I grab the remote out of my pocket and slip it into his hand.

Caz May

"Press it, hard and long when our girl is up on stage getting her diploma, stud," I whisper, suggestively in his ear.

"Fuck yeah," he says back, slapping me on the arse playfully as he takes a seat.

I take Ariel's hand to head to the other end, hating that we have to sit in alphabetical order by surname and our names are at different ends of the damn alphabet. I'm closer to her, with a 'C' surname and hers an 'F' but Briston is at the other end of the damn earth, and I'm already missing him.

That kiss wasn't the hottest we've shared but it had me on edge, so much that as I take a seat next to Aidan Chatman I have to adjust my dick in my slacks.

I glare down the row of seats, watching Ariel as she takes a seat. Her eyes find mine, and I blow her a kiss, mouthing, 'I love you, darling', to her. Aidan sees my gesture, and chuckles.

"Who you confessing your love to, bro?"

Slouching in the seat, my legs wide to hide my hard on, I reply confidently, "My girl, Ariel."

I don't give a shit if anyone knows she's my girl anymore —or if Briston is mine either. I'm owning my damn sexuality like a boss.

"Shit, bro. When did that happen?"

"Months ago, bro. Been in love with her for years, though," I confess, smiling wide thinking back to the first time I saw her walking into the art room, in a short skirt and tank top with a cat on it, her chocolate hair atop her head in a bun, like a croissant. I lick my lips at the memory.

Tamed Hearts

"Nice man. She's a quiet one, but the quiet ones are always the naughtiest, right?"

"You have no idea man. No idea."

He chuckles again. And then blushes with his next question, "You're also with Briston, yeah?"

I gulp, wondering if I should confess this time—but Aidan looks nervous, shifting in his seat—and I put a hand on his thigh to get him to look at me.

"Yeah, I am. Love that fucker too. Why you asking?"

"I...um...I..." he stammers, biting down on his lip.

"You got a crush on Briston?"

"Yeah," Aidan says with a laugh. "Been in love with him for years, but I was always too chicken to come out, and do something about it."

"Sorry, bro. That really sucks, but if being with him and Ariel this past year or so has shown me anything it's that you gotta own up to your feelings, and own your sexuality. It's freeing man."

He gives me a smile, and I add, "And a dirty, naughty ride. Best sex of my life."

"Thanks, Braeden. I won't steal Briston from you. And I wouldn't know, I'm a virgin."

"You'll find your sexy as sin dick, bro. Uni awaits! And I'm sure it's going to be a dickfest living in the dorms."

"I hope so," he replies, chuckling and smiling.

OUR CONVO ENDS there when Principal Reading steps up onto the stage.

Caz May

I honestly don't hear a word the fucker says, except for when he says, "Ava Darby Castello" and she saunters up onto the stage with a sexy shake of her hips.

No doubt Zeke is in the crowd watching his girl graduate.

I'm antsy about getting up on the stage, as there's only two others with 'C' names before me.

With the time flying by too quickly it's my turn, principal Reading announcing, "Braeden Devon Chappell."

I get up from my seat, strutting up onto the stage and getting my diploma from Ms Miller, shaking her hand.

Under her breath she says softly, "Well done, Braeden. I'm so proud of you."

"Thanks, Miss M," I reply, giving her a kiss on the cheek before I walk off the stage. As I descend the steps to head back to my seat, principal Reading calls out, "Aidan John Chatman."

As I sit back down Aidan reaches the stage, taking his diploma and facing the audience, making an announcement of his own, "I'm gay!"

Applause erupts for him and he descends the stairs, coming back to his seat with a huge grin on his face. I pat him on the back.

"Well done, man. That took guts."

"Thanks, felt good."

"I bet," I reply with a nod, glancing down the row of seats to count how many more classmates there are before my girl goes up.

There's five, and my heart is racing in anticipation.

Tamed Hearts

Time stands still, and then I hear the loud booming of her name being said, "Ariel Jane Findley."

She stumbles to her feet, walking up onto the stage like she has a stick up her arse—her thighs tightly clenched—or actually a vibrator in her pussy.

I snigger, hiding my laugh behind my hand when she takes the diploma from Miss Miller, and bends down a little as though she is losing her footing and is going to fall to the floor in a trembling heap.

Briston is really bringing it.

Ariel shifts uncomfortably on her heels, biting down on her lip as she nods at Miss Miller, and then stumbles off the stage, her legs obviously like jelly as she shakes a little.

Strutting past me, she mouths, "I'm going to kill you later."

I point at myself, mouthing back, "Me darling, why?"

"You know why," she says, stopping in front of me with her crotch in my face. I inhale the smell of her pussy, that's evident even with the gown covering her body.

"Not me, darling, Bris is in control right now."

She grunts at me, heading back to her seat.

The rest of the ceremony is a blur, the only other significant classmates being my sister, and Briston. It still feels weird calling Dakota my sister, but I wouldn't change the last months getting to know her for anything. She's the best kinda sibling, the one I always wanted who cares about me. I wish I'd gotten to know her sooner.

I wish I'd spent more time with all my friends, and my girl and guy, long before these last couple of years of high school.

Caz May

AFTER THE CEREMONY, as I'm heading over to our parents for the congratulations ,Ariel launches herself at me, almost jumping into my arms.

"How could you, Brae!" She screams at me.

"What darling? I told you it wasn't me."

"Doesn't matter, dickhead," she angrily grunts at me. "I fucking came in my knickers on the damn stage."

I smirk at her, laughing when Briston comes up beside us, his hand in his pocket, also with a smirk on his face.

"Did you now, baby?" He taunts, still smirking even when Ariel glares daggers at him.

"Yes, and it dripped down my thighs, fuckers!" She says still angry but with a sexy rasp to her voice which only means one thing. Briston had set off the trigger again.

"Oh, darling, that's so sexy," I taunt, kissing her hard to swallow the moans of her fourth shaking orgasm.

Breaking the kiss she shrieks, "I hate you both!"

"No, you don't baby," Briston says cockily, handing me the remote, and whispering to me, "that was so damn hot."

"Told you," I whisper back, licking my lips and adding a little louder so Ariel can hear, "dibs on licking her thighs and pussy first at the afterparty."

"Of course stud," Briston promises, kissing me, as our family and friends surround us.

We exchange hugs and congratulations, before Zeke and Ava rush off hand in hand, and Dakota leaves with Knox, not feeling up to going to Drake's afterparty.

Waving goodbye to our parents we toss our hats and gowns to Miss Miller as she comes around with a towel trolley to collect them.

Tamed Hearts

I take Briston's hand, and snake an arm around Ariel's waist pulling her closer as we follow our classmates to the carpark to hitch a ride to Drake's afterparty.

I have a feeling this party is going to be epic, his best one yet, and one of the best nights of our lives.

Chapter Sixty-Four

Ariel

*A*fter hitching a ride to Drake's with Logan—the boys teasing me with the vibrator—I'm so on edge I don't waste a minute at the party, before I'm dragging the boys upstairs. Braeden shoves me against the wall, his hand gripping my neck as he smashes a kiss to my lips.

"Fuck, darling," he groans, as Briston opens the door beside us and we stumble inside the bedroom.

Slamming the door behind us, I have a moment of panic hit me, but brush it off when I look at my boys who are stripping naked and staring at each other with lust.

Biting my lip I wait until their focus shifts to me, and Braeden rasps, "Darling, you're still dressed."

"Waiting for you to undress me," I tell him, smirking at him.

"Oh, really," he taunts, stepping closer to me, and gripping the tie of my wrap dress. Yanking on it, he tugs so it opens, and the front of my dress flops down. Briston steps towards us then, putting his hands on my shoulders to push the dress off my body. It falls to the floor, so I'm only in my lacy black underwear.

Both boys stare at me, their eyes full of lust roaming my body. Braeden leans in to kiss me, zealously, teasing me with his tongue, and then he whispers against my lips, "Are your knickers soaked, darling?"

I nod, speechless, gasping when his long fingers brush over my clit. He plunges my knickers to the floor, as Briston steps up behind me, unclasping my bra. My underwear finds the floor, and the boys sandwich me between them, Braeden kissing my lips, Briston brushing my hair aside to kiss my neck.

He whispers to me, raspy, "We want to fuck you at the same time, baby."

Breaking the kiss with Braeden, I gasp again, tipping my head back to kiss Briston.

"I...don't know if I'm ready for that," I admit, feeling a jolt of pleasure pulse through my core.

Caz May

Braeden yanks my face back to his, planting a soft, tender kiss against my lips.

"You're ready darling," he rasps, his finger pressing against my clit. "You've never been this wet for us. And you're going to come so hard, darling."

His husky words are making my pussy throb. Braeden yanks out the vibrator, throwing it on the floor and kissing me again. I can feel Briston's hardness pressing against my butt, and Braeden's against my clit. I want these boys more than my next breath.

"Ok, my B-boys, fuck me to the other side of heaven."

"Mmm, fuck, baby," Briston drawls behind me, taking a step back as Braeden pushes me down onto the bed.

He's smirking as he spreads my legs wide, kneeling between them as he starts to lick up my thighs, laving kisses over every inch of my skin, all the way to my pussy which he licks from the bottom up to my clit. Briston is watching, fisting his hard dick, and I grab it, yanking him closer so he's kneeling on the bed too, and I can take his dick into my mouth.

Braeden groans, glaring at me as he licks his lips, raspingly teasing me, "Fuck, darling, you taste delicious, and watching you with Briston's cock in your mouth is hot as fuck."

With my mouth full of Briston's velvety skin I can't reply, but no words are needed. This is all about feeling, and hell it's fucking amazing, especially when without warning Braeden spears inside my pussy, shoving my legs wider.

Moaning out in pleasure, I pull Briston's dick from my mouth, and he kisses me. My breathing is already laboured pants. And I know this is just the beginning.

Braeden pulls out, and touches my swollen pussy with his finger instead, rubbing my arousal down to my butt and teasing the tight hole with his thumb, coating it with my arousal to prep me.

Smirking, still teasing me with his finger, he grabs Briston by the neck, yanking him closer to kiss him passionately, their tongues battling each other. I could come just from watching my B-boys kissing like that.

Breaking the kiss, they both give me a wicked smirk, Braeden asking, "You ready, darling?"

"Yeah," I reply, raspy. "Watching you two kiss like that has made my pussy so wet, I'm dripping on the bed sheets."

"Mmm, baby," Briston murmurs, moving to behind me when Braeden pulls me down on the bed and lifts me up into his arms.

"Bris is going to fuck your pussy first darling," he tells me, his tone husky. "And I'm going to fuck your arse."

"Ok," I murmur, thinking about that first.

"Turn around, and get on Briston's dick, darling," Braeden instructs me. I give him a quick kiss, before following the direction, straddling Briston and sliding my wet pussy down onto his dick. Starting to ride him, he pulls me down for a kiss, whilst Braeden fingers my arse, pushing his thumb inside.

"You ready, darling?" he asks again. I arch back, kissing him.

"I'm ready Brae, take me."

Caz May

"Fuck, darling," he groans, pressing the tip of his dick against my unexplored hole.

He's straddling Briston's leg with one knee bent up and the other one on the bed, when he pushes inside my arse. And fuck! I have no words. The sensation is beyond incredible.

I kiss Briston again, fucking him whilst Braeden fucks me, our bodies bouncing and rocking together in bliss, our moans and panting breaths filling the room.

"Ahhh, fuck, darling!" Braeden calls out, pulling out and grabbing my waist, pulling me up for a kiss and off Briston's dick.

"Turn around again, darling. I want to fuck your pussy whilst Bris fucks your arse."

I follow the direction again, so turned on I'd practically do anything he asked. My pussy is throbbing and I know I'm going to come so hard.

In the reverse cowgirl position with his legs wide, Briston slides his dick into my arse, pumping in and out. Braeden stands on the bed a moment, and I take his dick into my mouth sucking it a moment before he kneels on the bed again, this time slipping his dick inside my pussy. My legs are in the air, and as he thrusts he gives me a kiss, a dirty teasing, dominating kiss.

"Feel good, darling?"

"So good, so fucking good," I rasp, moaning out a loud, "Fuck!"

"Ar's, fuck, baby. Fucking your arse is so...fuck!" Briston roars behind me, fisting my hair as he throbs inside, losing himself inside my arse.

Tamed Hearts

"Oh my god, fuck I'm coming," I call out, so close to the edge.

"Come for me darling," Braeden coerces, signalling my trembling as I start to let go. My pussy is throbbing with each of Braeden's hard thrusts, so much sensation with Briston's dick still inside my arse. With my whole lower body trembling, my thighs shaking I come, calling out, "Yes, fuck, my B-boys, I'm coming."

Braeden stills inside me a minute, giving me a kiss, and I say, "Brae, I want you to explode all over my pussy, and lick it off with Bris."

He rocks in and out one last time, pulling out and spurting ropes of come all over my pussy and stomach.

He grabs me by the waist again, lifting me into his arms for a kiss before I collapse next to Briston. They both kneel at my feet and lick the come from my pussy and stomach.

Sitting up after I laugh, jeering, "Well that was fun. I love you, my dirty, sexy B-boys."

"We love you too, Ar's," Briston replies, nodding to Braeden who is smirking.

"We do, and we should probably get to the other part of this party," Braeden says, standing from the bed, and starting to gather his and Briston's clothes from the floor. I do the same, about to pick up my underwear when Braeden shakes his head at me.

"You, my sexy girl are going to wear nothing under that wrap dress for the rest of the night."

I step up to him, with my dress in hand, taunting him, "And why would I do that?"

Caz May

"So Bris and I have easy access to your pussy, darling. You're still able to walk, so we haven't fucked you enough for the night."

I kiss him, stealing his breath away.

"I love you, Braeden."

"I love you too, darling," he replies, laughing when he adds, "Put that dress on now before I'm getting naked again."

I put my arms into the sleeves, and have only just tied the dress at the front when the door swings open, and two people stumble backwards into the room, kissing.

I gasp and glance around the room again. *Oh shit!*

I just fucked my boyfriends in my ex-boyfriend's room, in his bed.

"Oh shit, Drake," I stammer, elbowing Braeden and Briston in the side to stop them from laughing.

Drake breaks his kiss with the girl, and I realise it's Polly. He's clearly seeing her and wanted to have a sexy tryst with her in his room. If he'd been here moments before, things could've been bad. Or good? No, that's way beyond my limits.

"Ariel?" Drake questions, squinting as though he's trying to make sure I'm really standing in the middle of his bedroom with two guys by my side.

"What are you doing in my room?"

"Um, nothing," I stammer, feeling myself blush because I certainly wasn't doing nothing moments ago when I came with my B-boys dick's inside me, on Drake's bed.

"We were just leaving. Realised this was your room."

Tamed Hearts

Drake glares at me—a dagger eyes glare—that shows he's not believing my words at all.

"Well, get the fuck out of my room. I'm kinda busy," he seethes, yanking Polly against his side.

I don't say anything, as my B-boys and I exit Drake's room, Braeden's hand around my waist, and Briston's hand with mine.

The door slams behind me, and descending the stairs the panic hits me. I pull out of Braeden's arm around me, about to race back up the stairs when he stops me.

"What darling?" he questions.

"I left my knickers and the vibrator in Drake's room."

Braeden and Briston both laugh, smirking like devils.

"So, baby, he can sniff them and think about what he missed out on."

I smack Briston's abs.

"You're an arsehole, Bris."

He laughs again.

"Maybe, but you're the one who just got your arse hole fucked by two guys in your ex-boyfriend's bedroom. You're a dirty girl, baby."

"Our dirty girl, darling," Braeden says, kissing me, and adding against my lips with a whisper, "Let Drake have fun with his girl and your toy." He gives me another kiss that makes my pussy throb.

"We'll get you a new one, and one we can all play with."

"Fine, but I need to get drunk now. And you two fuckers can keep your hands to yourselves for the rest of the night."

"Aww, Ar's, baby, that's no fun."

Caz May

"Yeah, darling," Braeden adds, his hand on my thigh edging under the hem towards my pussy that is already throbbing and ready for his touch. "You've got nothing on under this dress, and I'm already thinking of fucking you again." He kisses me, taking my breath away. "Maybe right here, on the staircase."

I gasp, because that sounds so hot and dirty I consider it for a moment.

"As much as I'd love that, we can't. Behave, and get me on edge again by kissing each other."

I start to descend the staircase, the boys following with their gaze on my butt.

"That we can do," Braeden promises, playfully slapping my butt cheek when I turn around and taunt him by lifting the hem of my dress up.

They both groan.

I love my B-boys, and love teasing them until they're both on the edge. It's only fair.

Chapter Sixty-Five

Ariel

Four months later

*T*his moment is crazy, one of those you dream about your whole life, and it feels so surreal when it's actually happening.

After piling Briston's jeep up with our suitcases, and driving the three hours to Melbourne—whilst singing along to all manner of songs from our childhood at the top of our

Caz May

lungs—we're pulling up to the university dorms. Manor house is a huge dormitory for most of the inner city universities, co-ed but girls and boys levels.

Getting out the car, I stare up at the brick building that's covered in ivy. It's easily ten floors, and it's just window after window. I wonder which rooms will be ours. I'm a little upset I can't actually room with the boys, but honestly I can't believe we're all here together.

Hopefully Braeden will be in some of my classes, as we're both doing a Bachelor of Arts at Melbourne Uni, and Briston is surprisingly doing a Bachelor of Business. He still doesn't know what he wants to do, but thought that would give him some opportunities for good job prospects. Dad was beyond pissed that I'd chosen—as he put it—a simpleton's degree. He'd said I could do better, but there was no way I was going to do medicine and I want a degree so Arts it is.

The boys are out of the car now, and Braeden wraps his arms around my waist from behind, kissing the top of my head.

"Can't believe we're here," he says, as I turn around in his embrace.

"You did it, Brae. Believe it," I tell him, kissing his lips softly. "I love you."

"I love you, darling, and you're going to blow Melbourne uni away." He smiles at me, then turns to Briston who's yanking his suitcase out of the back of the jeep.

"You fuckers going to help me, or just going to stand there pashing all day?"

Tamed Hearts

Huffing I get my suitcase out, berating Briston, "I'm not the one who gets to live with my boyfriend Briston."

He hugs me.

"I know Ar's. I'm going to miss you too, but it's only for a year to get the whole experience."

"Yeah, I know," I reply, as we start to head into the building to find our rooms.

The boys drop me off at my dorm room, which is on level one. They stop a moment at the door of room 115 with me.

Braeden pulls me close, giving me a tight hug before he kisses me. I can feel the glaring gaze from my new roommate as I turn to also kiss Briston goodbye. He spins me in a tight hug, teasing me when he puts me down, "Be good, baby. Don't do anything we wouldn't."

"Haha, Bris," I jeer back, giving them both a final crushing hug before they head to the elevators.

I drag my suitcases into the room, launching them onto the bed with a grunt. My new roommate laughs, coming over to help me, after closing the door behind her.

She has a wide smile, greeting me, "Hi, I'm Chloe. Guess we're roomies."

I hold out a hand which she shakes softly, making me feel odd, but welcome.

"Hey, yeah, I'm Ariel."

"Nice," she says with a nod towards the door. "What's that about? The boys? Like is one your brother or something?" she fires the question at me eagerly, encroachingly almost staking a claim.

Caz May

I laugh, feeling my cheeks heat with a blush when I reply, "They're my B-boys. Neither are my brother, no."

Chloe gapes, then smiles when she enquires, "So like they're both your boyfriend?"

Again I laugh, feeling a little nervous to tell this stranger about my relationship status. But I like Chloe. She seems sweet, and welcoming. Plus I need to burst her bubble of the possibility of her getting to be with one of my boys, as her eye had definitely wandered Braeden as the boys left.

"Yeah, I guess you could say that," I admit, adding with a soft smile, "I love them both."

Chloe shrieks excitedly, practically jumping up and down on the spot.

"That's hot!" she screams out, adding a question with a wink, "Are they bi?"

"Yeah," I reply, my voice raising excitedly when I add, "watching them together is hot."

"I bet," Chloe laughs.

I laugh myself, unzipping my suitcase to start unpacking, knowing we'll get along great.

Chapter Sixty-Six

Briston

S tepping into the elevator, my heart is racing. Playfully I slap Braeden on the arse, telling him, "Get in, sexy. Our dorm room awaits."

The doors close behind us, but the elevator doesn't move as they're pried open by a guy calling out, "Hold up!"

Caz May

He drags a suitcase in behind him, and my eyes are assaulted with how fucking gorgeous he is. Like holy fuck me right here, right now delectable piece of ass. His gaze doesn't meet mine, even as my gaze takes in his outfit of a loose grey Nike t-shirt and white backwards cap that curls of chocolate hair are peeking out of.

The door shuts, and the elevator shakily starts moving. He doesn't make a move to press a floor button, and I glance to Braeden for a moment, elbowing him in the side.

He laughs, and shrugs at me. Leaning closer to my boyfriend—damn that's weird—I whisper in his ear, "He's hot. And going to the same floor."

Again Brae laughs, whispering back, "He's probably not gay, stud."

I lick my lips, biting down on my lip ring, as I glance back at the sexy stranger again. He's standing against the elevator wall—his hands behind his back—in a nervous stance.

I'm practically hyperventilating staring at him, and my dick is about to greet him, wondering if this elevator has cameras that would see me pounce and grind on him. Just fucking looking at him—with Braeden next to me as well— is giving me a raging hard on.

Sexy stranger shifts on his feet, and stopping my staring for a moment I glance down at my dick and adjust myself.

Braeden laughs next to me, and when I look up again I catch a fleeting glimpse of my sexy stranger licking his lips and smirking, a shy smile on his handsome as fuck face. And fuck his smile is the hottest fucking sight ever. It makes my stomach flip, and all that comes to mind is, 'Oh shit'.

Tamed Hearts

We're so close to our floor, and I'm so damn horny. Thank fuck Brae is next to me, because at least I can kiss him. Granted I want to kiss the sexy stranger, but he has a shyness and I'm intrigued by that, but not enough—yet—to overstep.

I tug on Brae's t-shirt, yanking him closer and smashing a hard kiss against his lips. My boyfriend deepens the kiss, taking my lip ring in between his teeth as he licks over my lips and teases my tongue with his. Behind us, sexy stranger groans, almost growls, and it makes my dick throb in my shorts. I moan against Braeden's lips, groaning out a loud, "Fuck!" just as the doors slide open and sexy stranger hastily grabs his suitcase, shooting out of the elevator without a backwards glance.

Braeden and me trip over our suitcases as we head out of the elevator, stepping out into the busy corridor to go find our room. I'm glancing around for him—my sexy stranger—wondering which way down the expansive corridor he headed.

Braeden is racing ahead of me, and stops outside an open door, his mouth aghast.

When I catch up to him, he asks, "Stud, what's our room number again?"

"1013, why?"

He laughs, and smirks at me.

"Seems we have a hot roommate," he tells me, before leaning into my side to whisper, "that you want to fuck."

I practically shove him aside to find my sexy stranger standing in the middle of the open plan dorm room.

Caz May

I just died and went to heaven, hello and welcome to uni life Briston.

Dragging Braeden inside, about to greet the sexy stranger he nods at us, when I call out, "Dibs on the double bed room!"

He doesn't even say a word, just looks horrified and darts to one of the bedrooms. I take Braeden's hand dragging him to the other. I've never been so turned on in my whole damn life. And right now I need to fuck my hot boyfriend, and get rid of thoughts of the sexy stranger who will be sleeping in the next room.

I don't even know his name yet, but fuck I want to know all about him, and see all of him under his baggy clothes.

I might be a fucking idiot to be thinking about another guy when I have Brae, and Ariel as well, but I have an overwhelming urge to make sexy stranger mine. Just one look at him, and my whole world flipped.

I love Braeden and Ariel, but I honestly want someone to look at me the way Braeden looks at our girl; with the look of unbreakable love in his eyes.

Epilogue

BRAEDEN

Five months later

Sitting on the couch—with Briston—in our dorm room, I can hear Ariel's feet padding across the tiles of the bathroom as though she's petrified to walk out and face the truth.

Caz May

The past months have been crazy, a rollercoaster of highs and lows. We've gone to classes, partied, and fucked each other more times than I can even count.

Briston has been a bit standoffish of late though, caught up on lusting after our roommate Jebediah when he's been pushed into the friend zone, even though our roomie gives off gay vibes. I feel kinda sorry for the guy, but he's not getting the message and at the same time it just means more sex for me because when Jeb brushes Bris off he comes to me, and sucks my dick or fucks me, loudly so Jeb can hear.

Bris is a dirty fucker, and I love him so much. But being honest, the sex I've enjoyed the most lately has been the sneaky nights with just me and Ariel curled up in her bed, with her roomie across from us. Being quiet whilst making love to Ariel—just us—is the best, most sensual sex of my life. She's fucking everything to me, and with her being really tired lately, and not eating because she's throwing up every five minutes my heart has broken for her. I know she's scared. I am too. She'd gotten on the pill, but there's been nights were all three of us were drunk, and we fucked all night in our room, like fucking idiotic bunnies.

I glance across at Briston, who's picking at the skin of his fingers nervously. I'm about to yank my hair out. I want Ariel to come out of the damn bathroom, so we can face this together.

And when she does come out of the bathroom, holding the pregnancy test I don't know what to think. She's sobbing as she crosses the room, not looking at either of us boys but staring at the test in her hands as though the

Tamed Hearts

answer it's presenting will change the longer she stares at it. She falls onto her butt on the couch between Briston and I, still staring at it. Catching a glimpse out of the corner of my eye I see the two pink lines showing it's positive.

Ariel glances up at me, and she's panicking, biting down on her lip when she looks into my eyes.

Fuck me, she's pregnant. We fucked up.

"I can't be," she stammers through her sobs, still barely looking at me. "My dad is going to kill me."

I take the test from her hands, prying it out from between her fingers and putting it on my lap. With a finger under her chin, I tip her gaze up to mine. And kissing her forehead, I calmly tell her, "He won't kill you, darling. It's going to be ok."

"How do you know that Brae?" she questions me, stammering on her words and letting out a sob before continuing without letting me reply, "We're not married, and you know he hates all three of us being together as it is."

Briston is quiet next to her, as though he doesn't know what to say. I'm honestly surprised I even have words myself, and all I honestly heard Ariel just say was 'married'. We're young, fuck I'm not even nineteen yet, but she's it for me.

"Then marry me, darling?" I ask, not hesitating at all.

She glares at me, mouth agape.

"You don't mean that Brae," she tells me as though she's in my head. But I do mean it.

"And we can't all get married," Ariel continues, thinking out loud. Her head turns to Briston, and then back to me as

Caz May

she shifts back, sinking into the couch so she can see both of us clearer.

"I still want both of you," she confesses, biting down on her lip to hold back a sigh of frustration.

Again I cup her cheeks and turn her gaze back to me.

"I know, darling," I start softly, watching her eyes that lock on mine. "But who says we can't get married and still all be together?"

She darts her gaze between Briston and I again, when he speaks suddenly, "Yeah Ar's baby, Brae is right. I always thought I'd marry a guy anyway."

She opens her mouth to protest, but no words come out and he shakes his head at her.

"Don't say anything Ar's. You and Brae belong together. I want this for you."

She doesn't reply, instead she kisses Briston softly.

"That means a lot, Bris," she tells him, just above a whisper. "I love you and no matter what you'll always have a piece of my heart."

He caresses her cheek, smiling at her. "I know Ariel, and I love you too." His gaze shifts to me, and he adds, "Both of you, no matter what."

I poke Ariel gently in her still soft, but slightly rounded belly, teasing, "So darling, you saying yes?"

She kisses me then, a sweet, dirty kiss that stirs my dick in my trackies.

"Yes, Braeden, I'll marry you," she purrs against my lips, and breaking it all caveman style I stand and grab her around the waist, throwing her over my shoulder.

"Ripper! Let's go celebrate as a throuple in bed!"

Tamed Hearts

Briston laughs behind us, as he gets up off the couch and we head to bedroom together.

Putting Ariel down on the bed, I kiss her lips softly.

"I love you, Ariel, my darling, my fiancee'."

"Mmm, Braeden, I love you, and can't wait to marry you."

"Back at you, darling. And Bris, man, I love you too."

"Yeah, I love you guys too. We're having a baby together."

"Yeah, I can't wait to see our girl fully pregnant, she'll look sexy as fuck."

Ariel laughs, then lets out a groan of lust when I kiss Briston.

We both look down at her sprawled out on our bed. She looks absolutely stunningly beautiful and she's ours.

I practically tear my clothes off, and kiss her lips as I strip her—all whilst Briston is behind me—getting naked as well. My heart leaps out of my chest when our now naked girl raspingly says, "Make love to me, my B-boys."

"Oh Ariel, darling. We're going to make love to you for the rest of our lives." And with those words I kiss her, more tenderly, more sensually and passionately than I ever have.

Briston steps up behind me, kissing my neck and my heart soars. It's true that our love is complicated—and our hearts were once wild—but now our hearts have been tamed by each other, and this—our love for each other—is no ordinary love.

It's unbreakable.

Caz May

The end...or is it?

Tamed Hearts

Acknowledgements

Well, here we are again, the end of another book and these never get easier. I'm always wary as I don't want to forget anyone.
But honestly this time I want to thank Samantha Wolf. She's not only a great friend, but fabulous beta reader, and I'd be lost without her. I can't wait for her amazing books to be out in the world.

And I thank all of you have read Ariel & her B-boys. This book was certainly a trip, a very dirty one...and I loved every minute of writing it, so I sincerely hope you did too.

Until the next book,
Caz May xx

Caz May

Stalk Me

Caz May is a librarian/teacher by trade, but was always destined to be an author from a young age.
In her spare time, she can be found devouring books or writing her own stories with characters that may not be the typical romance heroes but are loveable just as much.
Caz is married to her own real-life bearded hero and has two fur babies.
She lives for Iced coffee, especially from Gloria Jeans or a Farmers Union but pretty much just loves food in general.
When she's not writing, or reading a book most likely she can probably be found asleep or binge-watching shows on Netflix and Stan. And probably also drooling over her character inspiration on Instagram as well.
Check out her Instagram or other socials to get in touch.

Instagram- @cazmayauthor

Facebook- @CazMayAuthor

BookBub-Caz May https://www.bookbub.com/profile/caz-may

Spotify- cazcat25

Pinterest- pinterest.com/cazmayauthor

Goodreads https://www.goodreads.com/cazmay

TikTok- tiktok.com/@cazmayauthor

Tamed Hearts

Caz May